SEARCHING
FOR JAKUP

ROBERTA KAGAN

ISBN (ebook): 978-1-957207-82-7
ISBN (Paperback): 978-1-957207-83-4
ISBN (Hardcover): 978-1-957207-84-1

Title Production by The BookWhisperer

PROLOGUE

Blood covered his hands and soaked the front of his torn shirt. Tears stained his dirty face. "Open your eyes. Please Mila. Please don't die on me. I need you. You are my everything." The fetid odor of feces and urine permeated the stifling air in the bowels of the dark underground sewer. Pitor was trembling, a sick feeling coming over him. He held Mila close to him. So close that he could see the shadows of her facial features in the darkness. He put his fingers gently on her neck and felt the weakness of her heartbeat. *She's dying.* "Come Mila. Please open your eyes. We can get out of here. I will help you. You can lean on me. I will help you..."

He didn't expect her to awaken, but he begged anyway. He pleaded with her and with God, until finally by some miracle, her eyes opened. "Pitor. Where are we?" she asked.

"In the sewer. I had to get you out of the city. Do you remember anything?"

"No," her voice was weak. "I hurt, Pitor. I've never felt such terrible pain."

"I know and I would give anything if I could take your pain away. I wish it was me, and not you who was shot," He said, his voice cracking. "But at least you are conscious. That means everything to me. I love you so much. I want you to know that I have loved you since the first time I saw you." Tears ran like a river down his cheeks. It was as if he was shedding all of the tears he'd restrained his entire life.

"I love you too. But I'm very weak, Pitor. I can't talk much. You must listen to what I have to say."

"I am listening," he said. He was trying to carry her and walk through the filth that covered the slippery ground.

"I am not going to make it, my darling. I'm sorry to leave you this way. But you must promise me something. Will you?"

"Anything. Anything you ask. Just don't die, Mila. Will yourself to live. You can do this. I know you can."

"Pitor, I don't know if Jakup is still alive. But I can't go to rest in peace if I am not sure that you will search for him. You must do whatever you can to find out what happened to him, because if he is alive, he needs you. Promise me."

"I promise I will never give up. I will find out what happened to Jakup."

Her voice was growing softer, weaker, "And you... you are a young man, Pitor, with so much life and love inside of you. I want you to find a woman who will appreciate you and I want you to marry again."

"Never. You are my bashert. There is no one else for me."

"I don't know where I am going," she said, her voice barely above a whisper. "But wherever I am, I will always be watching over you and Jakup. And it would make me very sad to see you live your life alone. Promise me that if I die, you will marry again. Promise me that you will fight to go on living, in spite of the pain and difficulties. Will you promise?"

"Yes, yes, I promise. Anything you want Mila. Just please fight. Please don't give up. Please, live. Please." He fought to get the words out. "Please don't die. Mila. Please."

It felt like all the sadness he had been fighting against for so long had formed a lump in his throat. Pitor forced himself to swallow hard as he carried his dying wife in his arms. *Mila has been shot. Why God? Why was it her and not me? My Mila has always been an angel. She didn't deserve to be hurt like this.* There was a flicker of light that filtered through a sewer cover and, in the light, he could see the terrible pain in her eyes.

His eyes connected with hers, and he leaned down and kissed her. Although she was very light because before the uprising, they had both been starving in the Warsaw ghetto, she was growing heavy in his arms.

"I'm tired, Pitor," she whispered. "Leave me here. And go on without me, please. I know you very well, and I can see that it is hard for you to carry me. I've become a burden to you."

He looked down into her eyes, so dark against her pale face. "I will not leave you behind, Mila. I love you. You are not a burden to me. You could never be a burden to me. I would rather die than leave you here in this sewer."

"I can't bear it, Pitor. I just can't."

"Then let me bear it for you. You rest. I will get us out of here," he said, with more confidence than he actually felt.

It was a long walk. Many miles underground. And by the time Pitor was able to pull Mila out of the sewer, he could hardly catch his breath. He dared not rest, not even for a moment. He couldn't take the chance that they might be seen. Even though it appeared as if there was no one around, they must not be caught out in the open. They were close to the forest. A few more minutes, and they would be hidden by the trees.

"We'll be all right, Mila. You'll see. We're almost in the forest where we'll be able to hide. I will hunt and fish for us. The food will make you strong," he said through the tears. "You're going to be all right. You're going to make it." He kept repeating over and over. "You're going to be all right. You're going to make it."

His face, hands and clothes were covered in blood.

She nodded, too weak to answer.

CHAPTER ONE

The warmth of the golden rays of the sun caressed Pitor Barr's face as he watched his beloved wife, Mila. She was sitting with their son, Jakup, on a blanket under a large oak tree. Jakup, a solidly built toddler, who looked just like his father, had recently learned to walk on his own. And since then, he wanted to walk all the time. Pitor watched his son, whose face was firm with determination, and Pitor smiled. Jakup's blond curls danced gently in the wind as he giggled, while he wobbled on his short chubby legs towards his mother's open palms. *What a wonderful day for a picnic. I have never seen the weather more beautiful,* Pitor thought, taking a piece of thick bread from the picnic basket Mila had packed. *But nothing is more beautiful than Mila, my bashert. I can still remember the first time I saw her. She was still just a young girl. I stared at her stupidly, memorizing her face. Before my mother passed away, she told me that when I met my bashert, I would know it. And somehow, I did. I knew it was Mila.*

When Jakup reached Mila's arms, she snuggled him close to her. Then she began to tickle him. Jakup loved to be tickled, and he laughed loud and clear—filling the air with joy—the way only an innocent child could. Pitor smiled. He couldn't help himself; he had to be a part of this beautiful moment. As he walked over to his wife and son, he gazed into her dark eyes and a secret romantic knowing passed between them. Then he sat down beside her and ruffled Jakup's hair. Jakup hugged his father tightly and although he wasn't rich—he was just a humble butcher—Pitor felt as if he were the luckiest man in the world. His heart was full as he closed his eyes and thanked God for his good fortune.

"Pitor..." It was Mila. Her voice was strained. "Pitor?"

She brought him back to the moment, and he opened his eyes to the harsh reality that had befallen them both.

Her chin quivered and tears fell down her cheeks, and her eyes closed. He felt her neck for a pulse. She's still alive. Gently but firmly, he shook her. I can't let her go. I can't let her just disappear like this.

"Think of our lives together, of all the good times we shared. There can be more. This doesn't have to be the end. You must fight. Fight Mila. Please fight," he said, his entire body shaking.

CHAPTER TWO

APRIL, 1943

Pitor lay on the cold ground holding his wife Mila tightly in his trembling arms. Blood from the gunshot wound covered his hands and face. He had done the impossible. He and Mila had escaped the Warsaw ghetto, but not before he'd lost everything he loved. His four-year-old son was stolen by a Nazi officer, and in wild desperation Pitor and Mila had tried to find the boy, but it had all been for naught. Little Jakup was gone, and they had no way of knowing if he was alive or dead. Even worse, they had no way of knowing why a Nazi might take a Jewish child. And considering the possible reasons was chilling. This horrific loss might easily have dissolved many marriages, but not theirs. Mila and Pitor were bashert. They were so in love that nothing could come between them, not even the harshest grief. But now Pitor sat under the stars, looking to the moon for answers and begging God to spare his beloved wife, as she lay dying in his arms. He had been instrumental in the uprising in the Warsaw ghetto where they'd been imprisoned, and he did not regret his participation in the valiant fight. That was because, unlike some of the other Jewish residents in the ghetto, he believed wholeheartedly that the Nazis planned to murder every Jew on the face of the earth. So, he was certain that following their orders would not spare him or Mila. Besides, he was a fighter by nature and losing Jakup left him itching to get out so he could try to find his son.

After Pitor's mother died many years before this, he swore to himself and to God that he would never cry again. And until now, he'd kept that promise, but as he looked at the blood pooling around his beautiful young wife, his face was covered in tears. Pitor hated being powerless. His only hope was to beg God to save his Mila. As he wept, he apologized for all his sins and begged god to spare his wife. "Take me instead," he cried out in the dark of night. "Let her live. She is a good woman, a kind and gentle soul. And I love her so. I am begging you. I will do whatever you ask of me. Only let her live.

"If you would only return my wife and son to me, I swear I will follow all your laws. I swear to it." The rebelliousness that had been a part of him all his life now seeped out of him, leaving him weak, gasping for breath, and helpless as he lay covered in dirt and blood. Shaking and barely able to speak, he whispered now, "I swear to you I will change. I will be whoever you want me to be and do whatever you ask of me, if you will only spare my Mila. Please let her live. I beg you, Hasheem. Let her live." But the only answer he received was the hooting of an owl.

When he looked down into her eyes, Pitor saw that Mila had regained consciousness. "Mila..." he whispered as he began to plant kisses on her face, "Mila, my darling. My beloved." And for a moment, he believed God had answered his prayers. "Thank you, dear and merciful God," he whispered as he lay his head gently on her chest.

"I'm dying, Pitor," she croaked in a barely audible voice. "I am very weak, and I don't have much time left. So, please, you must listen to me now, while I can still speak."

"You can't die. I won't let you. Just be still and let your body gain strength."

"Pitor, shhhh, please just be quiet and listen to me. After I am gone, I want you to leave here. Then you must do whatever you can to find Jakup. I know he is alive. I have always felt it. Do you believe me? Do you feel it too?" She took his hand and squeezed it in her own cold one.

"Yes, yes, I believe." He wanted to give her a reason to live, but he wasn't sure if he believed it or not.

Mila continued to speak in a strained voice, "Now, listen to me, Pitor, once you find our son, I want you to marry again. We had a good marriage and a beautiful family. You are a good husband and father. And it is my wish that if I cannot be with you, you shouldn't spend your life alone. You will need a wife—a partner who will share your life with you—and Jakup will need a mother."

"You are my bashert. I don't want anyone else. I never have and I never will."

"I know that. But it will make my passing easier if I know you will not be alone forever. I want you to try to be happy again."

"I don't want you to go."

"It's my time, Pitor," she said as she grimaced in pain.

"No, I won't let you go," he said, desperation in his voice. "You can't leave me, Mila."

"Promise me Pitor. Promise me you'll try to find Jakup and then you'll marry again. Please, I am begging you to promise me."

"I promise, Mila." He said, holding her tightly, wishing he could change the course of things. If only they had left Europe years ago. But how could he have known that something like this was going to happen?

Pitor covered his wife's face with kisses. But he was a butcher by profession, and he knew she had lost a lot of blood. So, he knew she was right; she was dying. He lifted her into his arms and began to rock her as yelps of pain escaped his lips. Time passed. He did not know how long he'd been sitting there steadily rocking Mila. But when he looked down at her, he saw her face was white, her beautiful brown eyes were closed. And he knew she was gone.

A bloody war was raging through Eastern Europe, and the forests were not safe. They were crawling with deserters and profiters from both sides. And there were also bands of people who had somehow escaped the evil of concentration camps, and then went into the forests where they joined together with other freedom fighters, creating small armies. While the Nazis combed the forests in search of their prey. Pitor knew he was far too loud as he wept. If he wanted to remain hidden, he should have remained quiet. These were dangerous times. Enemies lurked around every corner. But with Mila gone, he lost all concern for his own safety. He was like a dying animal or a mother who had just lost her child when he let out a loud cry of pain that sounded like a warning bell in the darkness. Tears and blood covered his face as he raised his fist to the sky and cursed at God. "If you really do exist, how could you let this happen? You took my mother, then you let them steal my son. And now, you have taken the one person who made my life worth living. Well, I will never pray again, because I don't need you. I will avenge the death of my loved ones on my own without your help." Then he fell into a broken heap and wept until sleep overtook him.

CHAPTER THREE

Pitor did not know how long he'd slept beside the body of his beloved wife, Mila. But when he opened his eyes, there were two men standing over him. They were young. He decided they could not be more than twenty-five years old, and they were very dirty. Both wore the uniforms of German soldiers. Pitor was awake now, and he quickly reached for his gun, but before he could put his hand around the trigger, one of the men shot Pitor in the hand. White hot pain raced through him as blood oozed out of the wound. "Don't try to grab your gun again, or I will kill you," one of the young men said, as he nudged Pitor with the butt of his rifle. "Now, if you want to live to see another day, you'd better tell me who you are. And be quick," he said.

"Who are you?" Pitor asked. Even though he was in pain and blood was running down his hand, the German soldier's gun didn't scare him. Pitor had nothing left to live for. He had already lost everything that mattered to him, and now he found he was completely unafraid of dying. In fact, he wished that he'd been fatally shot rather than just wounded.

The man in the German soldier's uniform laughed, "I don't know who you are, but I must admit that you certainly are bold to make demands of us considering we have our guns pointed at your head."

"What do you want from me?" Pitor said. "I have nothing to give you, but my life. I have no food, no money. Nothing. You want my life? Take it. I don't care." But even as he said these words, Pitor thought of Jakup. And, if it were true that Jakup was alive somewhere, then his son needed him.

"I am telling you what I want. I want to know who you are."

"Why should you care who I am?"

"Because if you're on the wrong side of the fence, we're going to kill you."

"And I suppose that should matter to me, but it doesn't." Pitor said angrily.

"You're already bleeding. I'm sure you're in pain. If you want us to help you, then tell us who you are."

"My name is Pitor Barr."

"Very interesting, you have a Polish name, but you speak perfect German without any accent. I would have taken you for a German native. I'm still not sure that you aren't a German, with that blond hair and those blue eyes. You certainly look like one," the soldier said.

Pitor hadn't realized that he'd answered the soldier in German. He was so used to his father switching between German and Polish that it was automatic for him. "That should please you. You two are German, aren't you?" Pitor wasn't sure that they were. They didn't look German. They looked more Russian, or maybe Polish.

One of the uniformed soldiers laughed, "Actually no, we aren't Nazis. We just like to wear the uniform. It makes us feel like we deserve to own the world." The other soldier joined in the laughter. Then the two looked at each other.

"Now, tell me how you came to speak such perfect German, but you say you're a Pole," the other soldier said.

"My father was born in Germany. My mother was from Poland. I grew up learning to speak both languages. I speak other languages too."

"Like what?"

"Like Yiddish." Pitor said suddenly. He was feeling proud to be Jewish, and he wanted them to know that he was not ashamed. "If I am going to die here, I am going to die as a Proud Jew," he said. "And I don't know or care what you do to me. If it makes you happy to kill me, then go right ahead."

"I see. You sound as if you have been defeated. I think you were in the war. And I don't believe you're Jewish. I think you're a real German," one of the soldiers said.

"I think he is too." The other one sneered. "A Nazi through and through."

"Pull down your pants."

"What?" Pitor said.

"Pull down your pants."

"You'll have to kill me because I absolutely refuse to do anything perverted with you," Pitor said, wincing in pain as he tried to move.

"Don't worry. We aren't going to touch you. We aren't perverts who lurk in the forest looking for victims. We just want to see if you are circumcised."

Pitor stood up and pulled down his pants.

The two men looked at Pitor's penis, then they eyed each other. "He's a Jew," one of them said.

The other one nodded, "Yes, he is." Then the one who spoke first pointed at Mila and asked, "What happened here?"

"First tell me who you two are and then I'll tell you what happened," Pitor said as he pulled his pants back up. His hand, where he'd been shot, was burning and aching.

"We have the guns, so we ask the questions. That's the way this works."

"Not as far as I am concerned," Pitor said. "I told you already that I'm not afraid to die. Go ahead...shoot me. I don't care."

"Are you running away from something?"

"Aren't we all running away from something? Hitler made sure of that," Pitor said bitterly. Then he added, "I am a Jew and if Jews want to live, they have to keep running, don't they? That's what the German's have done to my people. They've taken our homes, our loved ones. Our lives. What else do you bastards want?"

The German soldier studied him for a moment. "I have to admit from your blond hair and blue eyes, I didn't believe you that you were a Jew. But the beautiful lady who is laying over there looks like she might be Jewish."

"I don't care if you believe me or not. I don't care about anything anymore. And, for your information, yes, my wife is Jewish," Pitor said. "You Nazi bastards killed her."

"I believe everything he is telling us," one of the soldiers said to the other, who nodded, indicating that he too was convinced that Pitor was telling the truth.

One of the two soldiers shook his head. Then he leaned his gun against the side of a tree. He looked over at Pitor as he sat down beside him and said, "We are partisans. Both of us are Jewish too. We stole these uniforms from Nazi soldiers we killed. My name is Szymon. I am a Polish Jew and my partner here is Dima, he is a Russian Jew who was living in France. But like you, we both have made a point to learn to speak perfect German."

"You're both wearing German army uniforms, so it fits that you should speak the language like natives," Pitor said.

"Yes, I agree. That's why we spend a lot of time learning how to speak the language without an accent," Syzmon said.

"You said you stole those uniforms?" Pitor asked curiously.

"Yes, we stole these uniforms a few days ago from two German soldiers who we found in the forest. They tried to kill us, but we killed them first. It goes like that; you've got to be fast with a gun if you want to survive. If you look closely these uniforms are full of blood stains."

"They are very dirty."

"We use the dirt to hide the blood. Anyway, Dima and I think the Nazi soldiers we killed were deserters. We figured it would be easier and safer for us to navigate these forests wearing these uniforms. So far, we've been lucky. We have even been able to convince farmers that we are German soldiers and because they were afraid of us, they gave us food." Syzmon cleared his throat. "Now, tell us everything about you. Did you kill the Nazi who shot your wife or is he roaming around in the forest?"

"My wife was not shot here in the forest. She was shot during an uprising in the ghetto where we lived. Before we were arrested, she and I lived in a village in Poland. One day the Nazis came, and everyone was arrested, and sent to a ghetto in Warsaw. The conditions there were terrible. When we came to realize that the Nazis meant to kill all of us, we organized and put together an uprising. It was bloody, and we lost a lot of people, but we killed a lot of the Nazis too. When our ammunition ran out and we knew it was just a matter of time before they got all of us, Mila and I escaped. However, we paid a very dear price for our freedom. My wife was shot as we were escaping. I carried her here." Pitor glanced over at Mila. "At least they didn't take her prisoner and torture her. She died here in the forest."

"I'm sorry about your wife," Szymon said. "We all have stories of loss, I'm afraid."

"It's true," Dima said. "My wife was arrested while she was working at a factory. They came in and took all the Jews. At the time, I was in the army. When I went home on leave my neighbor told me that the Nazis took her. She was sent to a camp. I tried to find out which one, but no one knew. I haven't seen her since, so I don't know if she is alive or dead."

"No point in going over our tales of woe. Why don't you come with us. Join us. We are freedom fighters, and we're not alone. We'll introduce you to the others. We have built a cabin for shelter, and we also have a doctor among us who will fix up your hand. It will heal in no time."

Pitor leaned over and kissed Mila's cold lips. His heart was broken and there was a hole in the pit of his stomach. The taste of bile burned his throat. He didn't want to go on. In fact, he would have been happy to lie down and die beside his beloved. But he couldn't help but think of his son and the promise he'd made to Mila to find Jakup. If Jakup was alive, he would find him, no matter where he was, and he would kill as many Nazis as he could along the way. He gently lay Mila down on the ground. Then he stood up and stretched his back and legs. As he walked away, he knew his life would never be the same.

CHAPTER FOUR

"This is Pitor Barr," Dima said when they entered a shelter hidden by trees that had been built from logs.

Pitor looked around him and estimated that there were about twenty men or so sitting on the earthen floor.

The men nodded and began to introduce themselves. "Ivan... Anatole... Nicolas..." and so on. Pitor doubted he would remember all these names, but it didn't matter. "This is Moshe. He is a doctor, and he'll take care of your hand," Dima said.

"Sit down, make yourself comfortable," Szymon said. "Have some food."

"Thank you," Pitor said, his voice sincere as he grabbed a hunk of raw fish and tore off a bite with his teeth.

Moshe walked over to Pitor and took his hand. He looked it over carefully, then shook his head and said, "You'll be fine, but I'm going to have to get this bullet out."

Pitor nodded. "I know."

"Go ahead and finish eating first. After you're done, I'll take care of it," Moshe said.

"What have you told him about us?" Ivan asked Dima.

"We told him the truth, that we are Partisans," Dima took a cigarette out of the pocket of his uniform, then lit it.

"Where did you get the cigarettes?" Ivan asked.

"They were in the pocket of this uniform when I put it on. I guess the German bastard who wore it was a smoker."

Ivan shook his head. "Eh, so now you are going to smoke too? Foolish mistake. Bad habit, smoking." Then he turned his attention away from Dima and faced Pitor. "So, they told you we are freedom fighters. It's true. We are. All of us have plenty of reasons to hate the Nazis, so we do what we can to help defeat them. We take every chance we get to sabotage the Germans in their war effort. As you might well imagine, our work is very dangerous. We all know this, and we don't care. We do it anyway, because we feel we must find a way to help the allies stop Hitler. Now that you know what we are doing, how do you feel about joining us?"

"I'm happy to join you, but I too have an agenda of my own," Pitor said.

"Go on, why don't you tell us your story."

Pitor nodded, then he sighed and in a small voice he began, "My wife and I lived in a small village outside of Warsaw. I was a butcher. We had a beautiful baby boy. My wife and I were so happy," Pitor sighed again. "Then the Nazis started bombing Warsaw, but we never thought they would come to our little village. It was so small and to be honest, I thought it was a place they would overlook. But they didn't. They came and arrested all of us. They put us in trucks and took us at gunpoint into Warsaw where they had walled off a small area. They imprisoned all the Jews in this area. It was a terrible place; they called it the Warsaw Ghetto. Because it was so over-crowded and soap was difficult to come by, the place was filthy. It was full of rats and disease. But, because my wife and son were with me, I could overlook so many things. And at first, I was sure we would be released. So, Mila, that was my wife," Pitor paused and looked down at the ground, "Well, she and I tried our best to make the best of it. I found work in the ghetto, and we did what we could to try and live as normal a life as possible. But, then one day while I was at work a Nazi stole my son. I don't know why they took him. He was just a little boy." Pitor balled his good hand into a fist.

"Are you sure it was a Nazi?"

"I'm sure. A woman who was a friend of my wife's saw the whole thing happen. She told us the story. She said a Nazi officer came into the ghetto and took Jakup. She tried to stop him, but she couldn't."

"I've heard of the Nazis stealing Polish children, but never would they take a Jew," Dima said.

"Yes, that's true. But look at him," Nicolas said, pointing to Pitor, "he's blond and blue eyed. That's what the Nazis want, that's what they look for. I am assuming your son was blond like you?"

"Yes, he looked just like me."

"But even so, the fact that he was in the ghetto would tell the Nazi that he had Jewish blood. I'm surprised that a Nazi would want him for any reason," Szymon said.

"Who knows why these Germans do the things they do. They're crazy. We know that for sure," Ivan said.

"I don't know where they took my son. But I am going to find him."

"Listen to me, Pitor. I understand how you feel. However, you must consider the fact that your little boy might well be dead already," Dima said as gently as he could.

Pitor drew his healthy hand into a fist and was about to punch Dima. For a moment he believed that if he could silence him, Dima's words would not be true. Then he remembered Dima was not his enemy. He had not wanted to hurt Pitor, and he had no malice towards Jakup. He had only wanted to warn him not to allow himself to be too hopeful, just in case Jakup was no longer alive. But for Pitor, it was too late. All he had left was hope. There was nothing else of importance in his life. The only reason he was willing to go on living was that he'd promised Mila he would do what he could to find their child.

"Pitor's wife was murdered as well," Szymon explained to the others. "There was an uprising in the ghetto, and she was shot." All the other men nodded with understanding. And by the looks on their faces, Pitor knew they had all suffered great losses of their own.

"We'll do whatever we can to help you," Ivan said. "But meanwhile, perhaps you can help us blow up some trains full of Nazis? What do you say?"

"Sure," Pitor answered, "killing Nazis would be my pleasure."

CHAPTER FIVE

Ivan sat on the floor near the door, with his back against the wall and a gun ready at his side. He coughed, then he took a swig from a bottle of whiskey. Then, in a thoughtful voice, he said, "I wonder if that Nazi who took your little boy thought he was a Pole. If he is blond and blue eyed like you, the German might have mistaken him, and it's possible he could still be alive."

"But the German took the child right out of that ghetto in Warsaw. We've all heard that these Ghettos are prisons. The Jews can't get out and other people can't get in. So, if he thought the child was Polish, wouldn't he wonder how the little boy got into a Jewish ghetto?" Dima said.

"Yes, that might well be true. The only thing I am thinking is that children are often ignored. They can sometimes come and go as they please. I wonder if that Nazi thought your son was a Polish boy who found his way into the ghetto to play with other children. Not knowing that this was a prison for Jews," Ivan said.

"But he was so young. I can't imagine that they thought he could have wandered into the ghetto alone. Getting in and out of that place was a feat that a child of Jakup's age could never have accomplished."

"In truth, I don't know why that Nazi took him. I can't imagine."

"I pray he is alive for whatever reason. And I wish I had some idea of where they would have taken him," Pitor asked.

Ivan shook his head. "I honestly don't know. However, we know for sure that for some odd reason these crazy Nazis have started to steal Polish children," Szymon said. "We've heard about it from several drifters who saw it firsthand."

"And the answer to that question is what I must find out. Once I know why they took him, it will be easier to find out *where* they took him." Pitor answered.

"Do you know how to use a gun?" Ivan asked. "If not, I'll teach you. You are going to need to know this."

"I can use a gun. I can hunt and I can fish. I will help out while I stay with you. But I can't stay forever, I must figure out where to go next in search of my son. Please understand that my priority is finding my boy."

"I understand." Ivan said, "We all understand."

CHAPTER SIX

Over the next week, Pitor's hand began to heal, and once he was able to hunt and fish again, he kept his promise. During the freezing days in early May, he did his utmost to help the other partisans. He hunted and brought small game back to the cabin, and he made a pole so he could fish.

Then, on a crisp Tuesday morning, the partisans found another Jewish man in the forest. He was young, skinny, half dead, and terrified. They brought him back to the cabin where he was confronted by Ivan. "Who are you?" Ivan asked.

"I escaped from a group of soldiers who captured me," the young man said.

Ivan told the man who he was and then he explained what the partisans were trying to do.

The young man realized that he was safe, and his face brightened for a moment. "Before I escaped, I overheard the German soldiers talking about a train that is going to be passing through this area tomorrow. It will be carrying an entire platoon of German soldiers."

"Are you sure?" Ivan asked the young man.

"I'm sure of what I heard," he answered. "I don't know if it's true."

"Well, this sounds like an opportunity. And since it has fallen in our lap, I say we should rid the world of those Nazis. What do the rest of you say?" Ivan turned to the other men.

"I think we are safe here. For now, we have shelter and food. Let's just lay low. If we blow up a train, they will start looking for us. Then we might have to leave this cabin and live outside," Szymon said.

"Yes, of course they will start looking for us. And, yes, it's easier to stay here and remain safe and quiet. However, do we want to just survive? Or do we want to make a difference?" Ivan asked them all.

"I know I am one of the newer members here. But I feel compelled to share my thoughts. I say we attack them when they least expect it. We go out and blow up that train," Pitor said, "and I am willing to do it."

"Who agrees with Pitor?" Ivan asked. "Raise your hands and let's take a vote."

A large majority of the men raised their hands. Ivan nodded. "It looks like a whole group of unsuspecting Nazis is about to meet their maker. Hmmm..." He grumbled, "I'd love to hear a conversation between one of them and God. I wonder what they would say to justify their actions." Then he cleared his throat. "Anyway, Pitor has volunteered for this mission. Is anyone else willing to go with him?"

"I'll go with him," Dima said.

"Very well, we have two who are willing to risk their lives. Anyone else?"

No one else raised their hands. "There are only two of you. Do you still want to do this?" Ivan asked.

Both Pitor and Dima nodded.

"Very well," Ivan said.

The following evening, in the middle of a dark night, Pitor and Dima set out to carry out their plan. On that moonless night, they carefully laid sticks of dynamite on the train tracks. Then, the following day, they hid and watched as the train came through. When it hit the dynamite, it exploded into a giant ball of fire. Dima was thrilled. He laughed loudly and excitedly at the success of their mission. But Pitor got no satisfaction from seeing the injured Germans screaming with their burned faces and seared bodies scattered like the dead leaves of autumn, around what was left of the train cars. There were so many dead men. For a moment Pitor thought about their wives, who would soon receive a letter telling them they were widows. He hated the Germans for all they had taken from him, and he believed they deserved to suffer and die. So, in his heart, he wondered how he was still capable of feeling any form of compassion for them. He decided it was probably because of Mila. He always thought of the wives of the men he killed, and it was for those women that he felt a small twinge of pity, but not regret. Pitor looked away from the disaster. He'd seen so much death, so many mangled bodies, so much blood. Oh, how he missed Mila. If he could have, he would have given up the rest of his life in exchange for an hour with her. But that was just a fantasy, and in truth, there was nothing that could make him smile again, except for finding Jakup.

"Dima said you did an excellent job with the train," Ivan said to Pitor, when Pitor and Dima returned to the cabin. "He told me that you're a true warrior. He says you're fearless."

"I'm not fearless," Pitor smiled wearily, then he shook his head. "But I am glad I was able to be a part of this mission." He looked away for a moment. *I suppose Dima is right. Maybe it's true that I am fearless. But it's only because I am not afraid to die. And I suppose I would almost welcome death. If I were dead, maybe I would be with Mila. That is if I could only make myself believe that there is really an afterlife. Right now, I can't believe in anything. And the only thing keeping me going is that promise I made to Mila. Even though this place feels safe, and I have met some incredible men, I must leave here and go to find Jakup. And if he is still alive, no matter where he is, or what they have done with him, I will find him.*

25

"Ivan, all of you have been very kind to me. But I must leave here. I appreciate all you have done for me. However, I must try my best to find my little boy."

Ivan nodded. "I understand. If I were in your position, I would do the same thing."

CHAPTER SEVEN

The next morning, spring had finally come to the forest. The blood that had been spilled on the white snow during the long winter months now soaked into the soil, nourishing it. As the snow melted, tiny blades of grass sprung up through the earth. Flowers grew wild in the forest. Their various colors painted the forest floor like an oil painting, and the trees began to fill with green leaves again. Pitor looked out across the land, and he knew the time had come. He went to Ivan and told him he planned to leave that day. Ivan nodded. "We will miss you," He said, then he left Pitor alone with his thoughts.

Life goes on. Pitor thought as he marveled at the way the forest had rejuvenated him. *My heart is still empty, and I am still filled with pain and loss. I know I will never be truly happy again. But even so, the world keeps turning. The flowers bloom again, just like they did last year, and the year before that. The frozen ponds defrost and when they do, they reveal an array of swimming fish that sparkle like silver as the rays of sunshine stream through the trees and land like tiny diamonds upon the water.*

Pitor didn't hear Dima as he walked up beside him. "So, today is the day?" Dima said, patting Pitor on the back.

"Yes," Pitor answered. "I'm going to be leaving here today."

"Ivan told me. I will be sorry to see you go, but I understand your need to leave and to search for your child. Until you know what has become of him, you cannot be at peace. You must find him."

"Yes," Pitor said.

"I brought you something," Dima laid a German soldier's uniform into Pitor's hands. "Wear this. If the German's capture you, you can tell them that your platoon was killed, and you were somehow left alive. You tell them that you were wandering through the forest in search of another platoon."

"They'll take me for a deserter."

"Maybe not. You'll have to be convincing. Tell them you were not with your platoon when they were attacked because you were sent into the forest to try and hunt for food. Since you are an excellent hunter and a good shot, they will probably believe you."

"Thank you," Pitor said, taking the uniform. "Which way is Germany? It's hard to tell. The whole damn forest looks the same."

"I know. You're right; it does. But," Dima pointed, "Germany is that way."

"Are you sure?"

"No, but I think so," Dima smiled. "It's the best I can do."

"All right," Pitor returned Dima's smile.

Dima nodded. "Good luck, Pitor. I hope you find your son. Be safe. And may God be with you."

"Good luck to you, my friend," Pitor said.

Pitor hated goodbyes. He had not let himself get close enough to any of the men in the cabin, except for Dima. This was because he didn't want to experience any more loss. As Dima turned and walked back towards the cabin, Pitor watched him. He felt that same emptiness in his stomach, but he pushed his feelings away. Then he went behind a tree and put on the uniform that Dima had given him. His heart was heavy as he strapped the rifle he carried onto his back. Then, without turning around to look at the cabin again, Pitor steeled himself. He had a mission to accomplish, and no matter what it took, he was going to find out what had happened to his son. So, he turned away from the safety of the cabin and began to walk through the forest.

———————

TWO DAYS PASSED, and Pitor kept walking. He hoped he was headed in the right direction, but he had no way of knowing for sure. Since he left the cabin, he finished all the food Ivan had given him to take along on his journey. Now he was hungry and desperately searching for water, because not only was he thirsty, but he preferred fishing to hunting. Hunting would require him to use bullets, and his source of ammunition was limited. He knew he must save as many of the bullets as possible, just in case he ran into danger along the way. He didn't know how far he'd walked, but it seemed like an eternity before he finally saw a pond. Pitor searched for fish to make sure that the water was safe. And once he saw them, he drank heartily. Then he leaned back against a tree trunk and began to make a fishing pole from a tree branch that had fallen to the ground. Using his knife, Pitor carefully made a hole in the branch, then took a piece of thread from the hem of his uniform jacket. He pulled the thread through the hole in the tree branch, then searched until he found a thorn on a flowering bush. Carefully, he pierced a tiny hole in the center. He pulled the thread through the thorn, then tied it tightly. Next, he began to dig through the dirt close to the water in search of worms or insects that he might use as bait. Since it was spring, there were plenty of worms near the surface of the ground. After he found one, he tied it to the thread. Then he dropped the worm into the water and held on to the makeshift pole as he leaned his back against a tree and waited. Rays from the warm sun filtered through the budding tree branches and caressed his head and shoulders. The soft sound of living things swimming and jumping in the pond's water gently soothed his lonely and aching mind and soul. It had been days since he slept for more than a few hours at a time. And so, before he realized it, Pitor fell into a deep sleep. He dreamed of Mila, as he so often did. In his dream, they were younger and newly married. She was outside in the back of their little house, hanging the wash on a line. Pitor walked up behind her and kissed her neck. He could smell the soap in her hair and feel the softness of her skin beneath his lips. In his dream, he sighed with the longing he felt. Mila turned to embrace him. Their eyes met, and he felt all the warmth of their love filling his body and soul. They kissed softly as somehow the two of them got tangled up in one of the wet bedsheets Mila had been stretching across the laundry line. They both laughed as they fell to the ground, wrapped up in each other. Then they began to make love. His heart ached for her. Even as this vision filled him, he knew he was only dreaming. And that made it painful. How he wished he would never awaken. Then he was shaken awake by the sound of a loud guttural voice speaking high German. The male voice said firmly, "Soldier, soldier! Who are you and where is the rest of your platoon?"

Pitor's eyes flew open. At first, he was confused, almost unsure of where he was. He had been so immersed in his dream that he forgot all his plans. He sat up, taking in the entire situation before saying a single word. For a moment, he wanted to grab his gun and shoot when he saw an SS officer standing over him. Then he remembered he was wearing a German soldier's uniform. *He thinks we are on the same side, but I must convince him I am not a deserter.* He thought.

"I said, who are you? What is your name?" The SS officer asked again, and Pitor could hear in the man's voice that he was losing patience.

At first Pitor's mind was cloudy, and he couldn't think of a German name to tell this man. He closed his eyes for a moment, then he heard Mila's voice in his mind. She whispered to him, *tell him your name is Gefreite Rudolf Ziegler. Tell him that your platoon was attacked while you were out hunting and now you are all that is left of your platoon.* "I am Gefreite Rudolf Ziegler," Pitor said quickly. "I'm all that's left of my platoon. We were fighting on the eastern front. I went off to relieve myself and hunt for food. When I returned all my fellow soldiers were dead. I didn't know what to do. So, I decided to go back to Germany so I can be reassigned to another platoon."

"I see," the officer said, "the eastern front, huh?"

"Yes."

"Ahhh, yes," the SS officer said as he relaxed and laid his gun on the ground beside him. "I hear it's a living hell. But I hear that the closer you get to the Russian front the worse it is. If you can imagine."

Pitor nodded.

"Not enough food, and the clothing is not warm enough. And those Russians are barbaric. They are animals. Not gentleman like we are," The SS officer said.

"Yes, that's right. The Russians are very brutal. But even though the war is rough, I have been proud to have an opportunity to serve the Fatherland," Pitor said, knowing this was what the Nazi would want to hear. *However,* he thought, *no one is as bad as the Germans. No one is more barbaric than the SS. The things they have done to the Jews are unspeakable. And their cruelty is unimaginable for any normal person.*

"It's a shame about your fellow soldiers," the man said. Then he lit a cigarette. "But of course, you must realize that I would be a fool to believe you. I am sorry to say this, but I think you just might be a deserter." the SS officer said confidently.

"And, although on first observance, I must admit that I do like you. However, I don't trust you. I can't, you see. There are so many shady people in this forest. I'm sure you understand. So, I am going to do my duty as a good German solider and escort you back to the Fatherland where you can explain your situation to the authorities. I hope we can do this in a friendly manner. However, if it is necessary, I will take you home to Germany at gun point. And once you are there, you will be judged by our military," the German spoke casually, taking puffs on his cigarette as if he and Pitor were old friends who were discussing something as unimportant as a recommendation for a local restaurant. But in fact, they were not discussing restaurants, and there was nothing casual about an accusation of treason.

And this man was quietly accusing Pitor of treason. With the slight threat in his tone of voice and in his accusing words, this Nazi let Pitor know he was not really being escorted to Germany by a friend. He was, in fact, being returned to the Fatherland by an SS officer to be tried as a traitor. Pitor knew that somehow, he must find a way to make this German officer trust him or he would be taken back to Germany, where he would be tried and executed. Then he would never have a chance to search for Jakup. *Be patient.* Pitor told himself. *I must wait and hold my tongue for now. With any luck, an opportunity will arise that I can use to make this man trust me.*

The German watched Pitor closely for a response. It seemed he was expecting Pitor to get up and at least try to fight him. Or perhaps he expected Pitor to pull his gun. But Pitor did neither. Instead, Pitor just smiled and as he took a fish off the hook he said, "I understand completely. If I were in your position I would do the same thing. And since what I have told you is the truth, I will do whatever I must to convince the army that I was always a devoted soldier. Never a deserter."

The Nazi smiled and nodded. "Fair enough," he said, "I'm Sturmscharführer Konrad Hoffmann. I'm on my way to Munich. I will drop you off at the headquarters there."

"Munich?"

"Yes, have you ever been?"

"I'm afraid not. But I have heard it's quite beautiful."

"So, it is." The Nazi said. "They used to serve the most exquisite beer during Oktoberfest."

"Yes, I have heard that too," Pitor said in a pleasant tone of voice. He was hoping to convince this Nazi that he was a friend.

"Where are you from?"

"Me? I'm from Frankfurt. How about you?" Pitor asked.

"Berlin."

"Ahhh, so you're from the big city."

"Yes, and I do love Berlin." Konrad Hoffmann said, "Not only is it home, but it's really such a wonderful city."

"So then, what brings you to Munich?" Pitor asked casually.

"It's really none of your business," Konrad said, and although his words were harsh, his tone was still casual.

"I didn't mean to offend you or to overstep my boundaries. I was only making conversation," Pitor said innocently.

"Ehhh, I suppose you're right. We're stuck here in this forest, so we might as well enjoy some conversation. As far as Munich is concerned, I am very proud to say that I received a letter last week informing me that I am to report to a special gala taking place at the Eagle's Nest next month," he beamed with pride then he winked and said, "You see, I am quite honored, because I am to receive a job promotion. I am being promoted to be a bodyguard for the Führer."

"That's very impressive," Pitor said. "I can see why you would be very proud and excited."

Konrad put his cigarette out on the ground. "It's only been a week that I have been walking through this forest on my way back to Germany, but I must admit, it has been rough, getting myself back home. These forests are so dense and it's easy to get lost. And finding food and water is quite a challenge."

"Yes, I agree with you on that," Pitor said, and he smiled.

"When I received the letter about my promotion, I was in Prussia. The letter stated that I was to make my way back to Germany at once, and I was to come back alone."

"Have you ever met the Führer?" Pitor asked.

"I haven't even met him yet, but I am very excited for the opportunity."

"So, you were chosen without being interviewed by anyone? They just chose you for this position, because you have a good record?"

"Yes, I suppose you could say that."

"You really must have quite a record."

"I do. I am proud to admit that I have a very good service record," Konrad said, "And, besides, it doesn't hurt that my father is very rich and terribly influential. He has a lot of important friends. And, although he has been crippled for as long as I can remember and therefore has been unable to serve in the military, he has made a lot of financial contributions to the Nazi party."

"I must admit," Pitor said, "I am in awe of you, sir. It's truly an honor to meet you."

As Pitor predicted, the other man was flattered and because his ego was stroked for a moment, he forgot to be skeptical of Pitor. Instead, he began to brag and tell Pitor all about his service in Prussia. Pitor listened quietly, nodding and acting as if he were impressed with Konrad's every word, until another fish tugged on his line. "Looks like we are going to have a good dinner tonight," Pitor said as he reeled in the fish. "I have a few small fish. It should be plenty for both of us."

"I must admit, I'm looking forward to it. I haven't eaten in a couple of days and I'm very hungry," Konrad said.

"The forest can certainly be tough if you aren't used to hunting or fishing. And forgive me for speaking so plainly, but you seem like a gentleman. You don't look like the sort of fellow who grew up fending for himself. You look like, well, like aristocracy," Pitor continued to flatter the Nazi. "But don't worry about a thing, because you are an officer. You needn't fish or hunt. I will do all the hunting and fishing for both of us. My father taught me these things when I was a young boy. He would take me out on hunting or fishing trips, and we would return with plenty of food. Often, we had so much that we were able to share with our neighbors."

"Well, as I said, my father was crippled so he wasn't a sportsman," Konrad laughed a little, "But because you have experience with survival in the forest, I think it will be beneficial for both of us that we are traveling back to Germany together. If I had tried to make it all the way back on my own, I very well may have starved to death," Konrad admitted, smiling.

Pitor returned Konrad's smile. Then he put the line back into the water. Konrad leaned his back against the trunk of a tree and closed his eyes, giving Pitor a moment to really observe him. He was close to

Pitor's height and had the same color hair and eyes. In fact, the two of them were so similar in looks that they could have been brothers. As he studied the Nazi, a plan began to form in Pitor's mind.

Konrad helped Pitor gather wood and then make a fire. They used tree branches to spear the fish and then cook them over the open flame.

"This is quite delicious," Konrad said.

"Fresh fish is always very good. I am glad you are enjoying it."

CHAPTER EIGHT

Konrad and Pitor slept or rested each day until one in the afternoon. Then, at two or three o'clock, when the sun was no longer high in the sky, they began to walk towards Germany. Pitor knew he must delay their arrival if his plan was to work. However, this was easy because all he had to do was suggest that they stop so he could either hunt or —if they were near a pond—fish, for their daily meal. Konrad was not in a hurry to arrive at his destination because he'd left Prussia with time to spare before he had to attend the gala. So, he was always in agreement.

At first, Konrad took Pitor's gun away and was reluctant to give Pitor access to it. Pitor protested, saying that if he did not have access to a gun, he could not hunt and therefore would be unable to provide food, unless they found a pond. Still Konrad refused to listen, and for two days they went hungry until they came upon a pond and Pitor began to fish. Konrad leaned his back against the tree and waited for a fish to bite. The cool breeze and the sound of birds singing lulled the two of them to sleep. But then, in his sleep, Pitor heard a noise. He opened his eyes slowly. And when he did, he saw a Russian soldier stealing their guns and ammunition. Konrad was still fast asleep. And the Russian was so busy that he didn't realize that Pitor had awakened. Unnoticed, Pitor took a small shotgun from a holster in the back of Konrad's coat, and without a second's hesitation, he shot the Russian in the face. The Russian's face exploded into a mass of blood and red tissue. Konrad's eyes flew open. "What's going on here?" he said, observing the situation and then grabbing his gun from Pitor's hand.

"You have no need for your gun, sir," Pitor said. "I already took care of him."

"What happened?"

Pitor told Konrad that the Russian was going to kill them both and take their weapons. "And you killed him?"

"Yes," Pitor said, "I took the gun you keep in the back of your jacket and shot him."

"You could have killed me," The Nazi looked at Pitor in disbelief. "But instead, you saved my life. I believe you just might be telling the truth about who you say you are, and what you say happened."

"Of course, I am. And of course I saved your life. I would again. You are a fellow German, like a brother to me. You and I are fighting on the same side. We want to see the triumph of our Fatherland. We are both good German soldiers who would gladly give our lives for the Reich. And because we share our love for our country, that immediately makes you my friend," Pitor said. He looked directly into Konrad's eyes and his tone of voice made him sound convincing.

Konrad shook his head. Then his face crinkled into a warm smile. "Here," he said as he handed Pitor a gun. "I guess I was wrong. You're one of us. You're no deserter. A traitor would have shot me. Or at least he would have tried to run, but you didn't."

Pitor smiled. "No, I didn't," he said. "That's because I am no traitor or deserter."

"I believe you."

CHAPTER NINE

Now that Konrad trusted Pitor, their conversations were different. They had a lot of time together and to pass the time Konrad began to tell Pitor about his life before the war, in Berlin. He explained that his family had always had plenty of financial resources, and that from the first time his father heard Hitler speak, he loved him and was a staunch supporter.

"Do you have brothers or sisters?" Pitor asked.

"No, I'm sad to say that I am an only child. How about you?"

"I don't have any siblings either. Both my parents are dead too. So, you could say, I'm alone in the world."

"Yes, it's hard to be alone. My mother passed away last year and now my father is too old and sick to recognize me. So, I suppose I am alone too," Konrad said.

Pitor nodded.

"You know, it's really rather funny, but you and I look so much alike that people would think we were brothers. Perhaps we should agree to be blood brothers. I know it sounds a bit childish, like something you might do with a friend at summer camp. However, right now, both of us could use a friend we could trust. And after you saved my life, I feel that I can trust you. For the first time in a long time, I feel that I can turn my back and not expect to feel the blade of a knife between my shoulders. If you know what I mean," Konrad said. "And...I'll to be quite honest, it's a darn good feeling."

A wide-open smile came over Pitor's face. "I couldn't agree more. It is a good feeling. I feel the same way about you," he said.

"Well," Konrad hesitated as he took a cigarette out of his pocket and offered one to Pitor, who shook his head to decline. Then he said, "You know, our chance encounter was meant to be. And I'm glad to hear that you feel the same way about our friendship."

Pitor smiled, then he changed the subject. "Anyway, I am going to see if I can't get my hands on some fish for our dinner tonight." Pitor began digging through the dirt with his nails in search of worms as they sat beside a small pond.

Konrad nodded. "Yes, fresh fish certainly would be nice."

"Yes, it will. I am going to do all that I can to catch us some dinner." Pitor smiled.

CHAPTER TEN

The following day, Pitor and Konrad got up in the afternoon, as always. Then they walked for several miles before they sat down to rest. "I'm glad I have a month to get myself back to Germany, and to that party at the Eagle's Nest. It's a long walk."

"Yes, it sure is. And once you get to Munich, isn't the Eagle's Nest high up on a mountain somewhere in the alps?"

"Actually yes, it is. I haven't been there before, but I hear the view is quite breathtaking."

"I'd love to see it," Pitor said.

"And I'd love to bring you with me, but unfortunately, I can't. The invitation is only for me. And, you know how strict this regime can be when it comes to things like this."

"Yes, of course I do." Pitor sighed as he placed a worm on the hook of his makeshift fishing pole.

"You look and sound very disappointed. I'm sorry. Truly," Konrad said. "I realize that I owe you a favor. After all, you saved my life and now as we are traveling together, you continue to provide food for us. But I don't have the authority to bring you to this party with me. It's just not in my control. I do hope you understand."

"Don't feel bad. I understand. And you don't have to feel like you owe me anything. We're brothers, united in the love we share for our Fatherland. Isn't that right?" Pitor said, but he couldn't hide the disappointment in his voice. He'd hoped by attending this gala he might find out if the Nazis had some kind of plan for stolen Jewish children. *Well, it's easy to see that Konrad has no plans of taking me with him. So, I'll have to find another way to get there.*

"Sure, of course that's right. We love our country and our Führer."

After they cooked and ate three small fish Pitor caught, the two men got up and dusted off their uniforms. They walked for a little while in silence, then Konrad turned to Pitor and winked before he said, "I may not be able to offer you an invitation to Hitler's private party, but I can offer you an invitation to something that will be almost as much fun. And definitely more satisfying."

"Oh?"

"Yes, I promise you that you will enjoy this."

"What is it?"

"I was thinking that you might like to come with me and spend a night or two at Heim Hochland. I was planning a visit there before going up to the Eagle's Nest. It's located in Steinhoring, not too far outside of Munich."

"What is it?"

"It's a home for the Lebensborn. Do you know what that is?"

"I know the word Lebensborn means fount of life. But I've never heard of Heim Hochland. Is it some sort of a hot spring or a health spa?" Pitor asked.

"No, not at all," Konrad took a cigarette out of the breast pocket and lit it. "Are you sure you don't want one?"

"No, thank you. I never started smoking."

"That's lucky for you," Konrad smiled, then he went on, "Heim Hochland is a rather special place. And, it just so happens I have papers from a friend of mine who was an SS officer. We knew each other from before the war because we both grew up in the same neighborhood in Berlin. Sadly, he was killed during a terribly bloody battle. But before he died, he made me promise him that I would deliver all of his things to his parents when I got back home. That's why I have his papers."

"So many good German men have died," Pitor shook his head pretending to be sorry, but he was thinking, *too bad they haven't all perished.*

"Yes, he died in my arms."

"I'm so very sorry."

"Me too. He was a good friend and a good soldier. Waffen SS actually. And since it is required that a fellow be an SS officer if he is to be permitted to enter Heim Hochland, I will allow you to use his papers once we arrive there. You see, in order to go to the home for the Lebensborn a fellow must be vetted to have pure German blood. And if a fellow is an SS officer, then he has already been vetted. I assume you are of pure blood, are you not?"

"Of course, I am," Pitor said confidently.

"I can tell by the way you look. You are a pure Aryan."

Pitor nodded. "So I am," he said proudly. "But you still haven't told me what this Lebensborn home is."

"Let me start by saying it's a wonderful way to serve our country. First of all, it honors our Führer and is also a place of great pleasure for our officers."

"Yes, but what exactly is Heim Hochland?"

"It's a program that was set up by Reichsführer Himmler, to increase the population of pure Aryan children. You see, once we have won this war, and I have no doubt we will win, we are going to need many more pure Aryan people to populate and run our new Germany. These superior Aryans will rule the world. And the rest of the people on earth will live to serve them."

"You mean the Jews?" Pitor asked carefully.

"No, I said people, not subhumans like the Jews. Once the war is over, all the subhumans like Jews, homosexuals, Jehovah's witnesses, and gypsies will be gone. They will have been eliminated. I mean people like the Poles or the French, even the Slavic's from eastern Europe. In the New Germany these people will be servants to our Aryan race, slaves if you will. This is as it should be."

"What do you mean the subhumans will be eliminated?"

"Well, this is top secret, so you must never tell anyone, but even right now, there are camps that have been set up where these subhumans are being disposed of."

"You mean murdered?" Pitor tried to hide the horror in his voice.

"Well..." Konrad hesitated for a moment, then lit a cigarette and took a long puff. "Yes. I suppose you might call it murder. However, I don't like to use that word. But getting rid of these destructive elements is a necessary evil. If we are going to build a strong country, we must address the Jewish problem. And this is the only way to handle it."

Pitor looked away. He couldn't risk having Konrad see the look of horror and disgust on his face. "So, you still haven't told me what this home for the Lebensborn is exactly. I don't understand where we are going."

"Ahhh, but you will. At Heim Hochland, fellows who are SS officers are treated like royalty. We have our choice of plenty of very pretty Aryan girls with blonde hair and blue eyes. These girls never refuse our advances, because they want our seed. They too have chosen to serve our Fatherland. And, they are doing their patriotic duty by having children that are fathered by pure Aryan SS officers. Do you know what I am saying to you?"

"It's a brothel then?"

"No, not exactly. It's more like, well, like a breeding farm."

"You mean you breed with these girls?"

"Yes, exactly. We mix our blood with the blood of other pure Aryan's to produce more Aryan children that will eventually take over the world."

"And the women agree to this?'

"Absolutely. They want this as much as we do. They will never show disinterest when you take them to bed. And, for a handsome devil like you, well, these girls will go crazy. You would have to fight them off."

"Me?" Pitor said, "Fight them off?" he really didn't want to go to this strange Nazi breeding farm, but he dared not say so.

"You look so much like me they'll be sure that we are related. And not to sound conceited, but whenever I have gone to one of these homes the girls have gone nuts over me. They love blond haired men who are well built and attractive."

"You are an attractive man, and an important SS officer too. Not me, I'm blond, but I am really just an average looking fellow. And besides, I am not a member of the SS. So, I am going to assume they won't let me in."

"You're right. They wouldn't let you in. But, as I have been trying to tell you, I have a solution for that problem. You haven't been listening." Konrad smiled, then he pulled a pile of things from his pocket. "These are papers that belonged to that friend of mine, the one I was telling you about who was in the Waffen SS. The reason I told you about him was because I was thinking you could use his papers and badges to get into Heim Hochland. Under my supervision, of course."

"Really? That would be so very kind of you. Fighting has kept me away from women for far too long. And I must say, it's rather hard to live without them, if you understand my meaning," Pitor said, trying to sound appreciative of Konrad's efforts.

"Of course, I understand," Konrad smiled.

Pitor smiled back at him. "These girls must offer a great deal of comfort."

"They sure do," Konrad laughed and nudged Pitor's shoulder.

As they walked in silence, Pitor's mind was spinning. He could see all the advantages of having Konrad's friendship. These papers and the numerous badges that belonged to the dead SS officer would provide him with a respectable identity that few would question when he was traveling in Germany. There were three problems with this visit to Heim Hochland. First, the thought of making love to a strange German woman left him feeling cold, and he was afraid that he would not be able to perform. But even if he could get past that, how would he hide his circumcised penis from this girl? Once he took off his pants, there would be no doubt in this girl's mind that he was Jewish, and she would most assuredly report him. And then if he, by some miracle, managed to hide his circumcision, once he and Konrad left this breeding farm, Pitor was sure that Konrad would take the fake papers back. The papers were of the utmost importance to Pitor. Although he still held papers declaring him to be a German soldier, he knew it would be far more advantageous to have the papers of an SS officer.

For now, there was nothing he could do but go along with Konrad's plan until he could find a way out.

"So, for the time being, anyway, you will answer to a new name. Your new name will be Emil Keller. And just to get into the habit you and I should start using this name now, so we don't slip up once we arrive at Heim Hochland."

"All right. I will remember to answer to my new name."

"He was a good man, my friend Emil. You should feel honored to borrow his name, if only for a short time."

"I am truly honored," Pitor said, his voice dripping with sincerity.

They walked a while longer. Then Pitor said, "Your family must be very proud that you are being promoted."

"I never see them." Konrad sighed. "My parents stay in Berlin, and I never married. Sometimes I get lonely and when I do I wonder if perhaps I should find a nice woman and settle down. But I have always been a playboy. I don't suppose I could stop now."

"Me too. I've always been a bit of a playboy. Of course, women never were as wild about me as they have been about you," Pitor said.

"How could you know that?"

"I can tell. You come from a wealthy family."

"I do."

"You speak high German. You don't speak like the working class."

"You're quite observant." Konrad laughed.

"And, you are far more handsome and cultured than I," Pitor said. "I think you have always had your pick of the women you met. Even before the home for the Lebensborn existed."

Konrad smiled, and Pitor could see that Konrad was basking in his flattery. So, Pitor continued speaking, but he was careful with his words. "You will be a bodyguard to the Führer? That's a very important job. Germany's safety and security rests on your shoulders."

"I've thought about that. And I will admit something to you that I don't often admit to anyone. However, if you ever repeat it, I will deny it."

"What is it?" Pitor asked.

"Sometimes I am afraid I won't be able to carry out my mission. I am afraid of failing. I mean, what if something terrible happened to our Führer on my watch? Even if I wasn't tried for treason, which I am sure I would be, I could never forgive myself."

There was a long silence. Then Pitor cleared his throat. "It's only normal to feel that way. You are only human."

"But we—you and I, and all the other Aryan men—are superior men. We don't have the luxury of being just ordinary humans. We must be more than that."

"And you are more. You are so much more. I have only known you for a short time, but I can see that you are a good example of a superior Aryan individual." Pitor said and he noticed Konrad puffed out his chest a little. *Good, this flattery is getting to him. He likes me. And if this is going to work, I need for him to like me and to trust me. It seems to be working. He seems to believe everything I am saying to him.*

They walked along quietly until they came upon a stream. "Let's stop and I'll see if I can catch a fish or two for our dinner," Pitor said.

Konrad nodded. "Fortunately, I have plenty of time before I am required to report to the Eagle's Nest. So, yes, let's stop. I could use some food."

Pitor smiled and sat down beside the stream. They both leaned against the large oak tree and waited. "I wish we had some beers," Konrad said. "It's been a while since I had a good German beer."

"Me too," Pitor said.

"Do you have a girl?" Konrad asked as he picked some leaves off the bottom of his boot.

"I did. But... she died." Pitor said softly, and he felt the bitterness rising in his throat.

"That's a shame," Konrad said. "What happened?"

"She got sick," Pitor lied, turning his face away so Konrad couldn't see his expression.

"I'm sorry."

"Me too."

There were several silent moments, then Konrad said, "I had a girl, but she left me when I was conscripted. I wasn't ready to get married, so I told her that she would have to wait until the war was over. I was just buying time. I don't know if I would ever have married her. But either way it didn't matter because she told me that she couldn't wait until the war was over to get married. So, she married another fellow."

"That's a shame."

"Yes, well it seems to me that women can be so fickle and even foolish when it comes to marriage. They want it now, regardless of who the chap might be." Konrad smiled. "Anyway, from what I have heard, her husband has gotten quite fat. And I suppose that is because he felt guilty as he had very limited vision which made him unable to join the military."

"I wouldn't worry too much. And a handsome fellow like you will have no trouble meeting a new girl," Pitor said. "And I am quite sure that whoever she is, she will be honored to marry a man who is not only handsome, but very successful."

Konrad laughed, "You do flatter me."

"That's because I admire you. Someday, I hope to be as successful as you are."

Konrad smiled then he sighed "Yes, well, I am sure that eventually I will meet someone who I will want to settle down with. That is, if this war is ever over. I can't see the purpose of getting married then leaving your wife so you can go off to fight. In my opinion the reason for marrying is to assure oneself of a nice warm bed partner. Don't you agree?"

Pitor laughed, "Of course." There was a moment of silence, then he added, "As we both know, you are about to be promoted to the very important position of bodyguard to the Führer. I am quite sure that your new job will attract more girls than you will know what to do with. So, you will have more fun than you would have if you had gotten married."

"I'm sure it will attract many women. But even if I were married, I would never have restricted myself to be faithful to one person. I couldn't do that. It's not in my nature. But you're right, I am about to have my pick of some of the prettiest girls in Germany. And that's because women love men who have power. They are like lambs willing to follow a powerful man anywhere."

Pitor nodded. "So, they are." He said, but then he thought of his wife Mila and how high spirited she was, and he missed her even more.

"How about you? Have you thought about your future? I mean once this war is over, what do you plan to do?"

"I must admit, I don't know. I have purposely not allowed myself to think of the future, just in case I don't make it," Pitor admitted, and that was true. He had no idea what he might do next if he found Jakup alive. And if he didn't, well...

"You'll make it through. You're a tough and resilient sort of fellow I can see that in you already, even though we have only spent a short time together. You told me that your father taught you to hunt and fish. Is that correct? Is that how you learned to do it so well?"

"Yes, he was very good at providing food. And he taught me everything he knew. We were poor. My mother and I needed to eat and quite frankly we couldn't afford to go to the market. So, we had to find ways to supply our own food. My mother was quite resilient as well. She planted a vegetable garden which she tended every day. I enjoyed helping her, not because I was a good gardener. I wasn't. I enjoyed being with her because I loved her. I was fortunate, although my father could be harsh at times, I did have a very wonderful mother." This was true. Pitor closed his eyes for a moment and remembered his parents. His father had not been a good man. But when Pitor was very young, before the grip of alcohol took hold of his father, his father had been an excellent hunter and fisherman. Not only that, but he was also a wonderful teacher. When he would take Pitor into the forest with him, Pitor learned survival techniques as they would stay out and hunt for a few days at a time. During this time, his father was young and still had some patience. So, he would try his best to teach Pitor the things he knew. However, Pitor was still very young and had not reached his full height yet. He was a small child and was always afraid of disappointing his father, who was not a warm or loving man. But somehow, even with all Pitor's fears, he had learned everything he needed to know in order to survive in the forest.

"Your father must have been proud to have a son like you. You are big and strong and very capable."

"Actually, I wasn't strong or capable when I was a boy. And quite often my father was disappointed in me." Pitor gave a quick laugh. "At that time, I was the smallest boy in my class at school. It wasn't until I hit puberty that I grew tall and filled out. But by then my father had started drinking and he was a rather mean drunk."

"We are alike in many ways. Not only do we look alike, but I was the same. I was small until puberty. Then boom...I shot up like a cannon." Konrad smiled. "My father was a heavy drinker too. The only difference is that he never taught me anything. Not even when I was small. In fact, I can't remember a time when he wasn't drunk. And..." he hesitated, "he and my mother were always fighting. Their fights would always end with a terrible beating for mother. I was just a child and far too small to help her. That drove me crazy."

Despite his hatred of the Nazis, Pitor found he liked Konrad. He hadn't wanted to like him. It certainly wasn't in the plan. But they had such similar backgrounds that Pitor found he understood him. *I must be very careful not to allow any emotions to get in the way of my plans*. Pitor thought.

The fishing line began to quiver in Pitor's hand. He felt it immediately. Then he felt a strong pull on the line, and he began to pull the fish in. "Looks like we've got one." Pitor said as he lifted the small fish up out of the water. "It's rather small and it won't be enough for the both of us for our daily meal. So, let me try to catch another one."

They sat quietly for a few minutes, basking in the warmth of the ray of sunshine that filtered through the trees. Then there was another tug at the line and Pitor said, "We've got another one."

To Pitor's surprise, Konrad got up and began to gather twigs and tree branches. Then he made a fire. Pitor speared the fish with a tree branch he had sharpened, then he held the fish over the fire and quickly cooked it. Both of their stomachs growled from the smell of charred fish. "Smells wonderful," Konrad said.

"It certainly does. And I am quite hungry."

"Yes, me too."

They sat and ate in silence, careful to avoid the fish bones. Once they were both finished, Pitor thought to himself that he could easily have eaten two or three more fish. But he didn't say anything about it.

"This was a wonderful meal. You know, I had never had such fresh fish until you and I started traveling together," Konrad said. "I'm glad I found you. I owe you a good time at the Lebensborn home. I'll see to it that you have whatever girl you want."

CHAPTER ELEVEN

Under the warmth of the sun, they both closed their eyes and slept. That afternoon, Pitor fished again, and he was fortunate to catch two juicy fish which they cooked and ate. After they were done, they began to walk again. "I think we're getting close to Munich. I can see the city from here. Do you see it?" Konrad asked.

Pitor answered, "Yes."

"Well, we are almost there. Perhaps we might need to walk for another day or two before we reach Steinhoring."

Pitor nodded. He was nervous about going to the Lebensborn home. He was terrified that if he was put in the position of having a sexual encounter, the girl would see his circumcised penis and know that he was a Jew. And that would mean he would be executed for not only impersonating a German but impersonating an SS officer. But he had no other choice but to play along, at least for now. Pitor was sweating as it was a very hot day, and the sun burned his head and shoulders through his uniform. For a moment he closed his eyes and thought about Mila and how glad he was now that he'd granted Mila her wish when she had begged him not to circumcise their son. Her reasoning had nothing to do with religion. In fact, when she had decided that she did not want to circumcise Jakup, she had been unreasonable, almost hysterical. He remembered how she had pleaded with him not to go to the Mohel and set up the circumcision. When he asked her why, she admitted she couldn't bear to see her baby bleed. They both grew up knowing that by refusing to circumcise their little boy, he would never be accepted into the covenant of Jewish men. But Pitor didn't care about what other people thought. He didn't believe any of the religious laws and had never been a follower. That was why he'd always had so much trouble fitting in with the other Jewish fellows in the small village where he met Mila. And so, because it didn't matter to him, and he would have done anything for his wife, Pitor had agreed not to circumcise Jakup. Now, at least wherever Jakup was, no one could tell that he was born a Jew. And this small fact might just save Jakup's life. It might not, but Pitor was hopeful, and he thanked God for this small glimmer of hope, because right now it might just be the only thing that was standing between Jakup and death.

"If you have the right bloodlines, it is a lot easier to get a woman into your bed." Konrad said. "You no longer have to make any promises to them, because they aren't doing it for you. They're doing it for the Fatherland. And when they get pregnant, they don't come looking for you to support the child. They are proud to be having a baby for the Führer. And to make things even better for them, once the child is born, the child is taken away from them leaving them without any responsibilities. So, most of them stay at Heim Hochland and try to get pregnant again."

"Do you have any children that were born at the home for the Lebensborn?" Pitor asked.

"Who knows. None that I know of. But the truth is I probably fathered several. I've been to Heim Hochland at least a handful of times. I try to get there as often as I can."

"I can see why," Pitor said.

"And to add to it, you can be proud of yourself because you are preforming your patriotic duty. You're doing it for your country."

"What happens to the children?"

"These children are given everything they need. They are fed and clothed and cared for. Reichsführer Himmler goes to the home a couple of times each year when he has a special ceremony to give the children names. Once they have been named, they can be adopted by an SS officer and his wife. Only the most reputable officers are permitted to adopt a pure Aryan child from a Lebensborn home. And rightfully so. These children are very precious, they are the future of our country."

"Is Heim Hochland the only home for the Lebensborn?"

"Oh goodness no. There are several in Germany and quite a few in Norway. I also know of a couple in Austria. I have frequented the ones in Germany and Austria. I have heard there is also one in Belgium, and another in France, and a few others scattered across Europe."

"That is a lot of homes."

"Yes, it is."

"Well, there must be plenty of children bred at these places and then adopted each year," Pitor said.

"Well, you see, that has been a problem. The girls are trying, but even so, it seems that there just aren't enough children produced each year."

"Really?"

"Yes, and I'll tell you a secret. Because we need more children, German officers have been sent into Polish neighborhoods to take Polish children who have Aryan qualifications away from their parents and bring them to the Lebensborn homes where we Germanize them."

"Do these Polish parents volunteer to give Germany their children?"

"Never, we have to take them."

"You mean like kidnap them?"

"I suppose you might say that. But, believe me, any child who is kidnaped from a Polish family and raised as a German is in for a far better life. Wouldn't you rather be a German than a Pole?"

"Of course," Pitor smiled. *So, it's true. This is good news for me. I hope that it's possible that some crazy Nazi may have taken Jakup and now they are Germanizing him. I am not happy about this, but at least it would mean he is still alive. But why would a German take a Jewish child? They hate the Jews. It doesn't make sense. Still, I am hopeful.* "Have you ever considered adopting one of these children?"

"I can't. There are two criteria that are necessary when considering adoption of a child from the Lebensborn. First of all, a fellow is required to be an SS officer. And of course, I am. But the second requirement is that a man must be married, and his wife must be as pure an Aryan as he is. Since I am not married, I would not be eligible. But that's all right. What would I do with a child? Once this war is over, I might decide to settle down and have a family. But I doubt it. I must admit there are times that I think I would like to be a family man. However, I know the truth. I really enjoy my freedom and women get in the way of that."

"Yes, I can understand how you feel." Pitor cracked a smile.

"However, this is rather interesting especially since we have been discussing the Lebensborn children," Konrad stopped walking and let a cigarette. He took a long satisfying puff then he went on to say, "From what I understand, a group of children from the Lebensborn home are going to be presented to the Führer at the gala I will be attending at the Eagle's Nest."

"I am assuming that someone is going to be bringing them there. Or have they been living there?"

"No, they don't live at the Eagle's Nest. They live at Heim Hochland. I would assume they will be brought to the gala by the little brown sisters."

"What is a little brown sister?"

"These are girls who live and work at the homes for the Lebensborn. But because they are brown haired and brown eyed, they are not suitable for breeding. Even so, they are required to be of pure

German blood. You see the Führer has a dream of populating his newly conquered world with beautiful blond-haired, blue-eyed children. That was how Himmler came up with this brilliant Lebensborn project. From what I understand, Himmler is going to be presenting these children to our Führer almost like a gift."

"So, you will see them."

"Yes. And, who knows, although I haven't been to Heim Hochland for a little over a year, one of these children could even be mine. However, I must admit, I would never know it."

I'm just praying that one of them is mine. Pitor thought. "Would they already be on their way to the Eagle's Nest?"

"Probably. But who knows. I have no idea when or how they are getting there, but they will be there when the Führer arrives and that is exciting. It will be good to see our Führer happy."

CHAPTER TWELVE

The following afternoon, after walking all night, Pitor and Konrad stopped to rest. They had walked for a long time and not found a stream where Pitor might go fishing. Now, even if they found a stream, it was too late in the day, and the water would be too hot to fish. The fish were more likely to bite at night. "Looks like we are going to have to go to sleep hungry." Konrad sighed, looking down at his stomach. "Well, no matter. We are less than a day's walk from Heim Hochland, and once we are there, they will be so happy to see us that they will treat us like royalty." Konrad paused for a moment, lost in thought, then he continued. "You know, I must admit. I am really looking forward to sleeping in a soft bed with a warm and willing woman. I have been out in the field too long and I am ready to be pampered by an Aryan beauty. How about you?"

"Yes. I am too," Pitor said as he lay down with his arm under his head. He had been careful never to allow himself to fall into a deep sleep since he'd been in the forest. Danger lurked around every corner, and he dared not let his guard down. Especially since he was concerned that Konrad's snoring might attract wild animals. However, it was apparent that Konrad did not feel the same way. He was not worried. He fell asleep almost immediately, as he always did. His snoring began as usual, just a few minutes later.

Pitor listened to Konrad for a while. His snoring was even louder than usual, and Pitor wondered if Konrad's breathing had been affected by his smoking. Pitor sat up so he would not be consumed by exhaustion. *If we are taken prisoner by a partisan group, they will never believe I am not a German. In fact, because Konrad and I look so alike, they would never believe Konrad is not my brother. I must admit that I do like him. He's been kind to me and doesn't act like a Nazi, but I must never trust him. I cannot forget who he is, and who I am. The Nazis killed my beloved, and therefore, I must not be swept away by my emotions. I must do what must be done.*

Pitor lay awake listening to Konrad snore for a long time. It was impossible to rest with everything on his mind, so he looked up at the star-filled sky and thought of Mila. Sometimes, in the summer, they laid together holding hands on a blanket behind their little cottage and counted the stars. *Mila so loved the moon and stars. How innocent we both were then. Never in our wildest imagination could we have thought that a day like today would come. We were certain that we would watch our children grow up as we grew old together. I can remember her teasing me that she would still love me once I was an old man who had lost all my good looks.* He smiled as he let the memory sweep over him, but his cheeks were wet with tears. It was a moonless night, and that made the stars seem to shine even brighter than normal. Pitor thought of Konrad. He knew that even though Konrad treated him like a brother, Konrad was his enemy. And if Konrad ever found out that Pitor was Jewish, he would not hesitate to report him to the authorities despite the fact it would result in Pitor's arrest, or perhaps even his demise. The thought of killing Konrad left his soul feeling conflicted. Staring up into the vastness of the sky, Pitor began to pray silently. He didn't pray for answers. He already knew what he must do. He prayed only for the strength to complete the task.

As the sun began to rise, he knew the time had come. If he did not act soon, it would be too late. Once the women at the Lebensborn saw him and Konrad together, it would become more difficult for Pitor to take on Konrad's identity and pose as him. In the future, when he went to search for Jakup, he would need to have Konrad's credentials to pass through the home for the Lebensborn without scrutiny. It was a long shot that Jakup had been taken to Heim Hochland, but it was the only lead he had, so he must follow it. Pitor sat up silently, then he slowly reached for his gun. The gun Konrad had trusted him with so he could hunt for them both. The metal was cool in his hand as his finger closed around the trigger. *I hate to use a bullet. I may need my ammunition to hunt in the future, and I wish I didn't have to risk sending the sound of gunfire into the atmosphere. It could attract an enemy. But I can't stand the idea of strangling this man, whom I have come to know so well, even though I know he would do it to me if he even suspected I was a Jew. I must force myself to be logical and not to act on emotion. I can see Konrad's knife, and I can easily reach it. If I am swift, I can cut his throat with a single slice. This should kill him quickly and keep his pain to a minimum. Once he is dead, I will take his papers and his uniform coat. Then I will leave mine. Anyone who finds him will think he's a Jew who was posing as a German soldier. And I will be on my way to the Eagle's Nest to claim my promotion as Konrad Hoffmann.*

Ever so quietly, Pitor stood up and moved over to where Konrad lay resting. His hand trembled as he reached for the knife that hung from Konrad's belt. As he quickly pulled the knife out of its sheath Konrad's eyes flashed open. "What is it?" Konrad asked in a whisper as he looked up at Pitor. "Has someone found us?"

Pitor didn't answer. He couldn't answer. This was going to be much harder now that Konrad was awake, and the sun was high enough in the sky for Pitor and Konrad's eyes to meet. Pitor held the knife, but he was shaking so hard he wasn't sure he could complete the task. Konrad was staring at him, still unsure of what was happening. He trusted Pitor completely and was unaware of the danger. *This man trusts me.* Pitor thought. *And now, I must betray his trust.*

There is no point in delaying this any longer. It must be finished soon. For a single second, Pitor looked at Konrad. Then there was a knowing in Konrad's eyes. Suddenly, he realized he had trusted the wrong man. Pitor was his enemy. Konrad let out a scream, but before he finished screaming, Pitor had cut his throat. Konrad lay on the ground dying. A river of blood poured from his wound and soaked the ground as he stared at Pitor, shocked, hurt, and accusing. Pitor felt sick and vomited. He knew he would remember the look on Konrad's face forever. The light of life had almost completely drained out of Konrad's eyes when Pitor lifted Konrad's uniform jacket, which was lying next to his body. Luckily, the blood had not soiled the coat. He put it on and quickly rummaged through the pocket. There was not much there. A few bullets which Pitor kept, Konrad's friend's papers and dog tags, which Konrad had planned to allow Pitor to use to get into Heim Hochland. Pitor decided to leave those papers instead of his own. When Konrad's body was found, it would be believed that he was Rudolf Ziegler. And whoever found him would probably assume he was a deserter. This would be more easily believed than if Pitor had left his own papers. Pitor continued to go through the pockets of Konrad's jacket until he found what he was looking for. Konrad's papers. *This is what I need. I am now Konrad Hoffmann, and I am on my way to the Eagle's Nest where I will assume the job of bodyguard to Hitler. And then I will have infiltrated their world. I will be close enough to their private files to find my little boy.* Pitor wiped the knife clean in the grass and took Konrad's belt off him and strapped it on himself. He slipped on Konrad's jacket and then took one last look at Konrad's body. "Goodbye," Pitor said, careful not to look at Konrad's eyes, which were dull but wide open. Then he added, "I'm sorry I had to do this to you. I know you thought we were friends. But it was impossible for us to be friends, because of who I am, and who you are. Maybe in another place or another time, we might have been real friends. But as fate had it, you hated Jews, and I hate Nazis. So, this is how it ends."

Pitor reached down and took Konrad's gun. Then he turned and disappeared into the blanket of trees that was the forest.

CHAPTER THIRTEEN

Pitor was hoping to find out what he needed to know at the party at the Eagle's Nest. He preferred not to go to the home for the Lebensborn. If he did go to Heim Hochland, the only reason he could give them for being there was to share his Aryan seed. And he wondered if he would even be able to perform, as he had no desire for any of the Aryan women there. His heart still belonged to Mila, and besides, he was circumcised, and it would be a feat to hide that from any girl he had intercourse with. So, he decided first he would go to the gala at the Eagle's Nest that Konrad had told him about. If he could not find out anything about Jakup there, then and only then would he go to Heim Hochland. *But how does one find a place called the Eagle's Nest? Will the people in Munich know where it is? If they do, I am sure they will be happy to direct Sturmscharführer Konrad Hoffmann to his destination.*

Pitor walked out of the forest and on to the open road. He had to take the chance of running into enemy soldiers in order to find his way into Munich. He was fairly certain that he would not come upon any partisans so close to the road. But if he did, he would have another problem. If they thought he was truly a German officer, they would kill him. So, he would somehow have to convince them he was not really an SS officer, and he wasn't sure he could make them believe him. A laugh escaped his lips. It was suddenly funny to him that there were enemies of all sorts surrounding him. And no matter who he met up with on his travels, there was always danger. He began to laugh uncontrollably. *I am going mad. I feel as if I am losing my mind.* He thought. *But if I am found by partisans and I am forced to convince them I am only using the name Konrad Hoffmann to survive, I will show them my circumcised penis. How strange this is, but it seems my penis has become the central most important thing to my survival. To the Nazis, it's evidence that I am a Jew, and they will kill me for it. To the partisans, it is evidence that I am not a Nazi, and it might be my only chance of making them listen to me.* He began to laugh again. Then he saw Mila's face in his mind's eye, and he missed her so much that he began to cry.

Along the way to Munich, Pitor remembered Konrad telling him that sometimes he'd stopped at farmhouses where he was either welcomed inside as an honored guest or permitted to sleep in the barn. Pitor decided it might be nice to sleep somewhere safe for a while. It had been a long time since he'd slept soundly. And it would be nice to do so at least one night. Since he'd left his friends, the partisans, in the forest, he had gotten used to sleeping with one eye open. This was not only due to the wild animals who roamed the forests searching for food, it was also due to all the other dangers he was constantly facing. However, Pitor had another reason he wanted to go to the house of a farmer. And this reason was more pressing. Before Pitor entered a large gala attended by the Führer and filled with Hitler's elite, people who were more dangerous than the wild wolves in the woods, he needed an opportunity to test out his new name and to see if the farmer believed that this was his uniform. If, while they were talking, the farmer questioned him about who he was or where he came from, he would need to be able to answer any questions as if he were really Konrad Hoffmann. So, this was a test. Pitor knew that if he failed, he might be forced to kill an innocent farmer and his family so that they could not turn him in. And he hated the idea of such a thing. But this test was too important to be avoided and so he began to search for a farmhouse.

It was easy to find what Pitor was searching for. There were plenty of farms to choose from as he walked along the road. But each time he saw one, his nerves got the better of him and he could not stop there. So, he kept walking. Finally, after he'd walked for over a mile, he saw a farm with a house set back away from the road. The house was made of brown bricks and wood that had begun to warp. It was badly in need of a paint job. The barn had once been red, but now the paint had faded, leaving the building a shade of pale pink. The farmland itself was overgrown with weeds, and Pitor could see that nothing had been planted there for a while. He walked up and knocked on the door. He should not have been surprised to see that a young woman answered. *By the state this place is in, I doubt that there is a man around. This place has not been tended to in a long time.* There was fear in the woman's pale blue eyes when she looked at him. And he found it strange that she was afraid of him until he reminded himself that he wore the uniform of a member of the SS with lots of impressive and intimidating awards on the shoulder. *I wonder how the Nazis have been treating their own people. I know they are horrible to the Jews. But I never thought a German woman would fear one of her own soldiers. Yet, this woman looks terrified of me.* The woman was young. Her blonde hair was caught up in a bun, and she was as thin as a reed. Pitor noticed her hands. Her nails were bitten to the quick, and she trembled a little as she held on to the side of the door. She was not a beauty by any means, but she was not ugly either. He decided she might have been pleasant looking before she had become so thin. "How can I help you?" the woman's lips trembled as she asked nervously. Tiny pieces of her hair stuck to her forehead with sweat. Her small, pale white hands were trembling.

Pitor realized he hadn't expected a woman to answer the door, and he felt bad because he hadn't meant to scare her. All he had planned was to ask for a hot meal and whether he might take refuge in her barn that night.

"Yes," Pitor said, his voice was gentle. "My name is Sturmschar-führer Konrad Hoffmann." He felt foolish when he said his newly acquired title out loud. "I am an officer in the German army." He saw her eyes flash with fear again. So, he added "And please know that I mean you no harm..."

She interrupted him with a shaking voice, "I already gave every-thing that I had from this year's harvest to the German army. I have no more food to give you. Everything I grew in my garden is gone. I have only what was given to me to use for my mother and myself. Please, won't you go away now?"

"Of course, I will go if you want me to. But I did not come to take your food. I came to ask for a place to sleep and maybe a meal if you can spare it. I would be happy to sleep in your barn if that would be all right. I will be gone in the morning." *I never knew that the Nazis took all the food that their farmers produced. But it doesn't surprise me.*

She seemed to look deep inside of him as she stared into his eyes for several moments in silence. He was nervous, because he had no idea what she might be thinking. Then her eyes softened, and she opened the door and said, "Come in."

Pitor entered the house. It was impeccably clean, but sparsely furnished. From what he could see, this woman had been poor even before the war started. "Where is your family?" he asked.

"My husband is a soldier," she said. "I haven't heard from him in over a year." Then he saw her eyes fill with tears.

"Please don't hurt me. I am just a woman with a sick old mother to care for."

"I would never hurt you," he said, feeling sorry for her. When he'd stopped at this place, he'd been hoping that whoever was behind the door was going to feed him and allow him to stay at least for the night. But now that he saw this skinny, helpless girl, he felt bad about asking her for food. Gently, he said, "I am an excellent hunter. I will go and see if I can bring back something for us if you can prepare it for dinner?"

She nodded. And he wasn't sure, but he thought he saw gratitude in her eyes.

When Pitor returned three hours later with two large possums, she was waiting with a pot in front of her. Inside the pot were two potatoes cut up in cubes, half of a head of cabbage, and an onion, both chopped into bite-size pieces. But when she saw the possums, the girl began to weep. "Are you all right?" Pitor asked.

The woman was shaking all over, but she tried to put on a brave front. Standing as tall as her five feet would allow, she nodded and said, "Yes, yes of course, I'm fine."

However, Pitor saw her tears continued to flow. "Can you clean these or shall I do it? I don't mind." he asked, remembering how Mila hated to clean animals he'd brought back when he went hunting.

"No, I'm fine, really. I'm fine, and I can do it," the girl said in a small voice.

He shook his head. "You don't look fine. You look upset," he said gently.

"I'm sorry. I'm a silly sentimental woman. Forgive me. It's just that it's been so long since my mother and I had meat of any kind," she said, shaking her head. "Oh, just listen to me go on about all my problems. I am sorry. I am sure that none of this matters to you."

"Don't say that. I understand how hard it must have been for you. It's been hard on everyone."

"Yes, it is so very hard," she apologized again. "I want to thank you. You did a wonderful job of bringing home meat for us to eat today. Forgive me for getting emotional. I am sorry. I will clean it right away."

"It's all right. I understand. I'll take care of it."

"No, no, really. I can do it," she said, wiping the tears away from her face with the back of her hand.

He smiled. "It's fine. Please don't worry about it. I'll tell you a little secret if you want to hear it."

She nodded, and he thought she looked like a little girl.

"I never enjoyed hunting. I hate to kill things, but I realize we must eat. If we don't eat, we will die."

She nodded again. Then she said, "I lied to you."

"Oh?"

"I am not married. I don't have a husband in the army."

He gave her a soft smile.

She returned his smile. "I did have a brother though. He died very young. I think it was because we never had enough food, and he was always so weak."

"I wish I could have been here to help," Pitor said honestly. "Losing a family member is a terrible thing."

"Yes, it truly is. I miss him, and I miss my father who died recently as well. Losing my father was hard, but he was old. My brother was so young. He had his whole life ahead of him. I don't know if I'll ever get over losing him."

"You might not. However, the pain will dull with time, and you will be all right. You'll find a way to live with it," he said, but he was thinking of Jakup and Mila, and he didn't think he would ever get over losing them. And even if he found Jakup, his life would not be the same without Mila. He was sure he would never really be happy again. However, he didn't want to upset this young girl any more than she was already, so he tried to change the subject. In a voice as cheerful as he could muster, he asked, "By the way, I don't know what to call you. What's your name?"

"Steffi." She said. "Steffi Seidel."

He smiled at her as she took the two possums from him. "My wife used to hate it when I went hunting. She couldn't stand the sight of the dead animals. So, I always cleaned them. And I don't mind taking care of it now."

She shook her head. "No. Please allow me to do it," she said as she began to skin the possums. Then she glanced over at him and asked, "I'll bet you can't wait to get home to your wife, can you?"

He looked away from her. He hadn't wanted to tell her anything about his real life. After all, he was living under an assumed name and when he arrived at the farmhouse, he'd had every intention of only sharing information about Konrad's past. But when this young woman mentioned his wife, something inside of him ached and he blurted out a truth that he had meant to keep. "My wife passed away." As soon as the words left his lips, Pitor chastised himself. *What is wrong with me? Why did I mention Mila? This should never have happened. How could I forget that when I am wearing this uniform, I am not Pitor any longer? I am Konrad and Konrad was never married. I must be sure that I remember that when I am at the Eagle's Nest. I doubt that this young woman cares. She is just trying to make conversation. But at the Eagle's Nest, a mistake like this could be very damaging. In fact, it could be fatal. I am sure that is because I am going to be doing a very important job. Everything about my life will be examined carefully. This is just a warning, but I must remember it and make sure it doesn't occur again at the wrong place or time.*

"What happened to her?" She asked gently, pulling him back to the moment and out of his own thoughts.

"I'm sorry? What do you mean?" He said, for the moment he'd forgotten their previous conversation.

"Your wife. What happened to her?"

"Oh, yes, my wife. She was sick," he lied, speaking quickly and trying to dismiss her question. He had made an error and now he did not want to discuss his wife any further. Then he was relieved when they were distracted by the sound of a woman's voice that called out from somewhere in the back of the house.

"Steffi. Steffi. Come here now. I need you," the voice said.

"Excuse me, please. It's my mother. I must go to her. I'll be back in a moment."

Pitor nodded and watched Steffi as she hurried out of the kitchen, then down a hallway and disappeared into a room at the back of the house. He sighed as he sat down at the kitchen table and continued to prepare the meat he had brought back from his hunt. Once he finished cleaning the meat and cutting it into bite-size pieces, he put it into the stew pot with the vegetables that she was simmering.

Almost half an hour later, Steffi returned to the kitchen to find Pitor standing over the simmering pot. A wonderful smell of food filled the house. She looked at him and full of gratitude. "Thank you for putting up the stew. I got tied up taking care of my mother. It happens rather often, I'm afraid. She is ill and very needy these days," Steffi whispered.

"Of course. I understand," He smiled, stirring the pot. "Everything is done. And you look tired. So, why don't you go and lie down for a bit. I'll keep watch on this pot while it cooks, and then I will call you when dinner is ready."

"Are you sure?" She asked.

"I'm sure," he said, smiling.

CHAPTER FOURTEEN

When the meat was fully cooked, and the vegetables were soft, Pitor knocked on the door to the bedroom he had seen Steffi walk into. However, there was no answer. He knocked again. Again, there was no answer. So, he opened the door and walked in. He hoped that his entering her bedroom would not give Steffi the wrong idea. Pitor liked Steffi, she seemed like a nice person. But even though he was a widower, his heart still belonged to Mila, and he thought it probably always would. *I am not looking for a lover. Especially not a German girl.* So, he was glad to find that Steffi was fully dressed and asleep on the bed beside her mother when he walked into the room. "Dinner is ready," he whispered softly, not wanting to startle her. She was sleeping so soundly that she did not awaken, and for a moment, he was afraid she had taken something and ended her life. Pitor shook Steffi's shoulder gently. "Steffi..." he said, "I hate to wake you, but dinner is ready." Because she was not used to hearing a male voice in the house, she was startled. Pitor could tell because she sat up quickly, her head darting around nervously. "It's all right," he assured her in a gentle voice. "It's just me coming to let you know that the stew is ready to eat." Steffi breathed a sigh of relief as she relaxed. She remembered who Pitor was, and what he was doing in the house. Then she climbed out of the bed quietly, so as not to awaken her mother.

"I have my own room, but sometimes I like to sleep beside my mother. Because she has been so sick, I know that she doesn't have long to live. I want to spend as much time with her as I can."

"Of course you do. It's understandable. Goodbyes are very hard. I don't think we ever get used to them," he said.

She stopped walking and looked up into his eyes for a long moment, then she said, "You aren't like any of the other SS officers that have come by here. You are kind."

He shrugged. He was glad to be kind, but he was disappointed because he'd failed his own test. Pitor was not passing for a typical Nazi officer.

Steffi followed Pitor into the kitchen. "Please sit down. You have done all the cooking. Let me serve dinner, and then I will clean up when we have finished," she said, smiling as she took a ladle off a hook and spooned out a bowl of stew for each of them. "If it's all right with you, I would like to bring a small bowl to my mother when she awakens. She doesn't eat very much. I promise you," she said.

"It's all right," he said. "I insist that you bring her a bowl." He sat down at the table across from Steffi, and they both began to eat.

"This is really very delicious," she said as she closed her eyes and smiled, inhaling the fragrance of the stew. "I can't remember the last time I had any meat."

"I can't remember the last time I ate sitting at a table," Pitor admitted. "It's nice."

"Yes, it is. It's also nice to have a man here to help bring food into the house. For a long time, it was only me bringing anything in, and all I had was what I could forge from my vegetable garden."

He smiled. "I'm glad I could be of help."

When they finished eating, Pitor asked if he might sleep in the barn that night.

"I know it's spring, but it still gets cold at night. You may prefer to sleep in the living room. I don't mind. I think you will find it far more comfortable," she said. "I'll bring you a warm blanket."

"Thank you. This is very kind of you." Pitor said as he began to take off his jacket and boots.

CHAPTER FIFTEEN

Pitor had meant to leave the following morning. But when he entered the kitchen, Steffi was standing at the stove. She had just prepared a hunk of bread with freshly made jam from berries she had picked this morning. His stomach growled as he looked at the plate of food. Pitor was hungry. He'd slept well for the first time in a long while. It was nice to sleep soundly without listening for animals or enemies who might kill him as he slept. Now, as he sat down at the table and began to eat, he realized he was not in a hurry to get back on the road. *I have almost a week before Konrad is expected to arrive at the Eagle's Nest for that party. I know that this is a big promotion and therefore I, posing as Konrad, must be sure to arrive on time. I doubt my son will be there, but at least once I am at the party, I might be able to find out more about the children that are being taken, and the Lebensborn program. I might learn if Jakup was taken to be a part of it, and where he might be now.* Pitor took a deep breath in and steadied himself. *I must remind myself that this is little more than wishful thinking. I can't be sure that the Lebensborn program has anything to do with Jakup. My little boy might well be with his mother. If it is so, I will take my own life and join them. However, in*

*case he was taken by a Nazi for this Germanization program, I will
search for him.*

"Have you ever heard of the Eagle's Nest?" He asked Steffi.

"Of course," Steffi said as she removed her apron and sat down
across from him at the table. Her plate was nearly empty, and he realized she'd given him most of the bread. He tried to control his
gobbling of the food, but it was nearly impossible. "Please know that
we don't have food all the time," she said, and he realized she was
nervous, probably afraid he would think she was hiding food from the
German army. And he assumed she probably was. But of course, he
didn't care. Now he knew the Nazis were confiscating most of the
produce from the local farms, he figured most of the farmers were
hiding whatever they could. If only he could tell her the truth about
who he was, she would relax. However, he dared not. It was far too
risky to trust her. Even though she was kind to him, she was still a
stranger. And he must never forget, she was, after all, a German.

"How far would you say we are from the Eagle's Nest?"

"I don't know. If you are walking, perhaps you are several days
from there. But I have a friend who owns a truck. He is my neighbor,
I am sure he will take you there, if that's where you need to go. It's no
more than a day's drive from here."

"So, we are in the outskirts of Munich then?"

"Yes, we are."

"I have been walking for a long time and sometimes it is easy to
get lost when you are not walking on the roads."

"I understand. The Eagle's Nest is up in the mountains. I hear it's
very beautiful. But I have never been there. Have you?" she asked.

"No, actually. I've not been there before. I am on my way to a
party there where I am expected, because I am to accept a job
promotion."

"Oh?" she said. And he could see that she was choosing her
words carefully. "I hope it is not rude for me to ask any questions
about your promotion."

"Not at all," he said, smiling.

"Well then, what will your new job be?" she asked.

"I am to be a personal bodyguard to the Führer."

She looked away. "My goodness, but that is quite an honor. You must be a very important man."

He shook his head as he thought about Konrad Hoffmann. "No, not really. I suppose you could say I am just a good solider."

"I would assume you are in a very high up position to be considered for such a job. After all, you are a Sturmscharführer," she said. He knew she was trying to flatter him, and he realized she was still afraid of him. She had given him bread, which he was sure was hard to come by. He assumed she flattered him so he would not look too closely for any food that she might have hidden.

"You needn't call me Sturmscharführer," Pitor said warmly. He hated to see her fear him, and he no longer wanted to convince her he was a dangerous SS officer. Pitor felt sorry for her. He wanted her to feel safe. "We are friends. You treated me very well, and I appreciate your hospitality. My name is Konrad. Please, won't you call me Konrad?" he asked.

She smiled, "I will call you Konrad."

"Good. And I will call you Steffi, instead of Frauline Seidel, if that's all right with you?"

"I'd like that," she said.

Once he'd finished eating, he stood up and carried his plate to the sink.

"No need for you to do that. You go and sit down in the living room. I'll clean up," she said.

"Are you sure?"

"Of course, I am sure. But thank you for offering. Your mother would be proud of you. She certainly raised you right."

The mention of his mother warmed his heart. It had been a long time since he'd thought of her, and Steffi's words melted him. "Thank you. That means a lot to me. My mother and I were very close."

She smiled. "I can tell. I can tell you are a good son."

CHAPTER SIXTEEN

The following morning Pitor went hunting. He brought back a rabbit and a squirrel. Then he cleaned and prepared the meat, so she might roast it for dinner. She brought a few soft potatoes and a carrot into the kitchen, where she cut them up and roasted them along with the meat.

After dinner, he and Steffi went for a walk. As they walked, they talked about their lives. But Pitor found that every word he said about his past was a lie. He was telling Steffi a life story, but he was not telling her about *his* life. He was sharing what he knew about Konrad's life. And he wasn't sure she was telling him the truth, either. Still, it was nice to walk amongst the newly flowering trees and the tiny blades of new grass. It all gave him a strange feeling of well-being. Pitor knew it was unwarranted to feel any degree of safety. Even so, the coming of spring was making him feel hopeful.

The following day, they ate early, so it was early evening when they took their walk. As they did, they came upon a pond. The sun was just setting, and it was not yet dark. In the last light of day, Pitor took a moment to look at the pond more closely. "I see fish," he said happily. "I can go fishing in the morning and try to catch something for our dinner."

"That would be lovely," she said. "I don't know if I have thanked you for all the hunting you've done over the past few days."

"You have. You have thanked me numerous times. However, no thanks is needed. We both have to eat."

"So, your father was a hunter?" She said as she smiled but he thought he detected nervousness in her voice.

"I wouldn't say he was a hunter. But he knew how to find food, and he taught me. He could fish, and he could hunt. He even kept a small garden by the side of our house when I was young." He longed to tell her how his father had been a decent man until he started drinking too much. But he couldn't tell her anything that was true about his past. After all, she must never know that he was Pitor, a Jew. She must always think he was Konrad Hoffmann, a German Sturmscharführer. It had been years since he'd thought about his parents. He'd told Mila a little about them, but he and Mila were so young and so much in love that the hurt he'd felt over his father's drinking no longer seemed important. Pitor remembered he experienced so much joy in his marriage, there had been no room for past pain. Now, with Mila gone and all the wonder and happiness they had once shared seeming so far away, he found himself thinking about his childhood, and wishing he could talk to Steffi honestly.

CHAPTER SEVENTEEN

Steffi seemed to have an easier time cleaning the fish than she did cleaning the animals that Pitor brought back from hunting. So, Pitor vowed that while he was still staying with Steffi, he would go fishing instead of hunting. He preferred fishing to hunting anyway, so he was glad to have found the little pond. He got up early in the morning, just before sunrise, and got dressed quietly. Then he left the house and walked to the pond carrying another makeshift fishing pole he'd fashioned from a tree branch.

The morning air was fresh and cool as he dug in the ground, searching for worms to use as bait. *I think I might have enjoyed living on a farm with Mila and Jakup. It's a demanding life, but I love the outdoors, and I think it would have been a wonderful place to raise a child.* A sadness came over him. *Ahh, but the truth is I would have loved any life at all, if I had my family to share it with me. Damn, I miss my wife and son.* He sat down beside the pond and threw his line in the water. Then he looked up at the sky as the sun made her morning entrance. The sky lit up with golden rays as they began to filter through the treetops and into the sparkling pool of water, making diamond-like reflections. Birds of all colors and all songs, chirped in the nearby trees. Pitor sighed. There was a peaceful aura that surrounded everything in the early morning. *Sometimes, when I am out here alone, even if it is only for a little while, I close my eyes and I make believe that the war was only a nightmare, and I will go home to my wife and son.* Pitor felt tears burning the back of his eyes and he was glad to be alone. There was a tug at his line, and he began to reel it in. But when it surfaced, it was only an old piece of wood which he quickly dislodged. Then he tossed the line back into the water and leaned back against a large oak tree where he waited, hoping a fish would begin to tug. Fishing had always been a time of quiet and sweet contemplation for Pitor. When he was just a boy and went fishing alone for the first time, he found he enjoyed it because it was a relaxing quiet time where he could easily lose himself in thought. When he was younger, his thoughts were always pleasant. However, today he was trying to resist the desire to become consumed by his loss of Mila. He wished he could turn back the clock to a time when she was still with him. Remembering her last words and the promise he'd made to her to find their son brought his thoughts to Jakup. Pitor remembered the day Jakup was born. His heart swelled with love and pain as he recalled Mila's eyes shining as he held Jakup in his arms. How they had both loved that little boy who had brought even more joy and laughter into their beautiful lives. Pitor felt alone and empty. "If he is alive, I will find him, Mila. I will find him and then I will find a way to keep him safe. But I will never get over losing you. Never." He whispered to no one but the birds in the trees and to the fish in the pond. He would have been happy to stay at this farm forever if he did not have a mission to accomplish. But tomorrow he was leaving. Tomorrow, he would be on his way to Eagle's Nest. A soft sigh escaped his lips as he watched a small brown sparrow pluck a worm from the ground. *Nature does not bow down in fear of Hitler. It goes on just as if there were no Führer trying to rule the world and destroy the Jewish race.* A little over a half hour later, as he was humming softly to himself, he felt a tug on his line and hoped he'd caught his first fish of the day. He'd learned early never to take more than he needed from nature. And so, he planned to take only two fish from the pond. The line tugged harder, and he reeled the shiny fish on to the shore. Then he threw his line back into the water and a few minutes later, he got his second bite. Now he had two fish, and he was ready to return to the farm. It was still very early morning when Pitor tossed the remaining worms into the pond and got up. After brushing off his uniform, Pitor began to walk back. Unfortunately, time was ticking and Pitor, who was usually calm, found that he was nervous about leaving to attend this social event where all the guests were high-ranking officials in the Nazi Party. He hadn't thought of this before, but it was very possible that someone could attend this event who knew Konrad Hoffmann personally. For a moment Pitor shivered as he imagined a Nazi in a uniform very much like the one he was wearing right now, standing up in front of Hitler and all the rest of Hitler's officials and pointing at Pitor, then calling out "Who is this imposter? He is not Konrad Hoffmann. I know Konrad Hoffmann personally. You see I served with Konrad Hoffmann in the army, and I tell you, this man is not him," Pitor shivered for a moment then he thought, *What am I afraid of? I am not afraid of dying. So, what will it matter if they find out that I am a fraud? The only thing that worries me is that if I am dead and Jakup is alive, what will happen to him? He will grow up to be one of them. And that thought is unbearable.*

Pitor really was not afraid to die. But he knew how cruel the Nazis could be. They were experts when it came to torture and suffering, and that made him hope he would never find himself at their mercy. Even if his son was not among the children who Hoffmann had said Himmler planned to bring to the gala, at least Pitor would be in the company of people who might be able to give him some information about where he might find Jakup. *I am walking right into the lion's den.* He thought. Pitor had always taken bible stories with a grain of salt, but right now he wished he could make himself believe the bible story about Daniel and the lions. A story his mother had told him when he was just a child. Pitor smiled as he remembered his pretty and gentle mother. His mother had made that story about Daniel so compelling that even though he didn't quite believe it, he asked her to repeat it over and over.

Since Mila died, Pitor had found that he was having a hard time believing that there was a God. When Mila was alive, her lovely reassuring smile and positive attitude convinced him that someday they would find their son again. But now he was angry and depressed, and he was fighting to believe that there truly was a God. He constantly asked himself if there was a God, how could he take Mila and Jakup away from him? *Perhaps God is vengeful. Perhaps he was angry, and he is punishing me for the early years of my life when I did not adhere to his laws. I was such a rebel. Maybe I shouldn't have been so willful. If I could go back, I would do anything to protect my family, anything at all.* Pitor sighed. He realized all this thinking was pointless. He was going to the Eagle's Nest and if there was a God, he prayed He would grant him a miracle and he would find his little boy alive. After he collected his two fish and his makeshift pole, Pitor made his way back to the farmhouse. He entered quietly without knocking because it was still very early in the morning, and he wasn't sure if Steffi would be awake yet. He took the fish into the kitchen, where he planned to clean them. But before he could begin to clean the fish, he heard shuffling noises coming from the living room. Thinking that Steffi was usually not awake this early, so perhaps a thief had entered the house, he took his gun with him as he carefully entered the living room.

That was when he saw them. Two young people, a boy and a girl, both very thin, dirty, and frightened. He thought the girl appeared to be about fifteen years old and the boy looked to be about nine, even though they were both small for their age. The girl turned and saw him. She stared at him wide eyed, her mouth gaping open with fear. She reached over and tugged on the boy's sleeve. Although she did not say a word, Pitor could see that she had started to cry softly. The boy stood up and bravely said, "Leave us alone or I swear I will kill you." For a brief moment Pitor smiled, because anyone could see that the child was so small and thin he would have had a difficult time killing an insect. The terror in the boy's eyes when he was trying to appear brave, made Pitor sorry and ashamed that he had wanted to laugh. He felt bad for these two children, even though he had no idea who they were. He wished he could say something comforting, but then he remembered he was wearing a Nazi officer's uniform, and he knew that was why they were so afraid.

"I am Konrad," Pitor said gently, trying to put the children at ease. "Who are you?"

Just then Steffi entered the room. When she saw the boy and girl, she shook her head and her shoulders slumped. Then, in an angry tone, she said to them, "What are the two of you doing? You know better than to just come out here. I told you to stay put. I told you that he was only going to be here for one more day. Why would you come upstairs? Why? You've caused us a lot of trouble. I wish you would have listened to me."

"I'm sorry, Steffi," the girl said. She was wringing her hands.

"I'll kill him. I'll kill him. I swear I will," the boy said.

"You will do no such thing, Asher. Now hush your mouth," Steffi said angrily.

"I think you should tell me what is going on here," Pitor said to Steffi. Then he noticed that the teenage girl wore a small but shiny Star of David on a thin chain that hung around her neck. He glanced over at Steffi, and he knew why she was nervous sometimes. Steffi had been hiding Jews. If he really had been a Nazi officer, this was an offence that would be punishable by death.

Steffi was shaking. He looked at her slender white hands with the prominent blue veins and he felt sorry for her. She tried to speak to him, but she was stuttering, unable to make a full and coherent sentence.

"I see what is going on here," Pitor said, shaking his head.

"Please, I am begging you. Please Sturmscharführer, let us be. Please just go away and let us be. You seem to be kinder than the others who have come here. Please, I am begging you, don't turn us in. These two are just children. They were my neighbors. When their parents were taken away, they didn't know what to do. They came to me. What could I do? I couldn't let them be arrested. I had to help them. Please, leave us. I am begging you. I will do whatever you ask of me. Whatever you ask," Steffi's face had turned crimson with embarrassment, and he could see that she was ashamed of the proposition she'd just made to him. She was wringing her hands, and tears had begun to stream down her cheeks. "Please, Sturmscharführer, have mercy on us. These two are young, they cannot pose any threat to you."

He sucked in a deep breath. *I wasn't planning on telling anyone what I am up to, but they are all so afraid of me I must tell them the truth.* "It's all right," Pitor said, softly and gently. "It's all right." Then he removed the jacket of his uniform, leaving himself standing in the living room wearing only a dirty white undershirt. "I am not a Nazi. My real name isn't Konrad Hoffmann. My real name is Pitor Barr. I am a Jew. I am wearing this uniform, because I killed Sturmscharführer Konrad Hoffmann and took it. When I leave here, I am going to a gala where I will pretend I am the Sturmscharführer so that I can infiltrate the Nazis. You see, one of them stole my son when my late wife and I were imprisoned in the Warsaw Ghetto. I must penetrate their group of elite SS officers so I can try to find out what happened to my little boy."

No one moved. The only sound in the room came from a woodpecker who was incessantly pecking at a tree outside. Steffi stared at Pitor. She did not speak, but she stopped crying. The teenage girl grabbed the little boy's hand, and they both stared in Pitor's direction. Pitor cleared his throat, then he said, "I am not going to hurt you. And of course, I will not turn you in. However, you two should know that you were very careless to come upstairs. Times are dangerous right now. You not only put yourselves in danger, but you also endangered Steffi. If I had been a real Nazi, the three of you would have been arrested. I know you two are young, but if you are going to survive, you must be more careful."

Steffi swallowed hard. "I had no idea," she said as she looked directly at Pitor. "But I should have guessed. You are too kind and too considerate to be one of them. Still, you look so very German in that uniform."

"Well, that's good to know," he smiled, "it means that hopefully I will pass for a Nazi when the time comes."

They all laughed. It was a nervous laugh, but also one of relief.

"What are your names?" Pitor asked the two young people.

"I'm Zita," the teenage girl said, "and this is my younger brother Asher."

"Hello, Zita and Asher. It's nice to meet you both. But like I said, you must not be so careless in the future."

CHAPTER EIGHTEEN

Zita and Asher spent most of their time hiding in the basement, under a floorboard in the living room. But that night they came upstairs to eat with Pitor and Steffi. This little makeshift family made Pitor miss Mila and Jakup even more. *Does the pain of loss ever subside, even a little?* He asked himself.

That night after everyone had gone to bed, Pitor lay on the sofa staring at the ceiling. He couldn't sleep. Every time he closed his eyes, he saw a room filled with Nazis and his blood ran cold. *Jakup? Where are you, my son? Where are you?*

In the light from the moon that filtered through the large picture window over the sofa, Pitor saw Steffi enter the living room wearing a robe. She walked over to the sofa and stood beside Pitor. He sat up to make room for her to sit down. But she didn't sit. Steffi stood in front of him and let her robe drop to the floor. She was naked.

Pitor shook his head remembering the promise she'd made to him that she would do anything he wanted if he would just not turn them in. "No," he said. "This isn't necessary. Really."

"I'm not doing it because it's necessary. I'm doing it because I want to."

He shook his head, but he didn't know if she could see that in the darkness. His hands trembled as he stood and picked up her robe. Then he helped her to put it back on. She cooperated with him, but then she whispered, "I know it must have been hard for you to lose your wife. You must be very sad and lonely."

"I am, but I am not ready to be with another woman. I don't think I ever will be. I miss my wife, she was my one true love."

"It must have been wonderful to have been loved by a man like you."

"You are a beautiful woman. Why did you never marry?" he asked.

"I never found anyone like you," she said, her voice barely above a whisper.

"That's the sweetest thing anyone has ever said to me."

"Make love to me Pitor. I won't expect anything else from you. I have been alone for a long time, and it has been so nice to have a man around. It would mean a lot to me. You see, Pitor. I am not so young anymore, but I am still a virgin."

"I don't know if I can, Steffi," he said honestly.

"Try? That's all I ask of you." She coughed. "I don't want to die a virgin, Pitor. And let's face facts. I could die any day. Death lurks around every corner."

He nodded in the darkness. "All right," he said. He knew that what she said was true. Life was very fragile, and in the world that they lived in, it was even more fragile. They were always just a breath away from dying.

Pitor began to make love to Steffi, and he was surprised at how responsive his body was to her. It had been a long time since he'd made love to a woman, and nature took over. He was gentle even though once he started, every part of him wanted to devour her.

Once it was over, she fell asleep beside him. But he did not sleep for a single moment the entire night. It puzzled him that his own physical needs could make him do this and betray the memory of his wife. *Mila, I am sorry. You are my love, my always and forever bashert.*

He reached around and felt that the sofa beneath him was wet. He dipped his hand in the wet part and then looked at it in the early morning light. What he saw was a small stain of wet blood. *I am not surprised. I knew she was telling the truth when she said she was a virgin.*

As the sun rose higher in the sky, Pitor finally fell asleep. When he awakened an hour later, Steffi was in the kitchen preparing food. He lay there quietly on the sofa and watched her as she carried a tray of food to her mother's room and then one to the children downstairs. On her way back to the kitchen, she stopped to check on Pitor. Steffi smiled at him when she saw he was awake. "Thank you for last night. It meant a lot to me," she said.

"It meant a lot to me too." He said, but then he added, "I want you to know this because I am leaving today. And...well...we probably won't see each other again."

"I know. I knew before anything happened between us. I knew it when I went to you last night. But please believe me, it's all right. It was what I wanted," she said softly.

"But why, Steffi? Why me?"

"Because you are the kind of man I want to spend my life with. And I won't settle for less. Even if I could only have one night with you, it was worth it."

"You amaze me. I am really not special in any way."

"You're kind, and you care about others. That's unusual these days. Most people only care about themselves."

He didn't know what to say. So, he turned away.

"Really Pitor, it's all right." She said smiling. "Now, come and eat before you leave. At least I will know you had a full stomach when you left here."

He nodded. "Thank you." He said sincerely. "Just let me wash my face first. I'll be right back."

"I'll have your breakfast on the table when you return," she smiled and walked into the kitchen.

CHAPTER NINETEEN

Steffi prepared Pitor's last breakfast with her. She tried her best to make it special. She scrambled the last two eggs she had saved until she was to receive her next set of rations, and she fried two potatoes that she had buried before the Nazis took most of the vegetables from her garden.

Pitor knew she wanted him to have the best she could offer because eggs were not easy to come by. She even poured him a cup of real coffee instead of the coffee made from acorns that most people had gotten used to since the war began. He wanted to say that she should not have given him all her best food, but it was so wonderful to have such delicacies that all he could muster was, "Thank you, this is more than I would ever have expected."

She smiled. "I had a little bit of coffee that I hid when the soldiers came. I wanted you to have it."

He returned her smile. "You needn't have done that," he said. But Pitor could see in her eyes that Steffi was falling in love with him. He thought that it would have been nice if he could have returned her feelings. Since Mila's death, he felt empty and alone all the time. *I am glad to have had the kind of love that Mila and I shared, even if I suffer harder for losing her. I know that no matter where I go or what I do for the rest of my life, my heart will always belong to Mila. Steffi is a good person, but I have no love to give another woman. Even though Mila said she wanted me to find love and marry again, I know that for me, that is impossible. Until I die and my wife, my bashert, and I are reunited in death, I suppose it is my destiny to walk on this earth alone.* "Thank you for everything," he said sincerely. "You are a good woman, and I hope that you find someone who is deserving of you." He took a sip of the coffee. It had been a long time since he'd tasted real coffee, and the rich flavor and aroma were wonderful. "Share this with me. Please. I don't feel right about drinking it all."

"All right." She said. Smiling, she took a cup and poured herself a small amount of the hot, dark liquid. Then she sat down beside him and said, "Thank you for coming here. Your arrival at my house has changed the way I look at things. Until you came, every day was dark and lonely for me. As you know, my mother is very sick. She is withering away. I can see that she is dying, and I have had to accept that it's only a matter of time before I will have to say goodbye to her. The only thing I had in this world to keep me going was the two youngsters I had hidden. But now that I have met you, I know that love is possible for me. Please don't take this wrong. I know you do not plan to stay, and I know that you do not choose to be the man I will love. But you have shown me that there are still good men in the world, and now that I have seen this, I have hope. I will search for someone like you. For a long time, I thought I was dead inside. Now I know I am not, and it feels good to be alive."

"Why, may I ask, would you be dead inside? You are such a young and very special woman."

"It's a long story. I don't want to burden you. I'd rather you leave here thinking of me as a good memory."

"You don't have to tell me anything you don't want to tell me. But if you need to talk, I will listen. And no matter what you have to say, the time I spent here with you will always remain a good memory to me."

"All right. I will tell you," she said, sipping her coffee. "When I was a child, I saw my father hit my mother all the time. He was very unkind to her. When I asked her why she put up with his terrible treatment of her, she said it was because she loved him. He hurt her, but she still loved him. This made me afraid to ever allow myself to love anyone that deeply. My father's behavior made me afraid of men. So, when I got old enough to marry, I avoided it. I dreamed of going to live in the city. I wanted to get a job in a shop or an office somewhere and make my own way. But life had other plans for me. My mother loved my father so much that when he died, she refused to eat, and she couldn't sleep. Then she got sick. I know it sounds crazy for her to have cared so deeply for a man who treated her so horribly, but she did. And once she became ill, she grew weak very quickly. I knew that she could not live here alone. She needed me to care for her. So, I couldn't just leave and move to the city. I had to stay and care for her. I planned to sell the farm when she passed. But then the Nazis came and that was when they rounded up all my Jewish neighbors and took them away. I am several miles away from the next farm and I probably wouldn't have known anything about the arrests of the Jews, had it not been for the children coming to me for help. I had always been close to them and to their parents. When they were little, they were sweet children. Their mother brought them by at least once a week to see me. Sometimes she would bring me a strudel she'd made; other times she would bring a pot of soup for my mother. Anyway, the night after the Nazis took their parents, I heard pebbles hitting my window. I had no idea what it was. At first, I just thought it was birds in my yard. But the pebbles were so persistent that I finally got up to look outside. I was shocked when I saw Asher throwing stones at the window. I got out of bed and went downstairs to see why he was in my yard so late at night. As soon as I opened the door Zita came out from behind a tree where she was hiding, and both of them came inside. They were wide eyed and terrified as they told me how they'd hidden in the back of a large closet when the Nazis came to their farm and arrested their parents. They said they didn't know where else to go, so they came to me. That was when I learned that if I couldn't love a man, at least I could love children. So I brought them in to live with me. Once this war is over, if it is ever over, and if God forbid, their parents don't return, I will keep them here with me and raise them like they were my own. They will need a home and so I will never fulfill my dream of moving to the city. But I will have a good life because I will love and be loved. And maybe I will be lucky, and I will find a man like you and finally get married."

"That's quite a story,"

"Thank you Pitor, you taught me that not all men are like my father."

He was blushing with embarrassment and didn't know what to say. So, he stayed silent. Several moments passed. Pitor finished his food. "I noticed that you cleaned and pressed my uniform," he said.

She nodded. "I know you are going to some sort of dinner with Hitler's elite. So, I wanted you to look as official and believable as possible."

"Thank you. I appreciate everything you've done for me. You really are a kind and wonderful lady. And I really believe that someday you will find a man who is deserving of you. A man who will love you forever."

She blushed, then looked away and shook her head. "I don't know. Perhaps I will."

He tried to put on a cheery smile, but he could see that she was ready to cry. "So," he said in a voice far too jovial, "do you think they will be able to tell that I am not really one of them? Or do you think I will pass for one of them?"

"You have the blond hair and blue eyes of a German. So, you look very realistic. In fact, the first time I saw you, I was afraid of you. Of course, that was because I was hiding the children. But even if I hadn't been, I know that the Nazis are cruel. Most of them are heartless. And a woman alone can never be sure what one of them might do."

"Yes, of course, you are absolutely right," he said, nodding. "And after I am gone, you must continue to be very careful."

"I know, you are right, and I will. I reprimanded the children for coming out of hiding without permission. They didn't know that anyone was here, but in the future, a move like that could prove to be extremely dangerous."

"Yes, that's true. And they need to realize how much is at stake." Then he sighed, "It's a terrible shame that young people are forced to hide like this. They should be outside in the fresh air and sunshine."

"I couldn't agree more. But right now, we have no choice," she said. "It's the only way that we might be lucky enough to survive."

"I realize that." He nodded.

"And that is only if this war ends, and Germany loses. If Germany wins, I don't know what the future might hold. I only know it will not be good."

He nodded, but did not speak. He knew she was right.

There was a moment of awkward silence.

"Pitor," she said wistfully.

"Yes,"

"Will you kiss me goodbye? I know I said I wouldn't ask you for anything. But...well...I want to remember your kiss after you have gone. Will you kiss me?"

He didn't answer. He took her into his arms and held her for a moment. The warmth of another living being in his arms gave him comfort. Then he gently pressed his lips to hers. A lock of her golden hair fell into her eyes. He gently moved it away. "Thank you again. For everything." He whispered.

"For what?" she said.

"Like I said, for absolutely everything."

A few moments later, Steffi walked over to the pantry. She took down a cloth bag. "Here, I packed this for you. I want you to take it with you. It's not much, I'm afraid, only two boiled potatoes and a bit of cabbage. I wish it were more, but it's not even close to rationing day, and I don't have a lot of food left. Of course, the children don't receive any rations. So, all we have to feed all four of us, are my rations and what I get for my mother. I must try to feed all of us with that."

"I can't take your food. I'll be all right," he said. Then he winked. "After all, I am a clever fellow. Don't you think?" He joked.

"Yes Pitor, I think you're clever. But I know that people don't have enough for themselves, so they won't be generous and help you. If you take this little bag I packed for you, at least it will get you through the rest of the day without being hungry."

He shook his head. "I'm all right, really."

"Please take it, Pitor. It will mean a lot to me."

"Are you sure you want me to?"

"I am very sure. At least I will know that I helped you as much as I could."

He nodded, and she smiled. She put the bag in his hand.

"Now, as for your ride into Munich," she said, "my friend, the farmer who will be driving you knows nothing about Zita and Asher. All he knows about you is that you are a Nazi officer. He is a nice man, but we live in a treacherous world. There are rewards for turning people in, so it is far too dangerous to trust anyone. That is why I have not told him anything. So, remember to be very careful what you say to him. His name is Emil Richtmann, and he should be arriving here in his truck any minute now."

Pitor nodded. Suddenly, he wanted to share something with her that he never showed to anyone else. "I have a picture of my wife and son," he said. "I hid it. I knew it was dangerous to keep a photograph of my family, but I couldn't part with it. Sometimes when I am alone, I look at it and I remember. I never want to forget their faces. Would you like to see it?"

"Yes, very much."

He took the worn photograph out of the breast pocket of his uniform and handed it to her. For a moment, she stared at it in silence. Then she said, "Your son looks just like you."

"Yes, he does."

"But your wife was such a dark-haired beauty."

"Yes, she was very beautiful," Pitor took the picture back and returned it to his pocket.

"Perhaps you should leave that photograph with me, for safe keeping," she said. "I will hold it for you."

He shook his head.

"Listen to me," she said, "if for some reason they find that picture on you, it will raise a lot of unnecessary and dangerous questions. I promise I will keep it safe for you."

He realized she was right and handed her the picture. "Hide it," he said. "I will be back for it."

Steffi nodded.

Then a horn honked outside. It was Richtmann.

True to his word, he arrived at exactly eight that morning. "Good-bye. I must go now," Pitor said as he glanced outside.

"I will keep that photograph safe for you. Come back and claim it when you can," she said.

He nodded and walked outside.

Emil opened the door to his truck for Pitor, as would be fitting for a Sturmscharführer. "Good morning Sturmscharführer," he said.

"Good morning," Pitor replied as he climbed into the cab of the truck.

The red truck was old and dirty, and Pitor could see that it had been used for farm work. "Thank you," Pitor said.

The farmer nodded.

Pitor turned and took one last look at Steffi. Her eyes were glazed over and she looked like she might cry, but instead she smiled and waved just a little. He waved back. Then the farmer got in beside Pitor and turned on the ignition, and the old vehicle belched and sprung to life.

They were on their way.

CHAPTER TWENTY

Emil, the old farmer who was giving Pitor a ride into Munich, was a weather-worn man with leather-like skin that was deeply lined from years of toiling in the sun. He had the strong body of a man who had worked the land all his life. He did not speak much to Pitor. Pitor assumed he might be afraid of him, because Pitor was intimidating as a Nazi in uniform. As they rode along the dirt roads, Pitor watched Emil and wondered what the old man thought of him. However, Pitor was glad that the farmer hardly spoke and never asked him any questions. When they arrived in the city of Munich, the farmer turned to Pitor and said, "Well, this is it, Sturmscharführer. We're here."

"Thank you," Pitor said confidently. The farmer got out of the truck and opened Pitor's door. Pitor easily climbed down from the cab and nodded to the farmer, then he began to walk towards the center of town. Once Emil Richtmann drove away, Pitor let out a sigh of relief.

Munich was a lovely, picturesque city, and Pitor wondered what it might have been like before Hitler. There were *biergartens* and chocolate shops. There were clock makers and toy makers with intricate and beautiful goods to sell in their windows. He walked the streets for a minute and looked around. Then he sat down on a bench and ate the lunch that Steffi had packed for him. There was a nice soft breeze in the air, and for a moment he closed his eyes, and his thoughts turned immediately to Mila. He wished she was there beside him, enjoying this city. And he missed the photograph that he had left with Steffi. But he knew she was right. It was too dangerous for him to take it with him to this party. *I will return to collect that picture someday.* There was no time to dwell on this. Time was ticking away, and Pitor needed to get himself up to the Eagle's Nest. So, he had to find someone to drive him there. But he had no idea who to ask. Sitting in the village square, he finished eating his lunch as he watched the famous clock that stood high above him on a building. When it struck noon, all the figures inside of it moved. There were angels and lions. He thought of Jakup and how much Jakup would have enjoyed seeing that clock in motion. People who walked by him averted their eyes. For a moment, he wondered why. Then he remembered that to everyone who saw him, he was Sturmscharführer Konrad Hoffman. They were afraid of him. He sighed. It was to be expected. If he and Mila had seen a Nazi sitting on a bench, they would have stayed out of his way.

I must get to the Eagle's Nest. I wonder if because I am a Sturmscharführer, I might be able to get one of the police officers to drive me there. I'll find the police station and try. I will tell them I am expected at a party at the Eagle's Nest by Hitler's highest elite. Perhaps the police will help me get there.

The idea of being in an automobile with a uniformed police officer made Pitor nervous. He felt sick to his stomach. Being in close quarters with this officer would give the policeman a good opportunity to observe him closely. And if he failed to be convincing as a Nazi, he would be arrested. Pitor recalled a time when he was living among the partisans, and he'd heard another man, who had posed as a

Nazi, say that the Nazi party members were not good friends to each other. They were always eager to turn each other in, because this could get them rewards as well as promotions. Therefore, Pitor knew he must appear to be beyond reproach as he rode to the Eagle's Nest beside this policeman. There must be no doubt in the man's mind that Pitor was Konrad Hoffmann, a high-ranking official on his way to meet with the Führer. Pitor forced himself to breathe deeply in an attempt to appear relaxed. *Well, this is just the beginning of my mission. It will be good practice. Once I get to the Eagle's Nest, I will be surrounded by them. The ones who will be there will be the elite. So, if I can't convince a lowly policeman, I will never convince Himmler or Goebbels, or the rest of these bastards.*

Pulling himself together and summoning all his courage, Pitor held his head high, as he knew an SS officer would do, and then he walked into the police station. *Act like a high-ranking Nazi and they will believe you are one. You are wearing the uniform. You have all the medals on your jacket. There is no reason they would think you are an impersonator. Just relax and act like you expect to be driven to your destination. A real SS officer would expect as much from a policeman, a man he considered to be his inferior.* He tried to comfort himself with this knowledge, but his stomach ached as he walked up to the front desk at the police station. A slender, middle-aged man with light brown hair and thick glasses looked up at him. "Can I help you?" he asked politely.

"I am Sturmscharführer Konrad Hoffman," Pitor delivered his line with conviction. "I need a ride up to the Eagle's Nest today. You see, I am expected to attend a party there. The Führer is awaiting my arrival."

When the middle-aged policeman behind the desk heard the Führer was waiting for this man who was speaking to him, his eyes opened wide. Pitor saw the officer's eyes scanning his uniform. He gazed admiringly at the stripes and awards on the shoulder and lapel. Pitor smiled, then he handed the officer Konrad's papers. The officer looked them over quickly and Pitor could see that he had convinced the policeman, who didn't doubt him at all. In fact, the officer was very nervous and trying hard to make a good impression on Pitor. "Of course I understand what you need. Of course, Sturmscharführer, I will see to it that someone will drive you to the Eagle's Nest right away."

"Thank you," Pitor said.

"I have never been there, but I've heard that the Eagle's Nest is breathtaking. I saw a photo once," he smiled. "And from what I hear, the ride there is lovely as well," the policeman stammered.

"I don't mean to rush you. But I am expected there today so, please hurry. I need to be on my way," Pitor said.

"Yes, of course. What was I thinking? I am talking far too much," the policeman giggled uncomfortably. "I'm sorry. I shouldn't be wasting your time. I'll arrange that ride for you immediately. Won't you please have a seat? Can I get you something to drink while you wait? A coffee? A beer perhaps?"

"No, thank you. That's not necessary, really. I must be on my way. As I said before, the Führer is expecting me, and I must arrive there as soon as possible." Pitor was becoming frustrated with this nervous man. He was trying to keep his patience, but he was about to explode with anger and yell at the policeman.

"Yes, yes, of course. What am I thinking? I'll take care of this right away, sir," The policeman stood up and several of the papers on his desk fell to the floor. He didn't stop to pick them up. Instead, he disappeared quickly down a hallway and into a room at the back of the station.

Pitor sat down on a chair in the waiting area. He quickly looked around him at the two other people who were also waiting. One was a young woman, blond, twenty years old or so. And the other was an old man. He wondered why they were here at the police station. But he chose not to ask. It was best to keep to himself.

I must remember that what I am doing right now is for my son. If more policemen come out from the back of the station and ask me questions, I will use the rank of Sturmscharführer to intimidate them.

It was less than five minutes later when the same middle-aged police officer returned with a younger officer. This one was a tall, blond, and extremely handsome man. He wore a clean, pressed uniform. Every blond and shiny hair on his head was frozen in place by a greasy pomade of some sort. His appearance was far too perfect. He looked more like a human size doll than a regular man. When the two police officers entered the room, Pitor rose from his chair and walked back up to the front desk.

"This is Hansel Scholz. He will be honored to drive you to the Eagle's Nest," the original policeman said.

Pitor nodded. Then he turned to Hansel Scholz. "Hello. I'm Konrad Hoffmann."

"Sturmscharführer Hoffmann," the original police officer said to Hansel Scholz.

Hansel nodded. "It's my pleasure to meet you, Sturmscharführer," he said.

Then Pitor heard the original police officer whisper to Hansel, "It would behoove you to make a good impression on this fellow. He is very high ranking."

"Yes, father," Hansel answered the middle-aged officer.

"He is your son?" Pitor asked.

"Yes, he is my son," the officer said proudly.

Pitor nodded.

"You should be going. You don't want the Sturmscharführer to be late on your account, do you?"

"No sir," Hansel said. Then he turned to Pitor, "Please follow me."

Hansel led Pitor to a shiny black automobile that was parked in front of the station. He opened the door to the back seat and Pitor slid inside. Then Hansel got into the driver's seat and within minutes, they were on their way.

As they drove through the beautiful alps, Hansel said, "My name is Hansel, but you can feel free to call me Hans."

"Very good, I'll call you Hans then," Pitor said, but he hoped

Hans didn't want to start a conversation. He was lost in his own thoughts and, quite frankly, the less he talked, the less he had to worry about being discovered as a fraud before he ever found Jakup.

"My father said that you are going to be attending a party with the Führer. That must be terribly exciting," Hans said. Then, as if he remembered Pitor's rank, he said, "I'm sorry. Please forgive me for being so bold. I have no right to ask you anything."

Pitor felt sorry for the young man who was so afraid of offending him because of his rank. "It's all right," he said gently. "Yes, I am attending a party with the Führer. I am going to this party, because I am to be promoted to bodyguard for the Führer."

"Really? That's wonderful," Hans said, and Pitor could hear a bit of jealousy in Hans' voice. "You must be feeling so proud."

"Yes, of course," Pitor said.

"I met the Führer once." Hans said.

"Oh?"

"Yes. Well, I didn't exactly meet him. I mean, I met him sort of. You see, a friend and I went to hear him speak at a rally in Nuremburg. After he spoke, on his way out, he walked through the crowd and shook hands with several people. I was one of those people. I actually shook hands with our great Führer."

"I see," Pitor said, not wanting to encourage the man to continue talking. But once the Führer was mentioned, Hans seemed to go into a trance. "His speech was enthralling. I found him to be quite amazing, brilliant really. Everyone was awestruck while he was speaking."

Pitor decided to take this opportunity to try and find out what it was about Hitler that his followers found so appealing. "What was it that he said or did that held you so spellbound?" Pitor asked.

"Everything he said. I mean, we are so fortunate to have such an insightful and intelligent leader."

"Yes, I couldn't agree more. But I was hoping to hear what you found so fascinating about his speech."

"Well, I was touched deeply by his love for our Fatherland. He wants to see Germany take her rightful place as the one and only world power. After all, we, the Aryan people of pure German blood, are the superior race. And if we are ever to prevent another loss like we experienced in the Great War, we must rid ourselves of the dangerous inferior sub-humans who live among us and caused us to lose that war in the first place," Hans said proudly.

"You mean the Jews?"

"Yes, most definitely the terrible and dangerous Jews who are only out to take what they can steal from the good German people. But also, the gypsies who pollute our society with their vulgar music, overtly sexual woman, and crude dancing. And the Jehovah's Witnesses who won't accept our Führer as their God. Then of course there are the filthy homosexuals and criminals who are poisoning our cities and corrupting our young people. Our Führer knows that we must eliminate these elements from our society if we are to flourish the way that nature intended."

"Hmmm, yes," Pitor said, "you seem to know quite a bit about our Führer and his policies."

"I do. In fact, I know that Germany will soon be a world power again. We will rule the rest of the world, and our Reich will last a thousand years. We will take over all the inferior countries, bit by bit, piece by piece. The lesser humans, like the Polish, the British, the American's, the French, will all serve us. They will be our slaves. This is the way nature intended it. That's why we are superior. Because Germany is destined to rule the world."

"Very good," Pitor agreed. He knew it was best not to challenge anything Hans said. There was nothing to be gained by it. Right now, more than anything, Pitor needed to play the part of the Sturmschar-führer. He needed to appear to be devoted to the party and above question. "You're right. This is our future. And it is as it should be," Although he'd heard all this nonsense before, hearing it again in the position he was in, posing as a high-ranking Nazi official, had shaken him up. He closed his eyes and remembered his goal. *I must find Jakup.* Pitor should not have been surprised by what Hans said. After all, he knew what they believed. But even though he'd heard their doctrine a thousand times before, he still found it shocking to hear someone say it aloud, and he wondered how an entire society of intelligent people could follow such a madman as Adolf Hitler.

Hans continued speaking, but by this time, Pitor had grown weary of listening. The young man's twisted convictions only angered him, and if he continued to listen, he knew that at some point he would no longer be able to control himself, and then he might say something to give himself away. So, it was far better to close his eyes and think of Mila and Jakup, and remind himself why he was going to this party filled with his enemies. He held the picture that he'd left with Steffi in his mind. As he remembered the look in Mila's eyes, he felt a wave of comfort come over him.

As the automobile inched its way through the winding roads at the edge of the mountain, Pitor glanced out the window. They were high up, and the view was breathtaking. However, if the driver did not pay careful attention, it would be easy for this car to go plummeting over the edge. Pitor and the driver would both meet their death at the bottom of a mountain. The height was dizzying. Hans looked in the rear-view mirror at Pitor, who had turned away from the window. "The height is a bit unnerving, I'm afraid. Actually, I was selected to drive you, because I have no fear of heights. A lot of the officers do, and the Eagle's Nest is located quite high up."

"I can see that," Pitor said, feeling a little nauseated.

Before they entered the actual Eagle's Nest, they were required to stop the automobile at a checkpoint. A young Nazi officer, in a crisp new uniform, wearing his hat and looking very official, walked up to the window. "Who are you, and what is your business here?" the young officer asked.

"My name is Hansel Scholz. I am a police officer in Munich. I am driving Sturmscharführer Konrad Hoffman here to the Eagle's Nest for a dinner party that is to be taking place this evening. He is expected. He has come because he is receiving a promotion tonight that will be awarded to him by our Führer himself," Hans said proudly.

The young Nazi walked back over to his station, where he took a clipboard off a countertop. Then he ran his finger down a list of names. Once he'd found what he had been searching for, he returned to the automobile.

"You are Sturmscharführer Hoffman?" The young Nazi ignored Hans and turned his attention to the back seat to speak directly to Pitor.

"Yes, I am."

"And why are you here?"

"As Hans told you, I am here because I have been invited concerning a job promotion," Pitor said.

"May I see your papers?"

Pitor handed the Nazi his papers.

The Nazi took the papers and went into his small booth, where he began to look at the list again. Suddenly, Pitor began to worry. He felt sweat begin to bead on his forehead, and he felt heat spreading down the back of his neck. *What if Hoffmann was lying to me? What if he was making up a story to make himself look important, and none of it was true? And now I am here. These people will not be pleased to find out that I have come here uninvited. I am sure I will be arrested on the spot. This crime might easily be punishable by death. After all, the Führer will be here and this road block is part of his security. If they even think I am coming to harm him, they will be out for blood.*

A few minutes later, the young Nazi returned. He smiled broadly as he handed Pitor his papers. "I had to verify your papers. But no need to worry, you are on the guest list sir. Enjoy the evening. Heil Hitler," the young Nazi saluted him.

"Heil Hitler," Pitor said, the words sounding bitter on his tongue.

The Nazi stepped out of the way, and Hans maneuvered the car forward.

Pitor sighed with relief as he glanced out the window again.

"You know, sir. I would like to ask you something," Hans said timidly.

"What is it?" Pitor asked, a little annoyed that he'd just gotten away from the roadblock and now his driver was pressuring him.

"Well, I can see that you are a very important man. And I feel honored to be driving a Sturmscharführer to a destination as beautiful and as private and selective as this one."

"All right. So, what is it you want?"

"Well, I was hoping that perhaps you might put in a good word for me. I mean, I know it's presumptuous to ask this of you. But I must ask because, well... as you know, it's often difficult to get ahead. I would like to move up in the party if I could. I have a wife, and she is going to have a child. If I can secure a better position, it would mean better pay. And well, I mean if your ride here was pleasant, and if you found me to be a pleasant fellow, perhaps, well, perhaps, you might mention this to the Führer or to one of the other important men at his party."

He's an idiot, but I feel sorry for him. He was taught all this doctrine, and he believes what they taught him. He doesn't know any better. My guess is that he's never had any contact with Gypsies or Jews or even Jehovah's Witnesses. I'm sure he's had contact with criminals, but he wouldn't see them as such. He would see them as Gestapo agents. But I'll wager that the Gestapo have murdered and tortured a lot more people than simple thieves. "I would be happy to help you. But I don't know for sure if I will have an opportunity to do so. I haven't even started my new job yet," Pitor said.

"I understand, sir. But perhaps later? Perhaps after you have established yourself? Maybe you will remember me."

"Yes, of course," Pitor said. He was glad when Hans pulled the car over into a parking area. Hans got out quickly and opened the door for Pitor. Then he pointed to what appeared to be a tunnel.

"This is as close to the actual Eagle's Nest that I have ever been. But I know that there is a tunnel right there. You go inside and walk to the end where you will find an elevator. Get on the elevator and it will take you up to the Eagle's Nest."

"A tunnel?" Pitor asked. He was surprised. He hadn't expected a tunnel.

"Yes, from what I understand they built it to protect the Führer in case of bombings."

"I see," Pitor said, nodding his head slowly. He smiled at Hans and then thanked him for the ride before he began to walk towards the tunnel.

CHAPTER TWENTY-ONE

Pitor entered the dark opening that had been carved into the mountain. His stomach felt sick with nervous anticipation. Without thinking, he turned back for a moment. It was then that he saw Hans watching him longingly. *He wishes I would take him with me. He thinks this is the biggest opportunity a man can get in this lifetime. For him, perhaps it might be. But for me, well, it's only a means to an end. Once I've found my son, I will find a way to take him far away from here, and far away from any contact at all with Hitler and his Third Reich.* Pitor turned away from Hans, and entered the dark, humid, and musty tunnel. The cobblestone floor was very uneven, and he had to take care not to trip on an irregular stone, or to catch his boot on a broken one. His heart raced as he listened to the sound of his boot heels echoing through the damp and windy chamber. An uneasy feeling spread over him, and he felt bile rise in his throat. But he refused to vomit. If they detected any form of weakness in him, they would attack him like wild animals in a snowstorm. The darkness and the loud clicking of his heels unnerved him as he made his way down the long corridor, and once he had to stop and close his eyes before he could keep going. He reminded himself again of why he had come here. *I must find Jakup. I must.* When Pitor reached the end of the long tunnel, he entered a large room with a dome ceiling. A few moments later, Pitor heard a door open, and there it was. The elevator. It seemed to know he was there. He stepped inside, where he found a gold panel on the wall with a button to press that promised to deliver the waiting occupant to the top of the mountain. When Pitor pushed the button, the door to the elevator closed slowly. For a moment he felt confined, as if he were being choked. Then the elevator began to rise. Pitor tried to slow down his racing heart as he took long, slow breaths. The tiny enclosure of the elevator trembled and shook until a few minutes later the door opened to the most magnificent sight Pitor had ever seen.

Pitor walked out of the elevator to find himself at the top of a glorious mountain overlooking a valley and the small towns below. For a moment, the beauty of the breathtaking view overtook him, and he forgot to be frightened. But his moment to admire the mountain was short-lived, for he was approached by a uniformed guard. "Heil Hitler," the guard greeted Pitor.

"Heil Hitler," the words still stung Pitor's tongue. *I will never be comfortable saying those awful words.*

"Who are you and what are you doing here?" the guard asked in a deep, guttural voice.

Pitor considered the fact that one of the guests at this dinner party might know Konrad Hoffman personally, and of course, that would expose him as a fraud. *I considered that before I came. But I had to come regardless of the danger, because this is the only possible connection I have to finding Jakup.* Although it was only a long shot that someone at this party might know where his son was, he had to take every opportunity, because he had no idea how else to begin to search for his son. He turned to the guard, and in a voice that sounded far more confident than he felt, he said, "I am Sturmscharführer Konrad Hoffmann."

"And your business here?"

"I was invited to this event, because I am to be promoted by the

Führer. I am to be awarded a position as one of the bodyguards to our Führer." Pitor took a deep breath and stood up tall, drawing on his six feet of height.

"One moment," the guard said, then he added, "may I please see your papers sir?"

Pitor handed him the papers. "I'll be right back," the guard said.

The guard, like the guard at the checkpoint, had a guest list. He checked it for Konrad Hoffman. Then he returned and handed Pitor his papers. "You're on the list sir. Several of the guests have already arrived. Some of them are in the dining hall, others are in the sunroom. The dining hall is right over there," he pointed to the right. "And the sunroom is over there," he pointed to the left. "If you need anything, let me know. And congratulations on your promotion, sir. I hope you have a lovely evening."

"Thank you," Pitor said, putting his papers back into his pocket. Before he entered the dining room or the sunroom, he walked around the perimeter of the mountain to enjoy the view. The sun was setting, and the sky was painted in watercolors of fuchsia and purple. As he looked at the sky, he saw a faint hint of a silhouette of the moon and, for a moment, he wondered if God was watching. And, if he was watching, why didn't he cause some sort of natural disaster that would destroy all these terrible people who would be gathered here all at the same time?

A vivacious young woman with blonde curly hair wearing a floral dress that flowed elegantly around her shapely calves walked over to where Pitor stood, "Hallo, and welcome."

"Hallo," he answered.

"The guard informed me that you had arrived. You are the new bodyguard for our Führer, am I correct? Konrad Hoffman, yes?"

"Yes, that's correct," Pitor smiled.

She smiled too. Her teeth were small and straight, and she wore red lipstick to show off how white they were. Pitor had to admit that even though she was a Nazi, she was quite lovely.

"I'm Eva Braun," she said in a soft singsong like voice, "won't you follow me into the dining room? There are a lot of people I'd like to introduce you to before the Führer arrives."

He nodded, "Of course. I would like that very much," he said, but he was dreading what might come next.

"Shall we go through the sunroom first? It's a bit out of the way, but it is so lovely, and I think you might want to see it before the sun sets completely."

"Yes, that would be nice," Pitor said, as he followed her to the entrance of a hallway that was surrounded by glass.

"This is the sunroom," she said. "Pretty, isn't it?"

"Yes, it certainly is." For a moment, he stood and looked at the sunset. He was up so high that it felt as if he were level with the clouds. Eva Braun stood quietly for a few minutes, to give him some time to enjoy the view. He gazed out at the large, encompassing glass windows and marveled at how beautiful the landscape was.

Finally, she said, "Come, you're going to love the dining room. Our Führer received a gift from Mussolini today. It's a beautiful red brick fireplace. It's in the dining room and I can't wait to show it to you."

Pitor smiled. Then Eva turned and began to walk down the corridor with Pitor following close behind. That was when he noticed a door to one of the rooms along the hallway was wide open. As he walked by, he looked inside. There he saw two dark-haired young women playing with a group of children. A man in uniform, with a pockmarked face, stood beside one of the women, smoking a cigarette. "You had better put that out, Horst," she said. "The Führer will be here any minute, and you know how much he hates smoking."

The man who she had called Horst nodded. Then he put out his cigarette.

"This is Horst." Eva introduced the pockmarked man to Pitor, who managed to smile but was very distracted by the children. "And this," she said proudly to Horst, "is the Fuhrer's new security guard, Konrad Hoffmann."

"Hoffman! Why I remember you." Horst smiled, then he turned

to Eva. "We attended boarding school together. That was before my father lost his position working at the school and we were forced to move. However, Hoffman was one of the most popular fellows in school. Everyone liked him."

"I can see why." Eva said. "You seem like you might have gone to an exclusive school, Konrad. What school was it?"

"It was Odenwaldschule. And it was a very exclusive school." Horst said.

"So, your father must have had a very important job, Horst. What did your father do?"

"Nothing special, I'm afraid. He had a small insignificant job, but it permitted me to attend the school."

"What was his job, Horst. You haven't answered my question." Eva said.

"He was only a janitor." Horst said, looking down at the ground.

"I see. Well, it's a good thing that the National Socialist government took over that school."

"Yes, it is." Horst said. Then he turned his attention on Pitor, who was only half listening to the conversation. "You look different somehow." Horst said, studying Pitor.

When Pitor heard Horst say that he knew he must say something clever to distract Eva from the possibility that he was an impostor. "Well, Horst. You don't look very much like the eight-year-old janitor's son that I remember either."

Eva laughed. Pitor laughed too. But Horst didn't laugh. He was studying Pitor even harder now.

"Come on, Horst. Go and throw that cigarette butt off the mountain so there is no evidence that you were smoking in here. I don't want the Führer to know," she said firmly.

It stinks of cigarette smoke. Pitor thought, *I don't know how anyone could miss that smell.* He thought, but he really didn't care about the adults in that room. His eyes were fixed on the children who were playing on the floor, and that was because one of those children was Jakup. *Am I dreaming? Is this really possible? Can it be that my son is alive, and he is here?* In his mind, Pitor called out to Mila. *Mila, look at this, my love, Jakup is not dead. He is alive. I have found him as I promised you I would! He looks healthy, as if he has been fed far better than he was in the ghetto. These lousy Nazis want him because he is blond, so it seems we have been blessed, and they have taken good care of him. But I vow I will find a way to bring him home. I promise you this, Mila. And I have never broken a promise to you.*

Then he heard Mila's voice in his mind, *"Be careful Pitor. Don't do anything rash. Think everything through carefully before you do it. Both for your sake, and for Jakup's."*

It was everything Pitor could do to restrain himself from entering that room and grabbing Jakup. But he knew Mila was right. If he tried to take the boy, he would be stopped at gunpoint and questioned. And in his haste, he might even jeopardize Jakup's safety. *I must be cautious if I am to get my son back. If I am not careful now, I will be discovered, and then Jakup will be one of them for the rest of his life. I will not be able to rescue him if they find out the truth about me.*

Eva noticed Pitor had stopped walking and was looking at the children. "These little ones are quite spectacular. Don't you agree? Perfect examples of Aryan superiority. They are part of a program that the Reichsführer has put into place to increase the production of Aryan children who will eventually populate the new Germany," she smiled proudly.

"Yes, they are quite spectacular," he managed to say.

"Blond, beautiful, strong," she said with admiration. "They are exactly the kind of people we will need to rule the world. As I said, perfect little Aryans."

Pitor suddenly remembered his conversation with Konrad in the forest regarding the Lebensborn, and the children that they produced being adopted by SS officers. "Are they available for adoption?" Pitor asked.

"Actually, yes they are."

"I love children. How does one go about adopting one?"

"Well, first, you must fit all of the criteria. Let's see," she smiled fetchingly. "You are an SS officer. And quite successful I might add. I realize that you've been carefully vetted, or you would not have been invited to this party to accept a job promotion where you would be responsible for something as important as keeping our precious Führer safe. The only question I have for you is, are you married?"

"No. I'm afraid not." Pitor said. "I've never been married."

"A handsome officer like you? That is a shame. And, I must admit, I'm rather surprised," she said, flirtatiously smiling up at him.

He tried his best to smile back at her. "Would an adoption require me to be married?"

"Yes, I am afraid so."

"I see," he said. He knew this already, but he was hoping it was not true.

"Why? May I ask? Do you like one of the children that you see in there?"

"I like that spunky little boy. The one right over there. You see, I've always wanted a son."

"Oh, yes, that one is rather adorable," Eva smiled. "I saw him when the two little brown sisters brought him in. They told me that he just received his name last week, when Reichsführer Himmler was at Heim Hockland for his annual naming ceremony."

"What is the name that the Reichsführer chose for him?" Pitor asked, trying to act as if he wasn't invested, only curious.

"Let me ask one of the little brown sisters," Eva said. Then she motioned to one of the girls. "That little boy over there. The one with the head full of blond curls. He was named last week when Himmler gave his naming ceremony. Do you recall the name he was given?"

"Yes, Fräulein Braun. The Reichsführer named him Liam. He said that it means protector," the little brown sister smiled at Eva Braun. She was impressed with herself because Eva Braun, Hitler's longtime girlfriend, had stopped to speak to her. "Liam is a big boy for his age. But he's very gentle. He treats the other children with such kindness, that I believe he will grow up to fulfill his name and be a protector," the little brown sister was eyeing Pitor shyly.

"He sounds like a good boy." Pitor said, wishing he could stay in this room with Jakup, but he knew he must not appear to be as invested as he was. *Of course, he is kind and gentle. He is my son. But what they don't know is that Jakup is not Liam, and he is a full-blooded Jew. Not a drop of Nazi blood runs through his veins.*

"I know he is young, but he is already very fair when he plays with the other children. Most of the children are unwilling to share their toys. But not Liam. If one of the others asks him to share a toy, he will. I have seen him fight with another boy once, and he was fierce for a little guy. But he chooses to be gentle whenever he can."

"He got into a fight?" Pitor asked, forgetting his position for a moment.

"Yes, he did. It happened when another little boy bit one of the girls. Would you believe Liam stood up and defended her? My coworker and I thought that was an amazing response for a child his age. But we both agree that he doesn't get into fights often. Liam is a good boy. He really doesn't give us any trouble," she said.

"This officer likes him," Eva said, indicating Pitor.

"I can see why. Liam is going to grow up to be a handsome man," the brown sister said. She was fidgeting nervously, and Pitor assumed it was because she was speaking to someone as important as Eva Braun.

"In fact, I think he looks a lot like you," Eva said to Pitor. "So, you have a sweetheart, you could get married and adopt him. Everyone would think he was your biological son." Eva was smiling broadly.

The little brown sister's lip was trembling and Pitor wondered why. Then Eva asked the girl, "What's your name?"

"I'm Heidi Nessler," the little brown sister said.

"And your partner, the other little brown sister. What is her name?" Eva asked.

"She's Gretchen Auerbach."

That was when an idea came to Pitor's mind. He looked directly at Heidi and her face broke into a smile. Pitor returned her smile. Eva noticed the interaction between the two of them, and because the girl was only a little brown sister, she put her arm through Pitor's arm, and led him away from the room. "Come, we must get to the dining room. The Führer will be arriving soon."

"Yes, of course," Pitor said. Then he followed Eva to the back of the building and into a large dining room. At the front of the room there stood a red brick fireplace. Eva pointed to it. "That's the gift from Mussolini. It's magnificent. Don't you agree?"

"Yes, it is,"

"I think our Führer will really like it," she smiled. "Now let me show you to your seat."

Pitor followed her and as he did, he noticed several women were looking him over, head to toe. He knew by the way they stared at him they were attracted to him. But it made him anxious. He didn't want or need any extra attention. He was here to take back his son and if he could have remained invisible, he would have.

"It seems you are quite popular with the ladies," Eva said.

He shrugged, not knowing what to say. *Eva is very observant. Nothing gets by her. I have heard she is Hitler's girlfriend. But I've also heard that Hitler had a love affair with his niece, who is now dead. There was a lot of talk that he might have killed her. But other people said she committed suicide. If I were Eva, I would be very careful of Hitler.*

"It seems to me, that you would have no trouble finding a wife. Every girl here has already looked you over," Eva said, pulling Pitor back into the present moment.

"I suppose you might say I am shy when it comes to women," he said.

"That makes sense to me. Sometimes men like you, strong soldiers, have trouble when it comes to the more romantic side of life."

He shook his head. "I don't know. Perhaps you're right. Perhaps that's what it is," he said, looking down at the floor.

"Well, if you need help finding a good woman, you can feel free to ask me. I know a lot of lovely Aryan women that would make wonderful *hausfraus*. And... since you are going to be a bodyguard for the Führer, you and I will be seeing a lot of each other in the future. So, I will have plenty of time to make the proper introductions."

He smiled.

Then she added, "You see, in case you didn't know, I am the Führer's fiancée."

"I had heard," he said. Then he added, "he is a lucky man. You are very pretty."

She smiled at him coquettishly.

"Well, that's quite an honor to be engaged to our Führer."

"It is, isn't it?" she said, forcing a smile.

But he frowned because he thought he heard a tone of underlying doubt in her voice.

CHAPTER TWENTY-TWO

The dining room was dressed in full Nazi regalia. Flags hung from the ceiling, and the main wall was decorated with a large, beautifully painted picture of Adolf Hitler. Across from the main wall stood a life-size poster of a young, healthy and attractive blond haired and blue-eyed couple. The man's arms were exposed to reveal bulging muscles. His face was perfectly carved, with high cheekbones and a strong jaw. The woman had an ample bosom and a small waist as she gazed up at the man lovingly. A large caption beneath the picture read: "The Future of our Fatherland, a perfect Aryan couple." Each of the round tables was set with fine china, sterling silver flatware, and fine crystal. A large round flower arrangement of golden sunflowers, the official flower of the Reich, sat in the center of each of the dining tables, except for the front table which had an arrangement of the same golden flowers that reached the entire length of the long table. In the corner, at the side of the room stood a five-piece orchestra. They were playing a waltz by Wagner as a few couples glided across the expansive dance floor. Most of the men in attendance sported their uniforms, but some were in dark tuxedos. The women wore elegant floor-length formal gowns and exquisite jewelry. Pitor glanced around him at the opulence and wondered how the Nazi party had so much money behind it. He'd heard rumors the Nazis confiscated and stole all the valuables from the Jews they arrested. He'd also heard that Hitler had backing from businessmen who used the concentration camp prisoners as slave labor. *It must be easier to make a lot of money when you don't have to pay your workers.* Pitor thought bitterly.

"This is your seat," Eva Braun said as she directed him to one of the tables. "Now, I am going to warn you that you must be prepared because you are going be called up to receive an award for your bravery in battle. That's when you will be awarded your promotion. But first, there are several surprises in store. I do think you are going to enjoy this party, Sturmscharführer," she said, smiling warmly at him, and from the look in her eyes, he thought she might be flirting with him. But just when he was certain he saw a look of desire in her eyes, her expression changed. Quickly, she regained her composure and her distance. It was as if she remembered who she was and what was expected of her. Eva cleared her throat, then said, "Well, enjoy the party. I must go now and greet some of the other guests."

"Of course," he said. "And thank you for showing me around. The Eagle's Nest is certainly a lovely place."

Eva smiled at him, then she turned and walked away quickly.

Pitor sat down at the table in front of a place setting that read: "Sturmscharführer Konrad Hoffmann." Then he kept his eye on the doorway and watched as some of the most frightening men in Germany entered the dining room. The first to arrive was Joseph Goebbels with his graceful light-haired wife, Magda, who wore a simple black dress with pearls at her throat. Goebbels limped, dragging his foot as he escorted Magda to their seats at the head table. Magda looked around the room quickly, and Pitor wondered if she was searching for Adolf Hitler. He'd heard that she had always been a friend, a confident and strong supporter of the Führer. But Hitler had not yet arrived. *He's waiting for everyone to arrive first, because he wants to make an entrance.* Pitor thought. He noticed that Magda

Goebbels was about to take her seat when she glanced down to the end of the long table where Emmy Goering and her husband Hermann were seated. Emmy was an actress, and she was Hermann's second wife. Magda forced a smile when her eyes met Emmy's. But even Pitor could see that Magda did not care for the other woman at all.

A young woman sat down beside Pitor, and before he could introduce himself, she boldly leaned over and whispered in his ear. "I see you are watching Emmy and Magda. They have been rivals for the unofficial title 'First lady of Nazi Germany' for as long as I can remember."

"Oh?" Pitor said, glancing over at the young woman who was speaking.

"Oh, absolutely." She leaned in closer and placed her hand on Pitor's knee. "Just look at Frau Goebbel's face. She is sneering at Frau Goering," she giggled.

Pitor watched as Magda Goebbels scoffed as she placed her small handbag on the table beside her place setting. Magda was far more attractive than Emmy, who was heavier built with coarser features. And although Hermann Goering had been handsome in his youth, *now* he was old looking and heavy set, just like his Bavarian wife.

"Just between us, of course, Frau Goering doesn't have as much class as Frau Goebbels. But then again, Magda Goebbels was born in the big city of Berlin, and I believe Frau Goering was a farm girl. However, I am not sure that's true," she said, smiling. "Still Frau Goebbels has given birth to six children, and she has maintained her lovely shape. She is an inspiration to all of us Aryan women."

Pitor smiled. *In fact, only the women here at this Nazi gala seem to look even remotely like that poster of the Aryan couple that is hanging on the wall. None of Hitler's important men look anything like that. Especially not Hitler.* He thought. But he said nothing.

Pitor took a moment to glance over at the woman who sat beside him and had been speaking to him. She was about five feet five inches tall, and slender. She wore a pale blue gown with sliver shoes. Her blonde hair was caught up in a silver and diamond comb. He didn't find her to be pretty, but she did look Aryan.

"By the way, my name is Alice," she said.

"I'm Konrad Hoffmann. Sturmscharführer Konrad Hoffmann."

Alice looked him up and down. "I've been to several of these parties, and I'm sorry, but I don't recognize you." Then she added, "And believe me, if anyone even half as handsome as you had ever been in attendance at one of these boring dinners, I am quite certain that I would have remembered him."

"Oh," Pitor said. He was glad she wasn't asking more questions about who he was and why he was here. "I'm flattered that you find me attractive. But the reason you don't recognize me is because I have never been to one of these parties before. I am here to receive a job promotion." Then he remembered he didn't know if Konrad Hoffmann had ever been to one of these Nazi galas, and he began to worry that what he just said might have been a mistake. He might have trapped himself. A cold sweat began to form on his brow. Alice didn't notice it. She was smiling broadly at him. "Look at the door," she said excitedly. "Look who just arrived" she whispered, "it's Adolf Eichmann. And in case you haven't noticed, he's alone. I have inside information as to why," she said.

He nodded and smiled.

"Do you know anything about him?"

"Not really." Pitor admitted, as he stared at the tall slender man with dark hair who had just entered the room."

"Well, I've heard that his wife Veronica is supposed to be very devoted to him. But as you can see, she's not here. Would you like to know why?"

"Sure," Pitor said. He didn't really care why Eichmann had come to Hitler's party without his wife. He felt a bead of sweat run down his neck. There was no doubt that he was nervous as he looked around at all the men in their neatly pressed Nazi uniforms. He felt like a lost lamb in the presence of a group of hungry hyenas, and he was desperately trying to control himself so as not to show any fear.

"Well," she whispered conspiratorially. "I'm going to share a bit of gossip with you. I can't say for a fact that it's true. However, this is what I've heard. And...you must not repeat it. Do you promise?" she squeezed his arm.

"Yes, of course." He didn't care about what she had to say. Pitor wished she would just shut her mouth and take her hand off of his arm. But he was trying to pretend that he was amused by her nonsensical and unimportant chatter.

"Well, first off her name is Veronica, but they call her Vera."

"Vera," he repeated. He was watching Eichmann who was smiling at some woman who sat across the room.

"Veronica is not living with her husband. She's living in Bavaria."

"Oh? And that's the gossip?" he smiled.

"No, not at all. The reason she is not here is the gossip. It's been said she had to go to Bavaria because she is a Jew. Her parents were both Jewish. Can you believe it?"

He was stunned, but intrigued now as he turned to look at her. "No, I can't. Why would he marry someone Jewish?"

"I can't tell you that. I don't know."

"It's probably just gossip," he said. "Probably not even true."

"Oh, I think it is. You should see her. She looks like a Jew. She has dark hair and dark eyes. I think it's true."

"Hmmm," he said, "perhaps." Then he thought, *most of Hitler's top men have dark hair and eyes and they are not Jewish. I am blond with blue eyes and I am one hundred percent Jewish. So much for their evaluations.*

"And..." she continued, " from what I have heard, Eichmann is terribly ashamed of the fact that she is a Jew. In fact I'm sure that's why he is so adamant about participating in carrying out the final solution. They say he's devoted his life's work to removing Jews from Europe by transporting them to concentration camps where they can be watched and safely contained. And then, from what I understand, he was present at the conference in Wannsee. You have heard all about the conference, haven't you? I know it was top secret, but everyone knows about it."

"Do they?"

"Of course they do. You know how fast news travels in these circles."

"Well, I don't hear much gossip, I'm afraid. I am too busy and I don't have a wife to tell me everything I need to know." He knew he was being flirtatious, so he wasn't surprised that her face lit up when he said he was unmarried.

"Would you like me to tell you all about the conference? It's about the future of the jews in Europe."

"Yes, actually, I would."

"Now, you must realize that even though everyone knows this, it's still supposed to be a secret." She said smiling. Then she winked, "Therefore, you mustn't tell anyone that I told you."

"No, of course not." He agreed. Pitor wanted to know about the conference. What he learned might affect him in the future.

"Well, like I said, there was a conference. It took place in the winter of '42 in a lovely little suburb in Germany called Wannsee. And it was at this conference that the Final Solution was born."

"What is the Final Solution?" he asked.

"It's the program that has been put into place to deal with the Jewish problem."

"What exactly is it? More work camps?" He asked

"No. We can't go on feeding all of these useless eaters now, can we? The final solution is the decision that all Jews must be eliminated." She whispered in his ear.

"Eliminated?"

"Yes, eliminated. You know, done away with."

"Murdered?" he asked. He was unnerved.

"That's such an ugly word." She shook her head "Let's just say, they must be eliminated."

Pitor felt his hands shaking. He had to keep his wits about him. He had to be very careful not to let his true feelings show. If he said the wrong thing or showed the least bit of disgust at what he'd just heard, he might raise suspicion and jeopardize his chances of rescuing his son.

Then a man who seemed to be lighthearted and a little better looking than the other's walked over to talk to Eichmann.

"That's Albert Speer." Alice said.

And then an unattractive man entered. His hair was dark, as were his eyes. He was tall, but not as tall as Pitor, and he wore thick glasses. The man seemed to be very proud, even arrogant, as he stood very straight and made his way to his seat next to the one that had been reserved for Hitler. Alice gasped. Pitor saw her hands begin to tremble as she leaned over and whispered in Pitor's ear. "That's the Reichsführer, Heinrich Himmler," she said in awe.

Pitor nodded, not knowing what else to say or do. Then, because he was uncomfortable and wanted to change the subject, he asked Alice if she would like to dance. She readily agreed. "I'm not much of a dancer, I'm afraid," Pitor said. "But I'll do my best."

"It's all right. I'm an excellent dancer," Alice said. "I promise. I'll make sure you don't look foolish," she laughed.

He laughed too.

The band played a waltz and Pitor swept Alice across the dance floor until the band stopped playing abruptly. Everyone stood up. "He's here," Alice whispered, trembling. "He's here." She glanced over at Pitor, her eyes glowing and glassy like she'd had too much to drink. A bead of sweat had formed at her temple. "Oh my!" she exclaimed, unable to contain her excitement. "Look, it's him. It's our Führer. Isn't he wonderful? He has always had this effect on me."

Pitor hid his emotions as he stared at the man he hated more than anything in the world.

A few minutes later, another man entered the room. Alice turned and whispered into Pitor's ear, "It's Martin Borman and his wife just arriving. They are late. The Führer doesn't appreciate it when people arrive late."

Pitor looked at the head table where a strong-looking man who seemed to rule his demure wife sat down. The woman wore her hair in braids wrapped around her head, and instead of a gown like the others, she wore a traditional Bavarian dress. "That's Borman's wife Gerda. She is very traditional. Most of the men in the party approve of that. But personally, I love fashion, and I don't know how she can wear that traditional Bavarian dress, with her hair in old-fashioned braids. I mean, she is lovely, but from what I've heard she won't wear a drop of makeup. Not even a little lipstick," Alice shook her head. "I can't imagine that."

Pitor smiled. He had nothing to say about Borman's wife. He didn't care whether or not she wore lipstick. He was nervous as he looked at all of them sitting together. How he wished he could somehow inform the allies that all the top Nazis were here in one place. But he knew he could not bear to have this place bombed right now because his son was in the other room, and his little boy meant even more to him than winning this war.

"You know this place? I am talking about the Eagle's Nest. It was a gift from Borman to Hitler. Borman is a good man, very devoted to our Führer. But I can tell you a secret if you promise not to share it with anyone," she whispered.

"Oh, and what's that?"

"You must promise first."

"All right, I promise."

She smiled and winked, then in a whisper she said, "Our Führer hates the Eagle's Nest. He doesn't like heights. Or at least that's what I heard. From what I hear he hardly ever comes up here. It's Eva who loves this place. She has been known to come here to sunbathe."

"Oh," Pitor said. *It's good to know that Hitler hates heights. Just in case I need that information later.*

And then a hush fell over the crowd as Adolf Hitler stood up. The rest of the crowd stood up. Adolf Hitler was a short man with a mustache that was too small for his face, which made him look cartoonish. A far cry from the Aryan man in the poster on the wall. Then the little man, who was intent on ruling the world, raised his hands in the air and smiled at the guests. Pitor felt his blood run cold. Then Hitler's smile faded, and his face grew serious as he raised his hand in a salute.

When they saw him salute, the entire crowd raised their hands in a return salute. They called out, "Heil Hitler," in unison. Pitor forced himself to stand up and raise his hand like the others. It was one thing to pretend to be an SS officer when he was driving with a farmer or talking to a woman. But now he was standing and saluting the Führer, and he felt uncomfortable. The crowd yelled, "Heil Hitler" repeatedly in a frenzy until Hitler raised his hands in the air and motioned for the crowd to be quiet.

The room was suddenly silent.

As he looked around at the rest of the guests, Pitor saw they looked wild-eyed. They were mesmerized, almost hypnotized in their obsession with the Führer. Sweat began running down Alice's brow. "He's marvelous, isn't he?" she said breathlessly.

"Yes," Pitor managed to say.

Now the room was so silent that Pitor felt his nerves about to shatter. Then, in a voice ever so soft, and ever so clear, Hitler began to speak. Slowly, careful, step by step, he drew his followers in deeper and deeper. Then once he saw he held them all spellbound by his every word, his face grew red, and he began to speak more loudly and wildly until he was ranting and his fists were flailing. Suddenly his small stature disappeared, and he seemed to grow tall and strong, even monstrous, right before Pitor's eyes. Carefully choosing his every word, he convinced his followers that they were part of a group of superior human beings. He somehow made them all believe that even though it was not true, they looked and were exactly like the people in the Aryan poster on the wall. Hitler promised them a better life, which he explained was their birthright, because they were born into this superior race. "We should have never lost the great war, my fellow Germans. We only lost because of the Jews. It was the Jews who lost the war for us. They stole everything from the good German people. But you must never forget who you are. Every single one of you is a member of a supe-rior race, and you must never forget that. You are the Aryans. And I have come to restore you to your rightful place as rulers of the world." His entire body was shaking as he said these words that made the crowd feel elated and privileged. Hitler spat as he spoke of his contempt for the *untermenschen*, the Jews who he called subhu-mans. "These untermenschen must be weeded out so they don't destroy our Aryan race. We gave them a chance to live among us in the past, and look at what they did to us. They have brought shame to our Fatherland."

The crowd was nodding their heads and roaring with approval. Pitor saw the looks on their angry and determined faces, and a shiver ran up the back of his neck as if a spider had crawled on him. For the first time, he understood how Hitler had taken control of a country as civilized as Germany had been before the Nazis came to power.

The crowd was still cheering wildly when Hitler finished his speech and called for Reichsführer Heinrich Himmler to take the stage. Himmler walked up to the podium, and the saluting started again, "Heil Hitler, heil Hitler, heil Hitler."

"As you know," Himmler said, after they'd all quieted down, "I've been working on an important project. A project to create a strong and plentiful pure Aryan population to rule our New Germany. And as a special treat some of the children who have been produced through this program are here with us tonight. They are looking forward to meeting you as I am sure you are looking forward to meeting them," he said. "So, without further introductions, it is with pride that I introduce you to the future of the Reich." Then he motioned to the two young women with brown hair that stood in the doorway. Gretchen nodded. Then she and Heidi led the group of five young, blond-haired, blue-eyed children into the room, three of them boys, two girls. The man who Heidi had called Horst stood back against the wall and watched carefully. His job was to make sure the children remained safe. Horst was an ugly man, tall and lanky. His hair was white, his skin was pale, and his eyes were very light blue, encircled by red. He wore his hair cut very short with short, uneven bangs.

Pitor's eyes were glued to the children. He watched Jakup, who was smiling broadly as he entered the room, bouncing as he walked with his fat little toddler legs moving quickly. Pitor felt a tightening in his chest. *Of course he is smiling. He doesn't understand what is going on here. He's just a child.* Pitor closed his eyes for a moment and saw Mila's face in his mind's eye. *He felt his heart ache. I found him, sweetheart. Now I have to find a way to take him away from here. Away from these people. I'm thinking perhaps I will try to find a way to adopt him if I can. That would be the easiest way.*

"And tonight, Dr. Goebbels, our wonderful Reich minister of propaganda, also has a surprise for all of us. Joseph, please stand up," Himmler waved his hand at Goebbels.

Joseph Goebbel's wife Magda was smiling broadly and clapping her hands as her husband stood up and walked over to the microphone. "Thank you, Heinrich," he said, turning to glance at Himmler as he took the microphone. "As some of you might know, our Führer is enthralled with the work of an American cartoonist by the name of Walt Disney. In fact, there are two American's that our Führer is rather taken with. Herr Disney, who is a wonderful creative cartoonist, and Henry Ford, a brilliant auto maker. Both these men have made quite an impression on our Führer. If you have followed either of the speeches of these men, you will know that they are very sympathetic to our cause. They both seem to understand what our Führer is trying to do, and they appreciate his efforts. Therefore, on Christmas, back in 1937, I wanted to present our Führer with a gift that he would truly enjoy. Since he already had plenty of automobiles," Goebbels smiled at Hitler. The crowd chuckled, and Dr. Goebbels stopped speaking until they were silent again. Then he continued, "therefore," Goebbels cleared his throat. "I decided to give our Führer a gift of twelve Walt Disney films. Since then, our Führer has admitted to me that he enjoys them so much that he watches one each night before going to bed."

"He's correct! I do," Hitler called out and everyone in the audience began to clap.

Goebbels smiled and pushed away a strand of his thin hair that had fallen into his eyes. Then he paused for effect and once again, the room grew quiet. There was a small squeak from one of the children and someone giggled.

"And so," Goebbels continued, "tonight, as a special treat, not only for all of you, but also for these beautiful children, our crew has taken the time to set up a projector so we can all watch a couple of these short Walt Disney films. How would you like that?"

Everyone in the dining room clapped again.

"Good," Goebbels said, nodding. "I'm glad. I really believe you will all enjoy this." Then he turned to two production men who were waiting for his cue. "Why don't the two of you take over from here," he said to the production men. "And while they are preparing the films, I will hand the microphone over to our Reichsführer," Himmler nodded, then smiled and took the microphone.

The projection men pulled down a large screen that had been set up at the front of the room. Himmler lifted his hand and said to the two girls who were standing beside the children, "Little brown sisters, please gather the children and have them sit down on the floor in front of the screen."

The two girls who Pitor had learned were called Gretchen and Heidi led the group to the center of the room. The women in the crowd oohed and aahed at the little ones as they sat cross-legged in front of the screen. Once all the children were seated, the two little brown sisters sat down in the middle of the children to keep them quiet, so they did not disturb the adults while the films were playing. Pitor watched the children closely. His heartbeat faster when he saw Jakup sit down beside one of the other little boys, crossing his chubby legs under him.

Himmler asked Heidi, "Are we ready? Are they all set now?"

"Yes, Reichsführer." She answered obediently.

126

"Then, can someone please dim the lights, and we will watch the first film."

Then the lights were dimmed, and the film began. A boy and girl mouse filled the screen. They were cute and funny, and they made the entire audience laugh, especially the children. When the Mickey Mouse cartoon ended, the lights were turned back on. Everyone in the audience clapped. Pitor clapped too. Next, Himmler nodded to Heidi, who whispered to Gretchen. Then the two little brown sisters stood up and motioned for the children to follow. Once the children had lined up in a single file, the two little brown sisters led them out of the room.

"I hope all of you enjoyed this wonderful entertaining film. And, more importantly, I really hope you enjoyed meeting with our young people this evening. I cannot stress enough just how important they are to the future of our precious Fatherland," Himmler said.

Everyone clapped again.

"Now," Himmler smiled. "I am sure we are all quite famished. So, shall we enjoy our dinner?"

Everyone clapped again as Himmler sat down.

CHAPTER TWENTY-THREE

The first to be served was Adolf Hitler, followed by Eva Braun. Next were the SS elite, who were seated at the head table. Pitor watched as two tasters each took a forkful of food from Hitler's plate and ate it. Hitler then watched and waited for several minutes before touching his food.

Once the head table had been served, white-gloved waiters entered the room carrying large platters of beef and poultry, which they brought around to each table. Steaming plates filled with vegetables and breads doused in real butter followed. Pitor knew, because of the time he'd spent with Steffi, that the Nazis took most of the food that the local farms produced. He had heard that they not only took the food from the German farmers, they also took it from the farmers who were in the countries they'd conquered. But here, in the Eagle's Nest, there was no evidence of the lack of food that Pitor had come to know not only among the farmers, but it had been even worse for the Jews in the Warsaw Ghetto. Hitler had put his German citizens on limited rations. However, at this gala, there were no shortages of anything. Dark German beer and bottles of wine flowed like water.

And more food was left on plates to be discarded than Pitor had seen in years.

When dinner was done and dessert had been served, the band took the stage in the back of the room. They played a single waltz while the wait staff cleared the tables. Once the tables were cleared, Dr. Goebbels limped to the stage and took the microphone.

"Everyone, please be seated," he said, and the band stopped playing. Then Goebbels continued to speak, "I hope everyone enjoyed their dinner."

Applause followed.

"Tonight, we have another special surprise for you. I am proud and honored to have been chosen to introduce you to some newly promoted members of our party," Goebbels looked around the room, nodding proudly, "so, if you hear your name called, please stand up." He went on to read off the names of three men. After each name was read, the crowd clapped. The third name Goebbels read was, "Konrad Hoffmann, please stand up. Sturmscharführer Hoffman is to be honored this evening. He is to be promoted from Sturmscharführer to personal bodyguard to our Führer."

The crowd cheered.

For a moment, Pitor forgot his name. He was too busy thinking of ways he might get to Jakup. But then Alice nudged him, "Konrad." She said in a strong whisper, "The Reichsführer called your name. Stand up."

"I'm sorry. I wasn't paying attention," Pitor whispered to Alice as he stood up quickly.

"Heil Hitler," Goebbels saluted.

"Heil Hitler," Pitor saluted.

Again, the crowd cheered. Dr. Goebbels was smiling as he said, "Come on up here Hoffmann. This is not a time to be shy or humble. You've proven yourself to be a loyal and trustworthy servant of the Reich, not to mention a brave soldier."

Pitor walked up to the podium. Even though he knew he had fooled them, his knees were threatening to buckle. His heart was racing, and his mouth was dry. When he arrived at the front of the crowd, Himmler was standing beside Goebbels. "This is a most important position," Himmler said, "you have a most crucial job. You have been chosen as one of the men who will be responsible for the safety of our Führer. What do you say to that?"

"I am honored," Pitor managed to say. "I will always act in a way that is best for the Fatherland. I will protect our Führer with my life."

Everyone began to cheer and clap as a badge was pinned onto the lapel of Pitor's uniform. Himmler turned to Pitor and whispered to him he must stand behind the head table as everyone began to leave the dining room. As Pitor stood quietly looking at the crowd who were leaving, he overheard Goebbels speaking to Hitler. "Your new bodyguard is quite handsome," Goebbels remarked. "What a remarkable lad, he is a true specimen of Aryan perfection. And from what the Reichsführer has told me about him, he is eternally devoted to you and to our Reich."

"Yes, I can see that," Hitler said confidently. "I have a good feeling about him." He cleared his throat. "I hardly know him. I mean we just met. But somehow, I feel confident that I can trust him."

Pitor's eyes met Hitler's and Pitor managed a smile. He had overheard the conversation between Goebbels and Hitler, and he was glad Hitler trusted him.

"Come Adolf, let's say goodnight to our guests," Eva took Hitler's hand and led him to the door of the dining room where a crowd had gathered waiting to leave.

Pitor turned away. He didn't want to take the chance that his face might reveal his inner thoughts. *The hatred burning in my heart is well hidden. None of them suspects a thing. And Hitler, that bastard trusts me. Well, if I have anything to say about it, I will be the last person on this earth he will ever trust.*

"Hoffmann," Pitor heard a male voice say. He turned around to see Horst, the boyfriend of Gretchen, the little brown sister.

"Yes?"

"I just wanted to extend my congratulations," Horst's voice was soft, and he attempted to sound genuine, but his eyes told a far different story. "We always knew you had potential back at school." Horst said, but there was sly tone to his voice. "But I just can't believe how different you are today. You are so quiet now. When we were boys, you were always so outgoing and friendly."

Horst made Pitor uneasy. He could not put his finger on what it was about this man that left him unnerved, but it was a distinct feeling that he couldn't shake off. "Thank you, we all grow up." Pitor said graciously, not sure of how to respond.

"The Führer is going to be staying in Salzburg tonight. Or so I've heard. So, you will probably be staying here for the night as well. Anyway, Gretchen, Heidi, and I are going down into town for a few beers before we return to Steinhoring. Would you care to join us?" he asked.

"What about the children? Will they stay be staying here at the Eagle's Nest or going to Salzburg?"

"Neither, they are already on their way back to Steinhoring. They will be at Heim Hochland in a few hours. We'll meet them there later tonight."

"I see," Pitor said. "Who took them back to Steinhoring?"

"Two guards. Don't worry. They will be safe." Horst patted Pitor's back.

Pitor nodded. Then he thought about Jakup, and then Heidi, and what the next best course of action would be. He didn't like Horst, and would rather not have any further contact with him, but he thought it would be best if he befriended him and the two girls. They might prove instrumental in his pursuit of his son. *Heidi has access to Jakup. Going out for a drink with this group is a good opportunity to find out more information about the adoptions at the Lebensborn home.* Then he said, "I would love to join you. But I must consult the Reichsführer first to see if I am required to be anywhere tonight."

"Of course. I fully understand," Horst said, with a twinkle in his eye. "But it would be lovely to have a few drinks with an old school chum. We could reminisce about some of our old teachers and class-mates as well."

Pitor waited until the Reichsführer was alone, then he forced himself to appear humble as he asked for permission to join Heidi and the others in town that evening. Pitor dreaded spending time with Horst. He wasn't sure what Horst might bring up from the past, and what he might discover about Pitor and the truth. But Pitor needed to get close to Heidi to learn whatever he could about Jakup's whereabouts. And he was willing to take any risk necessary to rescue his son.

"While we encourage you to have friends in the party, those young people who you are planning to spend time with are beneath your station," Himmler frowned. "Little brown sisters are not good marriage choices for a man like you. Of course, they have been checked out and they are of pure blood, but their coloring is all wrong. Besides that, you are expected in Berchtesgaden tonight. That is where the Führer will be staying. And he wants you to be there."

Pitor nodded. "Yes, of course. Reichsführer," he said, but he was disappointed at not being permitted to go with the little brown sisters. He'd been hoping that Horst and the girls would get drunk and tell him some secrets that would help him adopt or steal Jakup. But it was not going to be possible, at least not yet. He had to do what Hitler demanded, at least for now. So, he decided that he would have to wait until he had some time off from this job. Then he would find a way to go to Heim Hochland. It was going to be difficult, because he knew if he went to the Lebensborn home, he would be expected to have sex with one of the girls. They would think that he came to share his seed in order to produce an Aryan child for the Führer. Not only did he find the idea repulsive that a child he spawned might serve the Third Reich, but he also knew that if one of those girls saw his circumcised penis, his secret would be revealed, and he would be arrested. *This is going to be a very delicate matter.* He thought.

The Reichsführer was still speaking, but Pitor didn't hear him. He was lost in his own thoughts. Then, he was brought out of his thoughts when he saw Himmler pointing to the poster of the Aryan couple that hung on the wall. Himmler was telling Goring that he was so proud to be a pure Aryan. For a moment Pitor wanted to laugh. Not a single one of the top Nazi officials looked like the couple in the poster. They only imagined that they did. Most of them were dark-haired and brown-eyed. And for all of Hitler's criticism of the physical and mental handicapped, Goebbel's club foot was obvious in the way he limped when he walked. *The rules don't apply to them. In fact, the rules only apply some of the time. When it's convenient for them. This whole Aryan race is built on nonsense.*

Himmler saw Pitor watching him and he smiled. Then he walked over to Pitor and said, "Not only are you a perfect physical Aryan specimen, but you are smart, and you are now in a position to find a quality wife. I would recommend you start searching for a girl who is as perfect as you are. Our Führer is adamant about marriage. He would like every pure German couple to marry and have as many pure Aryan children as possible."

Pitor nodded. *Another contradiction. The Führer would like everyone in Germany to get married and have Aryan children. But he is not married. So, how is it he can make a demand like that? I remember one of the partisans telling me a story about Hitler. He said that he knew for a fact Hitler had an affair with his niece, the daughter of his stepsister. And, when Hitler grew tired of her, he murdered her. The papers said it was suicide. But I believe Hitler killed his sister's daughter.*

"Do you have an auto available to you or will you be traveling with us?" Himmler asked casually.

"I don't have an auto."

"How did you get here?"

"A police officer from Munich drove me. I went to the police station in Munich and asked for a ride."

"Brilliant," Himmler laughed. "Sometimes our men forget the importance of security up here, and they have a regular citizen drive them. That can be risky. It can put our Führer's safety at risk."

"I understand," Pitor said. "That's why I chose to ask a police officer."

"Well, that was an excellent choice. I believe you are going to do very well in your new position," Himmler smiled. "Now, go and get yourself ready to leave. We should be on our way to Salzburg in a half hour or so."

Pitor nodded.

It was exactly a half hour later when Pitor took the elevator back down to the road and then walked back through the dark tunnel. He had been told a black automobile would be waiting to take him into Salzburg with the rest of Hitler's entourage. As he waited for the car to appear, he noticed Horst was standing alone at the mouth of the tunnel. He was staring at Pitor, and when their eyes met, a strange and wicked smile came over Horst's face.

"Hoffmann," Himmler said to Pitor, pulling Pitor's attention away from Horst, "I'm leaving now, but your ride will be arriving here in a moment."

"Thank you, Reichsführer," Pitor said humbly. But he felt goosebumps forming on the back of his neck.

Once the automobile carrying the Reichsführer pulled away, Pitor turned to look back at Horst. But Horst was gone.

CHAPTER TWENTY-FOUR

It had been over two weeks since Pitor left the little farmhouse. However, for Steffi it was as if he had just walked out the door. The painful sting of loneliness she felt as she watched him walk away still lingered, especially late at night after the children were asleep and she was alone. He had brought her so much joy, more than she'd ever thought she was capable of feeling. She sat at the kitchen table sipping a cup of weak tea and listening to the rain as it clanged against the metal roof. The echo of her mother's loud snoring mingling with the sound of the rain made her feel sad. She closed her eyes and thought of Pitor. If only he had been hers to keep. If only he had fallen in love with her the way she had fallen in love with him. *Yes, it happened very fast. And I could hardly expect him to feel the way I did. But it would have been so wonderful if it had happened that way. As it is, I know he was only here for a short time and although I fell hard, he felt nothing. And I am pretty sure I will spend the rest of my life pining over him, even though chances are I may never see him again. The only hope I have is that he might return for that photo.*

Steffi took the picture out of her drawer and looked at it. She wished Pitor had been in the photograph. But he wasn't. Only his family was. Still, his little boy looked so much like him that Steffi imagined that this was what Pitor must have looked like when he was a child. She sighed. Then she returned the photo to her drawer.

Every night when Steffi was alone, she prayed to Jesus for Pitor's safety. Pitor had made it clear to her he was Jewish, and she knew that the two little ones she was risking her life to protect were Jewish as well. Most people would have thought of her as a fool to care so deeply for these people. But Steffi had grown up as a Christian. And she had been very good friends with a pastor from the local church who had once told her that Jesus, her lord and savior, was a Jew. So, she wondered how all these people who had also been raised as Christians could turn on the Jews the way they had. Steffi could not do it. Even though Hitler had declared himself more powerful than Jesus. She knew better. In her lifetime, Steffi had witnessed miracles. And even now, she was praying to Jesus for a miracle that would save the Jewish people.

"Steffi," she heard the voice of a young girl and she knew Zita was awake and had climbed out from under the floorboards.

"Zita, what are you doing up here? I've told you a thousand times that you must not come upstairs unless I tell you to. What if someone was here and they saw you? There are rewards for turning Jews into the Nazis. Our neighbors are poor, they would be hard pressed to turn down a reward. Besides that, the Nazis can come to our farm at any time. We must be so careful. It is light outside. What if someone was walking by the window and they saw you come out from under the floor? They would know something was not right. I know you hate it in the cellar, and I don't blame you—I hate having to keep you there. And, I've thought about bringing you and Asher upstairs, but I am afraid that any Nazi officers passing through who saw you might ask the neighbors if they knew who you are. And they might remember you."

"The neighbors were our friends. They liked our parents. They wouldn't turn us in," Zita said. "Besides, Asher and I hardly ever saw them. I doubt any of them would recognize either of us."

"You may very well be right. But we can't take a risk like that. Anyone who turned you two in would receive food and money as a reward for your arrest. People are starving, Zita. They are driven to do things they wouldn't ordinarily do because they are desperate," Steffi said. Then she added, "So, why did you come upstairs now, anyway? Is everything all right?"

"I had a nightmare," Zita said, with tears in her eyes. "Last night Asher was not feeling well before he went to sleep, and I had a terrible nightmare that he died."

"Is he all right this morning?" Steffi asked.

"I'm not sure. I hope so. He vomited last night. I am thinking that he ate something that made him sick."

"Is he breathing?"

"Yes, but he's wheezing. I think he is having trouble breathing," Zita said. "Can you come and look at him?"

"Yes, I wish it were dark outside. But I suppose I should come down there now. Let me go and get my blanket and I will be right back. By the way, have you two been warm enough down there in the cellar?" She asked as she walked towards the bedroom.

"Not really, but Asher and I know you don't have any more blankets to spare."

"I'll give you this one," Steffi said as she hurried back into the room with a worn gray blanket with a large hole in the center that looked as if it might unravel even more. It was her last available blanket. Once she gave it to Zita and Asher, she would have to sleep with her coat covering her. She knew she would be cold, but she couldn't bear to think of the two young people freezing in her cellar. When Steffi re-entered the living room, she looked around her quickly to ensure that all the shades were drawn, then she lit a candle before she opened the entrance to the cellar. It was always dark and damp down there. Zita went down the stairs first. Steffi followed her. When they reached the bottom, Steffi saw Asher was lying in his bed. "At least he is awake," she said, but she could hear his labored breathing. Steffi knelt beside the wheezing little boy and asked, "You aren't feeling well?"

"I can't breathe," he said. "It hurts in my chest when I try to breathe."

She put her hand on his chest, knowing full well that she couldn't do much for him. He needed to see a doctor. However, considering the circumstances, she knew that even if she had the money to pay a doctor, because of the risk of him telling the Nazis that she was harboring Jews, that was impossible. With her hand on Asher's small chest, she could feel him struggling and she almost let out a cry of frustration, asking God why he had added this terrible calamity to the rest of her troubles. But she didn't. She knew the children were frightened enough as they were. She must try her best to remain calm. "I'll go upstairs and make you some hot tea. That should help loosen up the mucus in your chest. Sitting up for a while might help as well."

"All right Steffi," Asher said. Then Steffi put the candle down on the floor and watched as Zita moved over to help her brother sit up a bit more. Asher was very weak, and being that Zita was small, she couldn't lift Asher, who had no power to continue to sit up by himself. So, before she went upstairs, Steffi went over to help her prop him up against the cold wall of the building.

"I'll be right back," Steffi said, wishing she had an abundance of pillows to put behind Asher to help him be comfortable. But she didn't. So, there was no other choice. Steffi watched him as his head flopped over to a side. She felt her nerves unraveling more every minute. *After all we have been through together, I can't let this boy die. I just can't. And look at Zita's face. Poor child, she is terrified. Her brother is the only person left from her family who she is certain is still alive. We don't discuss it, but I am sure both Zita and Asher are afraid that their parents are dead.*

Steffi turned and managed a strained smile as she opened the trapdoor and climbed out from under the floor. She stretched out her back and was glad that Asher and Zita were both young enough to still be flexible. It would have been very painful for an adult to stay cramped up in the cellar for a long period of time. After all, Steffi was not tall, and she had to hunch over when she was in the cellar. She sighed and said a silent prayer as she walked into the kitchen. Then turned on a light. A deep male voice whispered, "Fräulein..." Steffi was startled. She almost dropped the teapot. There had not been an adult male voice in her home since Pitor left. A shiver shot down her spine as she spun around, and her eyes searched the living room. Then she saw him and the room began to spin. She felt faint. Her hand went up to her heart and she let out a scream.

CHAPTER TWENTY-FIVE

Pitor had no choice but to do as the Reichsführer commanded. He would have preferred to go with the little brown sisters to see what he could find out about Jakup, but he had just been appointed to his new position, and any resistance to orders would surely give him away.

While waiting for his car to arrive, Pitor noticed Heidi standing off to the side of the tunnel admiring the view of the Eagle's Nest from below. "I'm sorry, I can't join you and your friends for drinks this evening. The Reichsführer demands that I go with him and the Führer. After all, protecting our Führer is my job," Pitor said, smiling warmly. *This little brown sister is my opportunity to get to my son. I must make her think I am attracted to her. If I can win her affection, she will help me.* "But if you would like, I would like to see you again. I mean, if you are interested," he said shyly.

"Of course I am, and I would love to see you again," Heidi said.

Gretchen was silent. She stood off to the side, watching them. Horst had his arm around her, his hand on her shoulder. Pitor sensed Gretchen was jealous of his attentions to Heidi.

"I will come to see you at Heim Hochland as soon as I have a day off from work. I can't promise when that will happen, but I hope when it does you will agree to have dinner with me."

Heidi was beaming. "Yes, I will, and I understand you don't know when you will be able to get away, so it might be last minute notice. That's all right. I will cancel any previous plans."

He smiled at her, then gently brushed his hand over her cheek. "I look forward to it," he said, wishing he could see Jakup at least once more before he left. But Jakup was already on his way back to the home for the Lebensborn. Although he would have liked to get more information from Heidi about Jakup, he dare not ask anything. Especially not under the earshot of Horst and Gretchen. Pitor had an intuitive feeling that he couldn't trust them. And right now, although he was fairly sure Heidi was smitten with him, he still couldn't risk trusting her either. "Ahh, well," he muttered softly, "I am glad that I met you. But unfortunately, I must go now." He said, as if it pained him to leave her. He saw in her eyes that she was stuck on his every word, and he hoped it wouldn't be too long before he had a day off from work.

CHAPTER TWENTY-SIX

The children had arrived and left the Eagle's Nest by car. They were escorted by security officers.

Earlier that day, Horst had driven to the Eagle's Nest with Gretchen and Heidi. He'd driven the automobile that he had so proudly purchased. So, he had his auto with him that night when the three of them stopped at a tavern in Salzburg for some beers. However, it had been a long night, and it was already very late. All three of them were expected to report for work in the morning, so they had to cut the evening short. The ride back to Steinhoring was less than two hours, but they were all exhausted. So, when Horst suggested Gretchen spend the night at his place, she declined. "I am tired Horst, and I must be here at Heim Hochland early tomorrow. Maybe on Saturday night since it's Heidi's Sunday to work, and I have the day off," she forced a tired smile at him. Gretchen and Heidi took turns taking Sundays off.

"I understand," he smiled. Then he got out of the car and opened the door to let the two women out. Horst leaned over to kiss Gretchen goodnight, but there was no passion in her kiss. In fact, it was devoid of all emotion, and even though Heidi tried to look away to give them privacy, she was able to see that Gretchen was not treating Horst with as much affection as she usually did.

The girls waved goodbye as Horst got back into his car and drove away, headed to his apartment, which was close to Heim Hochland. Heidi and Gretchen went inside and went up to their room. They immediately got ready for bed. These two women had been friends and roommates for years. So, Heidi thought she knew Gretchen very well. But tonight, Gretchen was not herself. Something about her was different. It was hard to explain, and Heidi would have liked to believe that it was because Gretchen was just exhausted from the day's activities, but Gretchen seemed colder toward Heidi than she'd ever been. "I'll be right back," Heidi said once she was ready to go to sleep. "I want to check on the children before we go to bed. They should be in their beds by now," Heidi said.

"Good idea," Gretchen said.

The children's room was quiet and dark, the little ones were asleep. Over the years, there had been arguments between Gretchen and Heidi, but never had Gretchen seemed so distant. And besides, they had not argued at all on this trip. In fact, everything had gone very well. Even the children had been exceptionally well behaved.

When Heidi returned to her room Gretchen was already in bed, but she'd left the light on for Heidi. "Is something wrong?" Heidi asked in a soft voice, hoping Gretchen would convince her that nothing was amiss. But when she looked into Gretchen's eyes, Heidi thought she knew what was bothering Gretchen. Gretchen was seething with jealousy. It was true Gretchen had a boyfriend. She and Horst had been together for a while now. However, Horst was unattractive and had a low paying position. And until now, both Gretchen and Heidi believed a boyfriend like Horst was the best that a little brown sister might hope for. But, for a man who was as attractive and successful as Konrad Hoffmann, to show an interest in a little brown sister was unheard of. A man like Konrad Hoffman could have his choice of athletic blonde Aryan girls. To have him show an interest in Heidi awakened a terrible serpent of jealousy in Gretchen that would prove to know no boundaries.

CHAPTER TWENTY-SEVEN

Gretchen lay in bed, unable to sleep. She heard Heidi's soft snoring in the bed beside her, and she cursed under her breath. *What would a man like Konrad Hoffman see in an unattractive girl from a poor family like her? Why would he even want to spend time getting to know her? I can't figure it out. All I know is, if he is attracted to little brown sisters, he should have chosen me. I'm far better looking than Heidi, and at least my father had a decent job. But for some odd reason, he's chosen her. And that makes me sick to my stomach. If he marries her, I will be livid. I don't think I will ever get over it. I just can't believe I'm stuck with Horst. I know Horst is a good man at heart, but Hoffmann has so much potential. And he is so handsome. Horst has mentioned to me that he sees something wrong with Hoffmann. He might be right, but it could just be jealousy. After all, Horst won't ever have the future opportunities that Hoffman will have. However, if there really is something wrong with Konrad, the party would reward Horst for discovering it. So, perhaps he and I should look deeper.*

CHAPTER TWENTY-EIGHT

"What could you possibly have been doing in the cellar, Fräulein?" He was an older man. From his Nazi uniform, Steffi could see that he was an officer. "Now, please don't tell me that a nice German girl like you has been hiding food from our German army. I would hope a good Aryan girl would understand how important it is that she be faithful to the Fatherland." He smirked. "I am quite aware that unfortunately, some of you farmers are too stupid to realize that by stealing from your harvest, you are endangering Germany's chances of winning this war. And thereby you are endangering your own welfare. What a pathetic thought. Don't you agree?" He shook his head as if he were talking to a small child. "Still." He sighed. "I might find it in my heart not to report you, so long as you don't give me any trouble and you make it worth my while. Do we understand each other?"

Steffi didn't know what to say. She felt nauseated, but it didn't matter to him, and she knew that. Even so, she had no idea how to answer, or even what he wanted from her. But she nodded her head, knowing that if he found out what was really in the cellar, it would be even worse than if he'd discovered that she'd stolen a head of cabbage or a few potatoes.

"Come here and sit beside me," he said, patting the sofa. "You're such a pretty girl. I think you and I should get to know each other."

She went willingly, because she was so terrified that he would find out about the children. And if he did, she was certain that he would arrest all of them. Steffi sat down, a little bit away from the old Nazi. But that did not deter him. He moved closer to her and put his hand on her upper thigh. She felt her body tremble with fear and disgust. Now, it all became clear to her, and she understood what he wanted. There was nothing she could do. She didn't know how to say no without causing him to become so angry that he arrested her. She closed her eyes and felt the heat of his hand on her thigh. It was riding towards her womanhood. She wanted to stand up and get away from his hot, snaking hand. But she dared not. Even if he didn't find the children, and he only arrested her, the two children would starve to death, because no one except Pitor and herself knew of their existence. And sadly, Pitor was far away. She felt the man's fingers slide under her panties and tears began to sting behind her eyelids. Pitor was the first and only man she had ever been with, and she certainly didn't want this one to be the second. However, there seemed to be no way out. His dirty fingers were inside of her now. She swallowed hard, trying to hold back the tears. But he didn't seem to notice. He was breathing heavily as he moved closer and began to kiss her neck. A thin bit of drool ran down her neck and then her chest. Vomit burned the back of her throat. Then he pulled her legs out from under her, and she hit her head on the armrest of the sofa. But that didn't stop him. He pulled her harder until she was lying flat on her back. He ripped off her panties and got up on one knee to undo his trousers. Then he entered her. Steffi could no longer hold back her tears. They flowed like a river down her cheeks. If he even noticed, he didn't say a word about it. He was pounding into her like a jackhammer and with each thrust, she felt her inner peace shatter a little more. And then it was over. Thankfully, he was done. He wiped his manhood on her sofa and then pulled up his pants. She lay there for a moment, wishing she could die, panting, her heart beating fast.

"I'm going to leave now," he said. "I am going to let you get away with it this time, but depending on where I am going, I may come back to see you again at some point. Next time, I suggest you make sure you aren't stealing produce from the Fatherland. Because, next time I won't be so kind and lenient with you."

She nodded, covering herself with her skirt, but unable to look directly at him, staring down at the floor instead. He stood and stretched and was just about to leave when the trapdoor slid open and Zita came rushing out. "I was worried that you might have hurt yourself. It took you so long to return. Asher and I were worried," Zita said, but then she turned around and saw the Nazi. Her face fell. Her skin turned white and she gasped in terror.

CHAPTER TWENTY-NINE

"What have we here? This is even worse than I thought," the Nazi said, clicking his tongue sarcastically. "And it seems from what this girl just said that there is another one under there. A boy named Asher perhaps," he pointed to the floor. "I just can't imagine living under a floor, can you?" he turned mockingly to Steffi, but it was a rhetorical question, as he did not wait for an answer. He shook his head. "This is bad. Yes, very bad. It seems to me that you are hiding Jews," he said to Steffi. "That's far worse than stealing food. I am afraid I can't let this go. I am afraid I must do something about this."

"No, please. Please," Steffi said. "Just go. I beg you, please."

"I beg you, please..." he imitated her. "I see you are an enemy of the Reich. Keeping Jews like pets under your floor," he shook his head. "You do realize that you are nothing special? When I want a woman, I can always get one. A man of my rank doesn't starve for affection. It just so happened that I was in your area, and you were available. But believe me, you were not worth overlooking a crime like this," he said, and a cruel smile came over his face.

Steffi felt the bitter taste of bile rising in her throat again and she had to swallow hard to avoid vomiting. This horrible man had just invaded her body and now he was threatening the lives of not only her, but the two children she had grown to care so deeply for. "I will do anything you ask, only please let them be. They've done nothing wrong. They are harmless to you. They are only just children, they cannot pose any threat to the Fatherland."

"They are Jews you idiot!" he bellowed. "This makes them dangerous to the future of our Reich. Right now, they are too young to be a problem. But if they are left alive, they will grow up and then they will remember what happened to their families. And you can be assured they will pose a threat to our country."

Zita looked at Steffi. Then she began to cry. Steffi put her arms out and Zita ran into them. Steffi held her tightly.

"I am begging you," Steffi said. "Please spare these two young people. I promise you that they will never try to do anything to hurt our Fatherland."

"Oh, but you are a poor little fool. And I have enjoyed my time with you. So, quite frankly, I would like to do this favor for you. But, alas, I cannot. We are forced, sometimes, to do things that are unpleasant. So, I must not allow myself to become sentimental, Fräulein. *Deutschland Uber Alles*. Germany above all else." He said, then he began to hum and then to sing the song *Deutschland Uber Alles*.

Steffi sat still and powerless. She held Zita in her arms. The Nazi was singing loudly now, clearly enjoying the power he held over them. His eyes were hard like glass. "Sing along with me," he said to Steffi, "you must know the words. I am sure you learned them when you were in the *Bund Deutscher Mädel*. Or were you too far away from the city to have an opportunity to attend the League of German Girls, out here in this rural area?" He taunted her. "It is truly a shame if you were unable to attend. Our Hitler Youth organizations are not only wonderful learning experiences for our Aryan young people, but they are also lots of good outdoor fun." He smiled, then he began to sing even louder than before.

Steffi's heart was pounding so hard that her chest hurt. She could not look at him, so she closed her eyes and began to pray. *Jesus, dear Jesus. I am begging you to please help me. I am not as concerned about myself as I am about these two young people who are in my care. They have their whole lives ahead of them, but they are helpless against this terrible government, and they are so vulnerable. This horrible man who has invaded my home is clearly out of his mind. I am begging you to please help me save these two precious young lives. I don't know what to do next. I am so afraid.*

"Girl," the Nazi pointed to Zita. "You go under the floor and get the little boy. The one who you referred to as Asher. He is the only other Jew here, is that correct?"

"Yes," Zita whispered.

"Good. Then go and get him, and bring him right back upstairs. Do you understand me?"

"Yes," Zita answered. She was still in Steffi's arms, and Steffi could feel her shaking.

"Go on. It's all right," Steffi said.

"And, just in case you plan to try and resist me by staying down there, I won't come after you." He smiled and his glass-like, emotionless eyes twinkled. "I'll just send this woman down there to be with you. And once you're all down there in the cellar, I'll start a fire, and you will be burned alive."

Zita stood up. Steffi could see Zita's legs were trembling as she walked to the entrance of the cellar. Before she went downstairs, she turned and looked at Steffi, who whispered, "It's all right. Do as he says."

"I knew that under all of that Jew loving behavior you had to have some common sense, because I can see by looking at you, with your blonde hair and blue eyes, you are a pure Aryan," the Nazi smiled at Steffi. "However, it wasn't very smart of you to allow these Jews to trick you into hiding them."

"I know." She said, trying to appease him, hoping it might soften the blow of what he was planning to do to all of them. "And, I must admit, you were right. They are like my little pets."

"Pet rats."

"Exactly," she smiled at him as fetchingly as she could manage.

"You are quite the prize. Such a pretty thing living out here without a man. I think perhaps I shall let you live, so I can come and visit you from time to time," he said. "But I am sorry, I know you will be disappointed, but I just cannot let you keep your two little pets. I must take them outside and dispose of them. It is, after all, what is best for everyone."

She felt her heart start racing again. Her chest hurt and her face felt hot. "I understand," she whispered. "I am disappointed, but I can see the error of my ways. I was lonely so I took them in. I know you must do what you must do."

"I'm glad we understand each other, because I am sort of intrigued by you, and I would like to be friends. I could come and see you again."

She smiled. "I would like that. But you look so tired. I am assuming you must have been traveling for a while before you found our little farm."

"Yes, I am actually quite tired."

"Lie down and let me rub your back," she said.

"Well," He studied her. "Well, I am rather achy and tired. So, I suppose it can't hurt to take a few minutes for a back rub."

"May I remove your jacket?" she asked.

"Yes."

Her hands were trembling as she removed his jacket. Then Zita and Asher walked through the trapdoor. "Go back downstairs," Steffi ordered them. They did as she asked. "I'll let you know when to return. But for now, stay down there."

Zita and Asher disappeared back down the stairs.

"Now I can put all of my attention on you," Steffi whispered to the Nazi in a seductive tone of voice. Then she said, "Wait here," and ran into the bedroom.

"Where are you going?" he bellowed. "Get back here right now."

She returned with a pillow in her hands. "I only wanted to make you more comfortable." She said, and he smiled as she began to rub his shoulders and neck.

He sighed, "That's good. That's good."

She didn't speak, but she continued to knead his flesh. And he began to relax.

"You must be terribly hungry. Before you leave, why don't I make you something to eat?" she asked. "Then, when you have finished eating you can lie down and sleep for a while before you go."

"Yes, that sounds rather pleasant," he admitted.

"Very good. Stay right here and I will prepare something for you."

"I would love to do that, but unfortunately, as much as I have come to like you, I cannot trust you not to poison me. So, I must watch you cook my food."

"But of course," she said, smiling, "it would be my pleasure to have you join me in my kitchen." *He suspected I was going to poison him, and he was right. Now I dare not even try. I must come up with another idea. But at least he is not fixated on killing the children right now. So, I've bought myself a little time.*

She stood up and turned to walk to the kitchen, but he caught her from the back, almost snapping her neck. She fell backwards into his arms. Her shoulders blazed with pain. But she didn't cry out or complain. He laughed heartily, "You weren't expecting that, were you?"

This is all a game for him. She thought, but she said, "No. You surprised me."

"Did I hurt you?"

"Yes, you did," she said in a matter-of-fact tone.

He laughed again. "But you didn't scream?"

"No," she smiled, "Would you have liked me to?"

"I would have, actually. I must admit that sort of thing excites me."

"Well, I am quite sure I can satisfy your wildest desires."

"You know," he said, taking a cigarette out of the breast pocket of his uniform, "I believe you can." Then he lit the cigarette and blew a large puff of smoke out of his mouth. "By the way, I don't know your name," he said.

"Steffi," she said. "Steffi Seidel."

"You really must explain to me why a good German woman has decided to hide these two Jews at a risk to herself no less? Don't you realize that they are your natural enemies?"

She turned and took his hand in hers. "I don't know your name," she said, looking into his eyes.

"Martin Huber," he answered.

"May I call you Martin?"

"You may. Now, why have you broken our law, Steffi?"

"I only took them in, because I was lonely. It's hard for a woman to be all alone on a farm with no one to talk to but her sick mother."

"You have a sick mother here?"

"Yes, she is in her bed in the back of the house," Steffi said. "She is sick and old. And I know she won't be alive much longer. That is why I took them in." Then she quickly added, "You were right when you said that they are little more than pets to me. I just kept them for companionship."

"You had to feed them. I hope you can see now that you have been wasting your rations. So, since I must eliminate your current pets, the next time I come to visit you, I will bring you a puppy. You see, I am not so bad," he smiled, then he added, "Would you like that?"

"Oh yes, of course I would," her hands were shaking as she cut up two soft potatoes and began to fry them up with a little cabbage and a single carrot in a pan. *I must make him trust me.* She thought.

Martin stood watching her as she prepared his food. "Please, won't you sit down?" she said. His standing over her made her even more nervous.

"Yes, thank you," he said almost civilly. "I can see you don't have much food. So, Next time I come I'll bring some with me. Would you like that?"

"I would," Steffi said, smiling at him. Then she began to sing softly as she stirred the mixture of vegetables in the pan. "I'm sorry but this is all I have left until ration day."

"That's a shame," he said, but he didn't seem to care.

"By the way," she whispered, "I must admit that I enjoyed that."

"Enjoyed what?"

"What we did earlier. On the sofa? I like to be dominated. I like the fact that you are a very powerful man."

"Do you now?" he beamed.

"I do," she smiled, "it was most, well, most exciting."

He laughed. "Rare to find a woman who is excited by such things. But this little farm of yours could turn out to be a pleasant retreat for me. I might just choose to make my way here to see you often."

"I really would like that," she whispered softly. Then she began to sing again. It was an old German folk song, and he knew the words, so he began to sing along with her.

When the potatoes, cabbage and carrots were fried, she put them on a plate. He gobbled them quickly, without asking her if she wanted any. And without concern that she might not have any more food left. *Selfish, sadistic Nazi.* She thought, but in as pleasant a tone as she could manage, she asked, "Is it good?"

"Yes, very good," he said, as he ate the last piece. Then he said, "Shall we have a go on the sofa one more time before I take the children outside and do what must be done?"

"I thought you were going to take a short nap," she said nervously.

"I'd love to, but I really don't have the time. I must be on my way. Alas, I will miss you," he said, his tone mocking her again.

Steffi felt a shiver run up her spine. *If I don't do something soon, he is going to kill them. And I don't know what to do to stop him.* "Martin," she whispered, running her hand over his manhood. "I would love to have another go. But I have a very small favor to ask of you."

"A favor? Again? You are a bold little thing, aren't you?" He said. "What is it now?"

She said a quick prayer in her mind before she asked, "Can you let me keep the children until you bring the puppy? Can you do that for me? Once I have the puppy, I won't mind if you do what must be done with them. However, if I don't have a pet, I'll be so alone here."

He looked into her eyes. Then he touched her cheek. "I do enjoy you. And I would love to please you," he said, and for a moment, she believed he was going to do as she asked and leave without hurting Zita or Asher. "However," he continued, and then his expression changed, and she could see that, once again, he was enjoying his power and the cruelty. "My dear...As much as I would like to grant your wish, I cannot allow this. I really am sorry." He smiled, and she wished she could wipe that wicked smile off his ugly face. "You see, what you don't realize is that these two children are not children. They may appear to look human. And I grant you, they do look human. But the truth is they are not. They are untermenschen, sub-humans. That is what makes these Jews so dangerous. They appear to be human beings. But if you observe them more closely you will realize that they are dangerous sub-humans. Now, I realize that living here on a farm in such a rural area, you don't have much contact with the outside world, so you didn't understand what you were dealing with. Therefore, I've decided not to turn you in. And please know that I am taking a big risk by doing this for you. But I am saving your life," he smiled, as he raised his eyebrows and waited. Several moments passed, then he said, "So...are you going to thank me?"

"Yes, of course," she stammered. "Thank you. Thank you so much. But please, I am begging you. Don't kill them."

"I would like to do this for your sake. But unfortunately, I simply can't put your needs above the needs of our Fatherland. So, they must be destroyed now before they have a chance to cause any problems."

Steffi felt the tears form behind her eyes. She had never been a strong woman. She'd always been subservient to her mother, and before her mother, she'd been subservient to her father. They had been in charge, and she had always done what she needed to do to keep them happy. Taking Asher and Zita in, against all the racial laws, had been her first act of defiance. She knew her parents would never have approved, but her father was dead, and her mother was bedridden, so neither of them knew about the children. Shana Goldberg, the children's mother, had been her friend. They had known each other since they were very young children. Before Hitler's rise to power, Steffi had attended Shana's wedding when she married Abram. And so, she was not surprised when Shana's two children appeared at her door, telling her that their parents had both been taken away by the Nazis. Zita explained that she and her brother saw the Nazis coming down the road. They told Steffi that their mother told them to hide, and then once they were sure the Nazis were gone, they were to go right to Steffi's house and beg her to help them. And that was how this all started. Steffi was no resistance fighter. Although she hated the Nazis and what they stood for, she would never have tried to defy them if the children had not come to her in desperate need of her help. She knew that some of the other farmers were stealing food from their own crops, which they were hiding by burying on their land. They would dig up the potatoes each time they needed them. And so far, no one she knew had been caught. Steffi had considered doing this, but she had been too afraid to even try it. Before the two youngsters arrived, she had managed to feed herself and her mother on the rations that the Nazis had allowed her. But without a man to help her farm her land, her harvest had been small because most of the land had gone unplanted. After her father died, she had tried, but she'd been unable to work the farm alone, and could not afford to hire anyone to help her. That was when, to care for herself and her mother, she had started a small and manageable vegetable garden. And although it had not produced enough to sell anything, it had been sufficient for the two of them. But then the Nazis began to come for her produce from the vegetable garden, which they said they needed for the war effort, and there was almost nothing left. Still, she had not tried to hide any of the vegetables. Then Zita and Asher arrived. With two extra mouths to feed, and tiny rations, she had to do something. That was when she began to steal small amounts of potatoes, cabbages, and carrots. She would never have been so brave had it been just her and her mother. However, she had put her fear aside in order to hide and feed the children.

"Oh, stop crying," the Nazi said, his voice filled with frustration.

Steffi hadn't even realized that she was crying. She reached up with her fingers and felt tears running down her cheeks.

"Please," she whispered helplessly. But he ignored her plea.

The Nazi stretched his legs and back, then he stood up. He avoided looking at her as he turned and walked over to the cellar. Lifting the trapdoor, he called down, "Come out now, you two or I will come down there and drag you both out by your hair," he bellowed, his voice echoing in the small room.

Steffi stood helplessly, her face blotchy from crying. He turned to look at her and then shook his head. "You are taking this far too seriously. In a few days you'll forget all about these two."

She couldn't speak. The horror of what was happening had silenced her. All she could do was weep.

"I'm going to finish this nasty business with these two little Jews you have in your cellar. Then you and I can go into your bedroom and have some fun," he looked directly at her with mock sympathy. "Steffi," he said, his tone of voice almost kind, "I know that right now you don't realize it, but I am doing you a favor. If another soldier or officer had found out what you were doing, they would have arrested you. So, by taking these children away from you, I will be protecting you from any danger that might befall you in the future."

She said nothing as she stood staring at him. Her stomach hurt and she doubled over for a moment from the pain, but she knew what she must do.

"These two may be young, but they are lazy like all the Jews I know. Just look at how long it's taking them to come upstairs," he complained. Then, in an even louder and more angry tone than before, he turned his attention on the dark cellar, "Get up here now. I am warning you. I don't have the time or patience to put up with this behavior. If you come upstairs right now, I will not harm you. In fact, I have candy that I will share with both of you. It's chocolate." He smiled and winked at Steffi. "Those Jews go crazy for chocolate."

She stared at him blankly. The children still didn't come out.

"Now you have made me angry," he called downstairs. "So, you have forced me to take action that I would rather not take. If you don't come up those stairs right this minute, I'm going to be forced to shoot your friend Steffi. I'm sure that is not what you want," he said firmly.

And...this worked. Single file, the girl first, followed by the boy. The two children shuffled up the stairs and into the living room. The Nazi slammed the trapdoor shut behind them, shaking his head at the inconvenience. It made a loud and final sound that made Zita jump. She reached over and took her brother's hand. He moved closer to her and the two of them curled into each other like two newborn kittens.

"Ahh Steffi, I am going to take pity on you again. Rather than making a mess by taking care of this in your living room, I will take them both outside and finish this job. You needn't accompany me. Wait right here, I'll be back shortly," he said to Steffi. "I suggest you don't look. In fact, on second thought, perhaps it is better if you just wait for me in the bedroom."

She nodded at him, and he smiled as he led Zita and Asher outside. Both Zita and Asher were crying. Steffi felt hot and itchy all over. She was nauseated as her heart raced like it was an animal trapped in her chest. But even though she felt sick and a little dizzy, she knew there was no time to sit around and wait for her nausea to lift. Quickly, she got up and ran into the bedroom. She opened the drawer of the dresser where she knew her father had kept his gun. Many times, she'd seen him take it out and clean it or load it before he went hunting. Now, she tried to remember exactly how he'd loaded it. There wasn't much time left. She had to think fast. Steffi knew she must get the gun loaded, then get outside before it was too late. Her hands were shaking so badly that the bullets were falling from her fingers and landing on the floor. Then the silence of the room was broken by the sound of a gunshot. A gasp of terror escaped her lips, but she forced herself to focus and put the bullets into the chamber. *Oh, dear God, please let me not be too late.*

Once the gun was loaded, Steffi ran outside. Asher was lying on the ground, and Zita was kneeling over him. Steffi felt her heart break. But she dared not take even a moment to mourn Asher, or to feel the horror she was experiencing. She had never shot a gun, and she had certainly never killed anyone before. The very idea of shooting another person terrified her, but she knew she must not stop and think about it because if she hesitated for even a second, this Nazi might fire a second shot and then she would lose Zita too. She crept up quietly. The Nazi was too busy taunting Zita to notice that Steffi was close behind him. Without allowing herself to think, she put the gun to his head. He must have felt the cold steel against his skull, because he trembled just a little and tried to turn around. But she didn't wait for his reaction. She didn't need to hear him beg. Steffi pulled the trigger and the Nazi's head exploded. Zita looked up from her dead brother's body. Her face was covered in tears. Steffi stood over the headless Nazi. There was dark red blood splattered all over her face and the front of her dress. Her eyes met Zita's as the gun fell from her hand.

Steffi and Zita were paralyzed with shock for several moments. "Asher is dead," Zita finally whispered. "My brother is dead. He killed my little brother."

"I know," Steffi said, "I know, and I'm sorry, it's my fault. I tried but I couldn't load the gun fast enough to save him. I tried. I really tried."

Zita nodded. Tragedy and pain had stolen her childhood, and in that moment, like no other before it, the loss of innocence showed in her face. "I know you tried. It wasn't your fault. You did what you could."

Steffi and Zita stood staring at each other for several long moments. The only sound were the birds chirping in the trees, and the sound of their heavy breathing. "We are going to have to bury them both as quickly as we can. I doubt anyone from the neighborhood will drop by to visit us today, but we can't take a chance. We must hurry."

Zita nodded. "Yes, we must hurry," she repeated, her voice empty and devoid of emotion.

Steffi knew Zita was in shock, so she said, "Zita, I understand how you feel. I know you are heartbroken about your brother, but you cannot collapse right now. You must keep your wits about you, if you and I are going to survive. And remember there is no one you can trust. You must never tell anyone what happened here, not even after the war, if this war should ever end, and we survive. No one must ever know that I killed a man today." Steffi shivered as she said, "You must promise me that no matter what happens, you will never tell anyone what I did."

"I promise," Zita said. Her slender body was trembling, and she looked like she might fall over. "Yes, I promise," she repeated as she forced herself to stand up straight. Then she wiped the tears away from her cheeks with her dirty hands, and in a calm voice, she asked, "Is there a shovel in the barn?"

"Yes," Steffi said. "There are two of them. They are hanging on the wall. My father put up a special hanger for them when he was still alive and doing all the farming. We must change out of these clothes first, they're covered in blood, and if anyone see's us they will start to ask questions."

"You're right. Let's change, and then I'll go and get the shovels," Zita said.

After they changed clothing, Zita returned with the shovels, and the first thing Steffi did was turn the soil to cover the blood that had been spilled. Then they began to dig the graves.

Digging up the earth was hard work, and it took the entire day for them to dig deep enough to bury the bodies. At the same time as they dug, they kept watch to make sure no one came by the farm. They had to be sure that no one saw them. Although neither of them said it aloud, they both knew that if anyone caught them digging these graves, they would be forced to kill that person. They dared not trust anyone else to keep their secret.

Steffi was surprised at how strong Zita was. For a small girl of a slight build, she did not shirk at the enormity of the task. She managed to be a big help. They stripped the Nazi of his uniform before tossing his naked body into the newly dug grave. Then they continued to dig a much smaller grave for Asher. This time, Zita was very tired. As they laid Asher's body into the ground, she was very emotional. "I'll put the shovel's away," Zita told Steffi. Steffi nodded, but because Zita was crying, her eyes were clouded with tears. Accidentally she hit her calf with the sharp side of the shovel. A yelp escaped her lips as her leg began to bleed. Steffi walked over to her to get a closer look and to assess how deep the cut was. When she saw the wound was only surface and Zita did not need a doctor, she put her arm around Zita's shoulder and took the shovel away from her hand. "I'll put these shovels away. You go on inside the house. I'll be right in to clean that wound," Steffi said.

Once Zita's wound was clean and dressed, they went back outside, and Steffi started a fire where she burned the Nazi's uniform. Now that all traces of what had happened earlier were covered up, Steffi breathed a sigh of relief. She didn't think her neighbors would want to turn her in, but she also knew that if they found out and turned her in, they would receive a large reward for bringing someone who killed a German officer to justice. That reward could be food, or money, or both. And Steffi knew everyone needed these things desperately. Desperate people often did desperate things. So, she was glad that the job was finished.

"We can go inside now. It's all over," Steffi whispered to Zita.

Zita nodded, but she didn't move. "I need a moment," she said. Then she knelt beside her brother's grave and began to weep. In a very soft and broken voice, she began to recite the Kaddish, the prayer for the dead. She could not remember the entire prayer, but she recited what she could recall from the time her father had said it at her grandmother's funeral. Steffi stood beside Zita in silence.

After Zita finished the prayer, she remained kneeling on the ground for a moment, rubbing the tears from her eyes. Steffi sunk down beside her and put her arm around Zita. They sat like that in silence for several minutes. Steffi finally asked, "Are you hungry?"

Zita nodded. "Yes."

"Come on, let's go in the house. I will try to find something for us to eat," Steffi said, as she helped Zita to stand up.

Without looking back, Steffi put her arm around Zita's slim shoulder and they both walked back to the house.

Steffi lit a candle, not wanting to turn on a light in case someone might walk by, see the light, and come up to the door.

"I'm afraid that lousy Nazi ate what was left of the potatoes. So, we don't have much left in the way of food," Steffi said as she scanned the mostly empty cupboard. "I do have this rotten cabbage. I think that might be all that we have left until I get my rations again. I can peel away the rotten leaves. But, unfortunately, it will be a day before I can get more rations. To carry us over, I'll see what I can borrow from one of the neighbors in the morning. I've borrowed food before, and they know I will pay them back as soon as the rations are distributed, so they aren't so reluctant to share it with me. Shall I try to cook this cabbage?"

"Yes, we have no other choice. And thank you," Zita said. Steffi could hear both of their stomachs growling. She glanced over at Zita. The girl's face, legs, and hands were covered in dirt and smeared with blood.

"Go to the bathroom and clean yourself up while I prepare this food. I still have a little bit of this fake butter, so I can fry the cabbage. It won't be so bad."

"I'll be right back," Zita said as she walked away.

When Steffi finished cooking, she brought a small plate of cabbage to her mother. "What took you so long?" her mother said. "It's dark outside. We usually eat much earlier. I've been waiting for hours."

"I'm sorry, mama. I was planting in the vegetable garden," Steffi lied.

"Oh. Well, all right," her mother said. "I suppose you must do that."

"Do you need anything else? Because if not, I'd like to go and clean myself up," Steffi said.

"Yes, you are quite dirty. There is not only dirt all over you, but there is some blood too."

"Oh," Steffi gasped.

Her mother didn't ask her why she had blood on her face. All the old woman said was, "Go and get cleaned up. I have everything I need."

Steffi washed her face and hands and then she returned to the kitchen, where she and Zita shared what was left of the cabbage. At first, they ate in silence. But when they were almost finished, Steffi said, "We must be more careful from now on. Oh, how I wish I had the money for us to leave here and start over somewhere where no one knows you. I could sell this place," she was thinking aloud now. "And then I could color your hair blonde and change your appearance. Maybe we could even live a normal life somewhere. But even if I did have the money to leave, I don't know how I could ever get my mother out of bed to take her with us. And I can't leave her behind. I know if she were younger and stronger she would go with us, but she is unable to walk. So, for now, we're stuck here."

"It's all right. It was my fault. I should never have come upstairs the way I did. I am the reason all of this happened," Zita looked down, "I was so worried about Asher, I forgot to be careful." There was a catch in Zita's voice when she said her brother's name.

"It's not your fault. You were upset and worried. But from now on you must never leave the cellar unless I come and get you. And I will only come when it's late at night and I am sure it's safe."

Zita nodded. Steffi saw Zita's hands shaking, and she knew it was going to be terrible for Zita to be all alone in that dark cellar all day long, every day. Steffi was sure Zita was going to be miserable because she would have so much time on her hands to think about nothing but her family, who had been ripped away from her so brutally. Steffi wished she could do something to make all this easier on Zita.

As if Zita read Steffi's mind, she forced herself to smile through quivering lips. "I'll be all right. Don't worry about me. You have enough to concern yourself with trying to stretch the rations and run this farm. I will be fine."

"Yes," Steffi said, "and meanwhile, I will try to think of a way to make this easier for you."

Zita nodded. And somehow Steffi knew Zita could see the truth. Unless the war ended and Germany lost, it would be almost impossible for Steffi to make things better for Zita.

She's just a young girl. Her life should be just beginning. However, she is like an adult, because of everything she has been forced to endure. Poor thing. I wish I could allow her to sleep upstairs. I know she would be so much more comfortable, but how can I? If one of the neighbors should drop by in the morning and see her, they would surely recognize her. And everyone in this village knows her parents were Jewish, and that they were arrested. It was the talk of the town that Sunday, when I went to church right after it first happened. I was so afraid that the fear on my face would give me away. So, I haven't been to church since. Of course, no one questions this loss of my religious connection anymore. That's because the Nazis have caused so many people to lose their faith in God.

"I am going to go to bed now," Zita said. "Can you please close the trap door for me after I go downstairs?"

"Of course," Steffi said, thinking Zita was very brave.

That night Steffi slept fitfully. She had dreams of Pitor and her longing for him was so strong that it woke her up. As she lay in bed, she thought of Asher and Zita, and how alone Zita must feel in the cold, dark cellar. When she was a child, Steffi had been afraid of the dark and now she considered how terrible it would have been for her if she had been in Zita's position. Then she thought about the Nazi and how he looked when he was headless. She shivered in the night, and she felt her blood run cold. Steffi knew she must change her thoughts if she was ever going to fall asleep. However, it was almost impossible for her to find anything that would distract her. She yearned to rest; she was so very tired, both mentally and physically. But when she closed her eyes and allowed her thoughts to ramble, she could see that Nazi's face vividly in her mind's eye. And sometimes his headless body, too. After an hour of restlessness, Steffi got out of bed and went into the kitchen where she filled a pot with water, then put it on the stove to boil for tea. While the water heated, Steffi sunk down into one of her kitchen chairs and waited. *I will miss little Asher. He was such a good boy. And, since they moved in here with me, I have come to care deeply for him and Zita. They became the children I never had. And now, because I did not move fast enough to protect him, he is gone. Just like that. In an instant, he is gone. Life is so fragile that it is frightening. I wish I could go back in time and change things. But I must face the fact that it's too late for anyone to save that poor little boy. He's gone forever. I want to still believe in heaven. I want to believe he is there. But it's hard to keep my faith alive with all the cruelty I've seen. So, all I can do in the future is to be very careful to protect Zita with my life.*

CHAPTER THIRTY

It was over two months after the party at the Eagle's Nest where Pitor received his promotion, before he was finally given a weekend off from work. During the time he was working for the Reich, he thought he might go mad. Every day was a challenge. He had to be very careful each time he spoke so as not to make a mistake and give himself away. That was why, as soon as he was given the message that he could take some time away from his job to enjoy himself, he instantly put in a request to visit Heim Hochland, where he knew that the little brown sisters had taken Jakup. Permission was granted almost immediately. "You are a beautiful specimen of an Aryan man," Himmler said, "and I like you. You don't talk too much or get on my nerves like some of the others. I suppose what I am saying is that you are what we are looking for in an Aryan man, and it's only right that you should do your duty and spread your seed for the Fatherland."

Pitor nodded. "Thank you, Reichsführer," he said. He knew Himmler had taken a liking to him, and he was glad because it made things a little easier.

The following Saturday morning, Pitor got up very early. He got a ride to the train station from one of the drivers at the headquarters in Munich, where he was currently stationed. Then he took a morning train out to Steinhoring. He'd spent the past month trying to devise a way to steal Jakup without putting his son in danger. But if he tried to take him, he knew it was going to be very difficult to get away from Heim Hochland. So, he decided that the best avenue to getting what he wanted was to marry Alice, the Aryan woman he had met at the party at the Eagle's Nest, and then to adopt Jakup. He would stay with her for a year or so and then file for a divorce or perhaps just slip away on a train with Jakup. He didn't doubt that he could woo and win Alice's hand. He knew by the way she'd behaved at the party that she already liked him. But he was worried about marrying her. He couldn't be sure of how she might respond when she discovered he was circumcised. He had already made up a story that he thought was plausible. He would tell her that his mother had been a progressive midwife, and she'd heard that circumcising a boy was good for his health. Pitor would explain that, of course, his ancestry was of pure Aryan blood, but his mother had him circumcised before she realized it could mark him as a Jew. He hoped Alice would believe this because if she didn't, he would be forced to kill her. And he didn't want to kill an innocent woman if he didn't have to.

This plan had formed in Pitor's mind almost immediately after he had returned to Munich and began working as a bodyguard. So, he made friends with several of the other Nazi officers who he worked with. Then, once they were friends, he asked them if they knew Alice. None of them did. Finally, after various quests, he met a young woman who had grown up with Alice. To his surprise, she was a plain-looking young woman who worked in the kitchen. Her name was Lotti, and her mother had worked as a maid for Alice's mother. When Pitor asked Lotti for Alice's address, Lotti had refused to give it to him. "I can't give you that information," Lotti said. "My mother could lose her job if I do. I have to write to Alice and get permission first. If she says it's all right, I'll give it to you."

"Of course. I completely understand your position, and I wouldn't want to cause you or your family any trouble," Pitor said gently. "Just let me know when you receive an answer from Alice, will you?"

"Of course," Lotti said.

TWO WEEKS LATER, Lotti found Pitor sitting alone in the garden and handed him a piece of paper. "Alice said she would love to hear from you," Lotti said, smiling. Then she blushed. "She certainly is a lucky girl. I wish a fella like you was interested in me."

Pitor smiled at Lotti and then took the paper with the address on it, and began his correspondence with Alice as soon as he had some free time that same day. It seemed from the address that Alice was living in Berlin. And he knew it would be difficult for him to get away to visit her. But he thought that if he were complimentary and inviting, she might come to see him in Munich. He explained to Alice that he was unable to get away long enough to go to Berlin, but that he would love to take her out sometime soon, if she could make her way to Munich. From the way Alice had behaved at the party, he was sure he would receive a positive response. She sent a return letter less than two weeks later saying she would love to come to Munich, but would be unable to do so for at least two months. Her sister was getting married, and she was expected to help her get ready, and then she must attend the wedding. He responded to her letter immediately, telling her to keep in touch with him, and they would schedule a meeting as soon as she was able to get away. And so, they began to send letters to each other, and as they did, Pitor put the beginnings of his plan into effect. He spun a web of romance that swept Alice off her feet.

But Alice's sister's wedding was delayed because her fiancé could not get a leave from the army, and in turn, Alice was unable to come to Munich. However, she promised she would visit Pitor as soon as she was able. He wrote back and assured her he didn't mind waiting. And so, they continued to correspond through letters.

Meanwhile, Pitor had received his time off from work and had scheduled his visit to Heim Hochland. He was so anxious to see Jakup, he could hardly wait until the train stopped in Steinhoring. He disembarked from the train, then walked the two miles to Heim Hochland.

It was late morning when Pitor arrived at Heim Hochland. As soon as he entered the building wearing his clean, pressed SS officer's uniform, he was greeted warmly by a woman at the front desk. "The ladies are out for exercise right now," she said. "Would you like to have something to eat?"

"Oh, no, thank you," Pitor said to her as he put on his most charming smile. "In fact, I was wondering if I might go upstairs and see the children while I wait." This turn of events changed his plans. The little brown sisters were nowhere to be found. If Horst was gone as well, Pitor thought that if this woman would allow it, he would be alone with the children. Then perhaps all he would need to do was go upstairs to the children's room and take his son.

"Of course, you may go and see the children. I didn't realize that you were here for an adoption. I thought you were here to visit the girls," she giggled, but she was blushing, "Forgive me."

"No need to forgive you. Your pretty face has made my morning quite pleasant," Pitor said, hoping that his flattery would help when he tried to escape with Jakup in his arms.

She blushed. Then she stood up and said, "Follow me, please."

He did as she asked and was led up a staircase to a set of rooms. "Are you looking for a child of any particular age or sex? We have infants all the way through young children."

"I would like boy. A toddler. Perhaps three or four years old," Pitor said.

"Of course. This room is all infants. They are the most popular. But a toddler *is* easier to care for. So, I can understand why your wife might prefer a child that is a little older," she smiled, "the room with children of that age is right down the hall. Follow me."

Pitor did as she asked, but not before glancing into the large room filled with bassinets. Most of the infants were red faced and crying. "These babies are crying, and no one picks them up or rocks them to sleep?" Pitor asked the girl. He was astonished. "There is no one here watching them either?"

"Yes, that's right. It is our responsibility to make them strong, and the only way to do that is to teach them to depend upon themselves for comfort. So, it's quite all right to leave them alone. You see we never pick them up, when they cry. They are fed and changed every two hours. So, they are not hungry, and their diapers are not soiled. They are just whining. And they must learn at an early age that whining will do them no good."

"I see," he said. Pitor was appalled as he walked by the room of screaming infants. For a moment, Pitor thought back to the time when Jakup was just born and he and Mila felt so blessed to have Jakup in their lives. Mila was a loving and attentive mother. When Jakup cried, she checked his diaper to make sure he wasn't wet. Then she fed him, thinking he might be hungry. And finally, once all his needs were satisfied, Mila held him in her arms and rocked him. She sat in the rocking chair that Pitor had bought her, holding Jakup in her arms and cuddling him until he stopped crying. The love they had shared, he and Mila, was reflected in the way they had raised their little boy. And even now, a day did not go by that he didn't think of his family, and how much he missed them. They had been snatched away from him for no good reason. And for this, and for all their sadistic and insane behavior, Pitor despised the Nazi party. If he could have, he would have killed all of them single-handedly. But he knew that this was impossible. There were too many of them. If he even attempted it, he would lose, and they would imprison him. And if he were imprisoned, it would be impossible to know what fate might await his precious son.

"The babies are quite loud and often very annoying," the young woman said, indicating the infants. "I can understand why your wife would prefer an older child. They really are far less work. Although, it would not be difficult for a man of your stature to hire a nanny to help her."

"I'm sorry. I didn't hear you," Pitor said. She had been rambling on for several minutes now, but he was lost in his own thoughts.

"Oh, it's all right," she smiled, then she led him to the room at the end of the hall where a small group of young toddlers were sitting on the floor and playing. His eyes scanned the group of children, but he did not see Jakup. His heart began to race. The young woman was speaking to him again. He nodded his head, but did not answer because he didn't hear her. Then he saw the two little brown sisters that he'd met at the party walk into the room through a door in the back. They were followed by the ugly white-haired fellow, Horst. Pitor racked his brain until he remembered the names of the little brown sisters. One was Gretchen and the other was Heidi.

"This is the room," the young woman said, smiling at him, "And it looks like you're just in time. The little brown sisters who work with these children have just arrived. They will be able to give you more information about each of the toddlers."

"Thank you for your help," he said, turning to the young woman who had escorted him to the room.

"You're quite welcome," she said. She was about to leave when she turned to Pitor and whispered, "If you are interested, I would love to spend an evening with you."

He smiled but didn't answer. Then he opened the door to the room where the children played and walked inside.

The two little brown sisters saw him and recognized him immediately. They both approached him with a warm greeting. "Heil Hitler, Sturmscharführer."

"Heil Hitler," Pitor said. He remembered Himmler had renamed Jakup. He'd called him Liam. Pitor's hands were shaking as he spoke to the two girls. It was so difficult to remain calm. He wanted to cry out and say, "*Where is my son, what have you done with him? Direct me to him now!*" But of course, he could not do this. He must keep up this façade if he hoped to find his son.

"How are you both?" Pitor asked in the friendliest tone he could manage.

"Fine," Heidi said flirtatiously. "We have both been doing very well."

Horst was standing in the corner, staring at Pitor.

Pitor was unnerved by the look in Horst's eyes. "Heil Hitler," Horst said.

"Heil Hitler," Pitor echoed.

"Well, welcome back," Horst said. "I was thinking about you the other night. Do you recall that afternoon when Herr Muehler got angry with you for bringing that creature with you to class. He had you go to the headmaster's office. Do you remember what kind of animal it was? I can't seem to recall."

Pitor shrugged, "I don't remember."

"But you do remember the incident, I am sure. After all, you were suspended for almost a full week."

"Yes, yes of course I remember." Pitor said.

"Ahhh, do you? Well, now that I think about it. I don't think it was you. I think it might have been someone else. Or perhaps it never happened at all, Konrad. Did it?"

"I don't know what you're talking about." Pitor was unnerved. "But you're starting to sound a bit mad."

"Do I now? Well, you said you remembered the incident. If you remembered it and it didn't happen, then who is mad? You or me?"

"Horst, I have no idea what you are talking about. There were several times that I was suspended when I was at school. And it was many years ago. So, I certainly don't remember why. What is the point of all of this anyway?" Pitor said, his voice rising with anger.

"What took you so long to come back to visit us?" Gretchen interrupted the conversation.

Pitor was relieved to have the focus turned away from Horst. She was looking at Pitor with glassy eyes and batting her eyelashes at him.

I thought she was Horst's girlfriend, and that she knew I was sort of courting Heidi. I wonder if these two are always in competition with each other. And if they are, how can I use that to help me find Jakup?

"I wanted to come sooner. But I was unable to get away from work. This is the first time since the party at the Eagle's Nest that I have been able to leave."

"And you came to see us," Heidi beamed. Her face was glowing.

"I came to see you," Pitor said. He noticed Gretchen was wearing a wedding band, so he assumed that Gretchen and Horst had gotten married. That meant he had made the right choice in putting his energy towards Heidi.

After Pitor said that he'd come to Heim Hochland to see Heidi, Gretchen stopped hiding the fact that she was jealous. Pitor shivered when he saw the way Gretchen looked at Heidi. He didn't want to cause trouble between the two girls, so he tried to appease Gretchen by paying her some attention. "I see a ring on your finger. Is Horst the lucky fellow?" He asked, thinking that Gretchen would not be as offended that he had chosen Heidi over her if she thought it was because he knew that Gretchen and Horst were together.

"They were married last month," Heidi interjected. "You should have been here. They had a nice wedding at one of the local bier halls."

Again, Gretchen turned to Heidi. She gave her a look of disdain. The raw hatred beaming from Gretchen's eyes made Pitor shiver. *These are the women who have been caring for my son.* He thought, hoping they had not been as cold and heartless to Jakup as they seemed to be to each other. *Keep your guard up. Don't let them suspect how you really feel about them. Smile, act cordial. Act like one of them.* Pitor smiled, "I'm sorry I missed the wedding." He said, then looking directly at Gretchen, he said, "I'd wager that you were a beautiful bride."

Gretchen beamed and for a moment Pitor thought he had calmed the war that was starting between Gretchen and Heidi. Then he said in a soft and very calm voice, "Whatever happened to that adorable little boy who was at the party at the Eagle's Nest?"

"Which one?" Heidi asked.

"The little blond boy with the curly hair? I believe his name was Liam?"

"Oh, yes, Liam. I remember him. How could we forget. He was quite the character."

"Yes, he was funny. He made us laugh," Heidi said.

"But he required a lot of discipline. He was one of those children who required a tremendous amount of reshaping. A very difficult child, I'm afraid. However, lucky for us, he's gone from here. He was adopted," Gretchen said.

"By whom?" Pitor asked. He was trying to keep his emotions under control, but he was distressed by what Gretchen had just told him. These crazy Nazis had disciplined Jakup harshly. Pitor prayed they had not broken his spirited little boy. And now, Pitor had arrived too late. Jakup had already been adopted by one of them, and Pitor had no idea how they were treating his son, or if he would ever be able to find him. "Who adopted him?" He tried to sound calm.

"I'm afraid we can't tell you that. It's against the rules. But, I can assure you he has been sent to live with a very well-vetted Aryan family. All the couples who are considered as prospects are good German people. You see, Sturmscharführer, there are very specific criteria for those who wish to adopt one of these special children. Not just anyone is a candidate. First off, the fellow must be an SS officer who is married to a woman who is of pure blood. They both must be of sound mind and body. And it goes without saying that this officer must also be in very good standing within the party," Gretchen said, sounding as if she was reciting a speech she had memorized.

"I see," Pitor said, but he could hardly speak. This was going to be more difficult than he'd hoped, and right now, he felt as if the wind had been knocked out of him.

"Perhaps I have no right to ask, but why? Do you want to adopt a child? You are young. You and your wife could have one of your own?

Or perhaps your wife cannot bear..." Heidi, realizing she'd said too much, stopped speaking mid-sentence.

"No, there is no one else to blame. You see, I'm not married. But I find that I am very lonely, and I thought that if I had a child, I might have someone that I could share all my knowledge with," he said carefully.

"Oh yes," Gretchen agreed, "That is the whole reason that a man must be an SS officer to be permitted to adopt a child from Heim Hochland, or any of our Lebensborn homes. We need to be sure that the children will be properly educated in all our teachings."

"But..." Heidi hesitated for a moment, then she looked away, not meeting Pitor's eyes, "It's very important that the officer is married. Family is important to our Führer."

"Yes, I am aware of that. However, must this officer be married to a blonde haired, blue eyed woman? Or is it acceptable for him to be married to a woman of pure blood who is not blonde?" Pitor asked. He was going to need her help, and he knew this question would spark her interest.

"Well no, actually. She doesn't have to be blonde," Heidi said, blushing. "I mean of course the lady in question would have to have pure German blood."

"Of course," Pitor said, "I completely understand."

She smiled shyly.

This woman has access to the records that list the name and address of the couple who have my son. I don't care if I have to marry her to get what I need. I will do whatever is required.

"Would you like to have dinner with me tonight?" he asked, his eyes fixed directly on Heidi. She looked away, blushing even harder now.

"Dinner? With you tonight?" She asked, and it sounded like she was asking because she could hardly believe he was considering a serious relationship with her.

"You were supposed to go into town with me tonight. I have to go to one of the clock shops to purchase a watch as a gift for my grandmother. Don't you remember? We discussed this just last night before we went to sleep," Gretchen said. "We had planned to go as soon as we got off duty."

"I remember," Heidi said, "Would it be all right if we went tomorrow?"

"Heidi, you promised to go with me tonight. I can't go tomorrow."

Pitor watched Gretchen. He was certain that Gretchen was behaving this way out of jealousy. After all, he remembered her husband, Horst, who Pitor thought was one of the most unattractive men he'd ever seen. "It's all right. I understand that you have previous plans, and I wouldn't want to interfere. I have a couple of days before I have to return to Munich. Perhaps you can get away to have dinner with me tomorrow night."

"Yes, of course I can. And, I would love to have dinner with you." Heidi stammered.

"All right. That will be just fine." He smiled as charmingly as he could muster. "Can I meet you here at the front of the Heim Hochland building at say, eight o'clock tomorrow evening?"

"Yes, I'll be here waiting for you."

Pitor smiled, but inside he was upset and nervous. Every minute until he held his son in his arms again seemed like a lifetime. And not only that, but he was very concerned about how this Nazi couple was treating Jakup. *Were they torturing him? Were they letting him cry alone in his bed at night, so he might grow up to be strong, the same way that the little brown sisters were ignoring the infants in the other room? I must not think about this. I must focus on finding Jakup. Once I know where he is, I can find a way to rescue him. And right now, this girl, Heidi, has the information I need. So, I must court her, and even marry her if need be, to find out what I need to know.*

CHAPTER THIRTY-ONE

Before he left Munich, Pitor had just received his pay, and so he would have enough money to take Heidi to a nice restaurant. But he hated to spend his money on her. *Ahhh, well, it's only money.* He thought as he headed into town to check into a nearby hotel. *I must treat her like she is special to me. I must pretend to be smitten with her. I tell her and everyone else that my reason for not staying at Heim Hochland and spending the night in bed with one of the blonde girls is because I am falling for Heidi. She will be ecstatic when she hears this, and it will save me from having to find a way to hide my circumcision.*

Pitor took off his jacket and wore plain clothing as he wandered the streets, looking for a room to rent for the next few days. He checked into the least expensive hotel he could find. It was small and lacked cleanliness. Pitor knew he could have gone to a nicer hotel and demanded their best room for free because of his ranking with the Nazi party, but because it was so inexpensive, he was forced to share his room with a stranger, and he would have an excuse to not bring Heidi back to his room this trip. His roommate was a young German man who smiled at him when he first entered the room. Pitor didn't mind sharing his room. At least he had a bed to himself, and besides, it was only going to be for a couple of days. Down the hall, there was a communal bathroom that was shared amongst the other men who were staying at the hotel. Although Pitor had slept outside in the forest, he had never stayed in a hotel like this before and at first, the smell that radiated from the unclean bathroom caused him to gag.

His roommate, Alex, was a soldier who had been maimed on the battlefield. He invited Pitor to join him for dinner that night. Pitor agreed. Then the two of them walked downstairs to the café to have a quick and inexpensive dinner. While they shared sausages and beers, Alex, who was friendly and open about his life, told Pitor that he was on his way home to his family in Munich, because he could no longer fight in the war. "I know I should be ashamed to admit this, but I was glad to be done with battle. I saw so many of my friends fall on the battlefield."

"Did you say that your family lives here in Munich?" Pitor asked.

"Yes. Not far away," Alex admitted.

"Then why stay here at a hotel? Why not go home?"

"I hate to admit this. But because I hardly know you, I can tell you. You see, I am ashamed of my body. I am worried that when my girl sees what's happened to my leg, she will turn away from me in disgust. I suppose you might say, I am prolonging the inevitable by not returning home. But it's difficult to face everyone in this condition."

"I understand," Pitor said.

"Were you a soldier in the war?" Alex asked.

"Yes," Pitor remembered Konrad had been a soldier, and he told him a little about some of the battles he fought.

"You don't have to talk about it," Alex said. "I know how hard it is to talk about it."

Pitor nodded. "Yes, it is." He was glad he didn't have to remember anything else that Konrad had said about fighting in the war.

"Anyway," Alex sighed, "when I got back to Munich, I was so happy to be here. Every day on the Russian front, as cold as it was and as hungry as we were, I thought about my girl, Marie. She was all

I could think about, actually. When I was freezing in the bitter cold, I spent all my time remembering how warm it was to lie in bed beside her. But then I had this dream that she took one look at my wooden leg and shook her head. In the dream, I tried to kiss her and she refused to be intimate with me. She admitted to being repulsed by me. It hurt so badly that when I awoke, I just couldn't go home," he said sadly. "Marie is a pretty woman. But I am sure that the war has taken its toll on her too. I'm sure she blames me for not having achieved a higher rank, because maybe if I had been more successful, she and her family would have had an easier time. Better food perhaps."

"Perhaps," Pitor said.

"But who knows what I would be doing right now if I had been of a higher rank. Anything is possible. I might have been in a different place. I could have been killed. The bullet doesn't discriminate, if you know what I mean."

Pitor nodded. "Yes, it's true," he said, then he added, "you've had a tough go and I'm really sorry to hear it. But you don't know for certain that your girl will reject you. She might be very happy to have you home with her."

"Yes, I'd like to think so. But I keep reliving that dream, and then I don't want to go home, so I stay here in this hotel for a day or two longer. It's cheap enough, but the little bit of money I was given is going to run out soon anyway. Then I'll have to go home, or end up living on the street like so many other returning soldiers. This war is certainly taking a toll on us," he said. Then, as if he suddenly remembered that he was speaking to an SS officer, he added, "But of course, Sturmscharführer, we must do whatever is required of us by our Fatherland. This is Deutschland and we are Germans. And like all my fellow citizens, I love this land."

"Yes, of course you do. And so, do I. But I understand how hard it must have been for you to lose a leg"

"It's been terrible. I don't know what the future will bring, but I am trying to remain hopeful. Eventually I will have to face Marie."

Pitor nodded. He had no answers for this man, and besides, he was tired and had plenty of concerns of his own that were ever present in his thoughts. He had to make Heidi trust him enough to tell him who had adopted Jakup and where he could find them. *Heidi has a coveted job. And because she is not blonde or beautiful, but only a little brown sister, and there are plenty of them in need of work, she is easily replaceable. Therefore, it might be difficult to convince her to break the rules.*

"You look like you're lost in thought," Alex said, as he poured himself another beer. "Want some more?" He asked, pointing to the pitcher and Pitor's empty glass.

"No, I'm exhausted, I want to get back to the room so I can get some sleep."

Alex chugged what was left in his glass, and they paid the bill, then walked back to the hotel and headed upstairs to their room. Pitor watched Alex limp as he climbed the stairs. But he didn't try to help him. He was afraid that if he did, Alex would be offended.

CHAPTER THIRTY-TWO

At promptly eight o'clock the following evening, Pitor arrived at Heim Hochland. He stood outside, and a young woman in a dark uniform approached him. "Can I help you, Sturmscharführer?" she asked.

"Yes, I'm here to see Heidi."

"Heidi? I am afraid we have lots of girls by the name of Heidi. Which one are you speaking of, and is she expecting you?"

"Heidi, the little brown sister who works with the toddlers in the children's area. And, yes, she is expecting me."

"A little brown sister?" The woman looked surprised as she repeated what Pitor told her. Then she turned and looked away as if she was ashamed for him. If he could look into her mind and read her inner thoughts, Pitor was sure she was wondering what a blond-haired, blue eyed, high ranking SS officer would want with a little brown sister when he could have the company of any one of the lovely blonde, athletic female residents who would be more than honored to allow him access to her bed. The woman's expression seemed to go blank, and it was as if she had recovered from her initial shock of Pitor's choice of women. Smiling warmly, she looked directly at Pitor.

"Yes," Pitor replied. "She's a little brown sister." He managed a smile, and in a conspiratorial whisper he said, "I can't help it, I suppose. I'm just attracted to brunettes."

The woman seemed to understand because she did not say another word about his choice of girls for the night. But she ran her hands over her brown hair, which she wore neatly placed in a bun at the nape of her neck. Then she said, "Come inside and wait in the lobby. Or if you would prefer, I'll escort you upstairs."

"No need. I am fine right here. We have planned to meet in front of the building."

"Very well, but if you need anything, just let me know. I am the receptionist. So, I am sitting at the desk right inside the front door."

"Thank you for your offer. And, if I need help, I will come to your desk."

"Very well. Good evening then, and Heil Hitler."

"Heil Hitler."

Heidi arrived a few minutes later dressed in a traditional German outfit. She wore a bright blue dirndl skirt and a crisp white blouse. Her hair was plaited into two perfect braids that were then twisted and pinned, circling her head. Even though the Nazi party frowned on cosmetics, Pitor noticed that many of the girls wore some makeup. And tonight, Heidi was no exception. Her lips and cheeks had a healthy pink glow. Her eyes were dark with mascara.

"Hallo," she smiled shyly when she saw him.

"Hallo," he said.

Then a middle-aged woman walked by and looked at Heidi, who had hooked her arm through Pitor's.

"Ahhh, isn't she a lucky girl?" she said to Pitor, then, turning to Heidi, "Now, if I were only twenty years younger, I'd go after him myself." The woman said, surprising both Pitor and Heidi with her boldness. They looked at each other in shock. But the woman didn't seem to notice. She turned to walk inside the building. Pitor freed himself from Heidi and opened the door for the middle-aged woman. He held it open until she was inside. That's when Pitor and Heidi burst into laughter.

"Do you have a favorite restaurant in the area?" Pitor asked Heidi, after they were both spent from laughing.

"Yes, it's right down the street," she replied.

"Good, shall we go there?" Pitor said, offering her his arm again. She beamed, and he knew she was excited and proud to be seen walking arm in arm with an SS officer. After all, it was rare that any SS officer would choose to spend an evening with a little brown sister. And even more unusual for a man who was as handsome as Pitor. He was the kind of man that every one of the perfect blonde Aryan women at Heim Hochland waited for.

The people who passed them as they walked arm in arm down the street, through the center of town, smiled approvingly as Heidi led Pitor to the restaurant she chose. Neither of them spoke as they walked. But each time Pitor glanced down at Heidi, she was smiling up at him.

Once they were seated in the small tavern that Heidi had chosen, which served inexpensive food, Heidi began to speak. "I do hope you enjoy the food here," she said. "I suggested this place because the food and beer are very good and it's not expensive."

"Oh?" he said.

Then she put her hand up to cover her mouth as if she'd said something wrong. "I didn't mean to offend you. I mean, I realize you are an officer, and you can afford to eat anywhere," she hesitated for a moment, then she said, "Oh dear, I talk far too much. I hope I haven't spoiled things."

"No, of course not," he said. "I am impressed that you are a frugal woman. That's a wonderful trait for a good German hausfrau to have." He felt sorry for her. She was so smitten with him, and he was playing her. He'd never in his life played a woman. He believed in treating women fairly, but he had to do this. It was the only way she would ever divulge the information she was hiding concerning

Jakup's whereabouts. He thought of Mila. In normal circumstances, she would never have approved of this. But he knew she would agree that he must do whatever was necessary to find Jakup. How he wished Mila was alive, somewhere safe, waiting for him, somewhere just waiting for him to find Jakup and reunite them all once again. Mila, his beloved bashert. How he longed to hold her in his arms again.

"So, I know you have just recently started your new job, but do you enjoy your work?" she asked him.

"Yes, actually. I find it fascinating," he lied, thinking about how he had to face high ranking Nazi officials every day, and sometimes he found it to be unnerving. Then he smiled, "And you? Do you like your job?" he asked.

"I do like it. The children can be a handful sometimes. But I know that is the way children are, and I am very fortunate to have an important position like this one. It is essential for the future of our thousand-year Reich, that we build a population of Aryan children who have been taught to be strong. These children are the future of our nation. They will take over the Reich when this generation dies off."

"It is certainly a noble endeavor," he said.

She blushed and looked away. "Yes, I believe it is. I like to know that even if I am not blonde and beautiful, the work I do matters to the future greatness of our Fatherland. I am sure you must feel that your work is very valuable. After all, you have the most important job of all. You are guarding our Führer. Our entire nation's security lies in your hands. Your very capable hands, I might add."

He smiled. "Thank you for your kind words, Heidi. I do my very best to ensure the safety and prosperity of our country. However, I must admit to you that I am not as important as you might think. You see, I am not alone. I am one of many bodyguards. The Führer's safety is far too important to entrust to just one man." *If she only knew the truth, that if I was given even a single moment alone with the Führer, I would kill him. Even if it meant certain death for me. I wouldn't care. That man deserves to die. But I can't leave Jakup alone to grow up as one of them, so I don't try to murder Hitler. It's such a dilemma that it forces me to question everything I feel in my heart. Of course, I wish I could rid the world of that crazy monster. But not at the expense of my innocent son.*

"Even though you are not working alone, I am still very impressed with the work you do, and its importance," she said, her eyes shining with affection.

He smiled at her. Then reached across the table and took her hand in his. "Sincerely, I thank you," he said.

Her face was beaming by the time the food arrived. It was nothing fancy, just a simple dinner of slightly spicy sausage served on black bread with sauerkraut and spätzle. The waitress put the food down in front of them, then went to the bar, where she retrieved two large mugs of dark beer, which she placed in front of each of them. Pitor lifted his glass and was about to take a drink when Heidi lifted her glass and said, "To our Führer."

"To our Führer," Pitor repeated.

"And...to you, and the wonderful job you are doing for Germany."

He blushed. Then he smiled and took a long gulp of the beer, practically emptying his glass.

She sipped her beer delicately.

For a few moments, there was an awkward silence. The only sound was the clinking of the knife against the plate as they cut their sausages. Then Heidi cleared her throat and said, "I have something to say to you."

He looked up, foolishly hoping it had something to do with Jakup, but knowing it could not. "What is it?" he asked gently.

"It's just that I'm so honored that you chose me. I mean, I am not stupid. I know you could have had your choice of the lovely women at the Lebensborn home. And there are certainly some beautiful women who are just waiting for a fellow like you to spend the night with them. So, well, can I ask you something?"

"Sure."

"I'd like to know why? Why me?"

"Because I find you very attractive and very desirable," he lied. Pitor had not been even remotely attracted to any woman, not even Steffi, since Mila died. "I happen to like dark haired girls. I actually prefer them to blonds."

"You do?" she beamed. "That is so unusual."

"Well, perhaps it is for other men. But not for me. I love the way dark hair looks on a beautiful girl like you. That's why I chose you," he said, tearing off a piece of his thick bread. "And you should never doubt the fact that you're a very pretty girl."

"I never thought of myself that way."

I almost feel bad about using her to find my son because she seems like a nice girl, rather shy and humble. But, I must remember that she is only behaving this way because she likes me. I must never forget that she is an enemy of my people. And I am sure that if I bring up the subject of Jews, she will bare her teeth and turn into a hyena. I've seen it so many times before. "I realize that dark hair has become unpopular among our people, because it is considered a trait that is primarily Jewish or Romany, both of them being enemies of our Reich," he said, waiting for her response. In a moment, he knew he was right. Just as he predicted, her hatred towards the Jews was immediately unveiled. Any good qualities he'd seen in her a few moments ago now fell by the wayside. He had brought up the Jews, so that he would be reminded of who she was. And it worked. Her face turned angry and mean. Her eyes turned heartless and uncaring.

"I hate having Jew hair," she spat out the words. "When I was growing up, my mother would say that I was an unfortunate, because I had Jew hair. The popular girls in the Bund Deutscher Mädels were the blondes. Always the blondes. One day, I decided to take drastic measures. I took bleach and put it on my head. It burned like crazy. But I didn't care. I would have done anything to be blonde. However, it didn't work. My hair turned bright orange. The next day at school everyone laughed at me. I went home weeping. You see, I would have done anything not to look like a Jew," she said, shaking her head. "They are such ugly people."

"Do you find them ugly?" he asked. He couldn't help but be amused by her answer. After all, he was Jewish. His hair was blond. And he knew that she certainly did not find him to be ugly at all.

"Oh yes. They are very ugly."

"Do you think they are all ugly?"

"Of course. They look like trolls."

"Have you known many?" he asked.

"Well, not many, really. But our Führer says that they are ugly and that not only are they physically ugly, but they are terrible people. They are out to destroy the purity of our race, and to ruin our Fatherland. Besides, have you ever seen the articles about them and the horrible pictures in *Das Reich*?"

Pitor had seen *Das Reich*. He knew it was a propaganda newspaper that was published by Joseph Goebbels, Hitler's minister of propaganda.

"I have seen it," he said.

"And what did you think of the pictures and the articles in that paper?"

"*Das Reich* is informative. It offers viable explanations of the Jewish problem in Europe," He was having a difficult time trying to keep up his façade.

"When I was still in school, a book called *Der Giftpilz*, the poison mushroom was released. It was a very scary children's book all about the dangers we Aryans face from the Jews. I read it and it frightened me, but I think it's very important to read this book to our children. They should have this knowledge. They will need it if they encounter any Jews as they go through life," she said, self-righteously. "But, fortunately for us, our Führer is locking the Jews away. So, at least they won't have any more power to destroy our Fatherland."

Pitor smiled and nodded. Heidi's face had turned red with emotion. The more she spoke of her hatred for the Jews, the more she became passionate and emotional. Pitor forced himself to nod. He wore a smile that seemed to be plastered unnaturally on his face. Heidi had become so caught up in all she was saying, she didn't notice his disconnection from her.

Pitor closed his eyes for a moment. He had to be careful to hide his true feelings if he was to insure her that not only did he have charm and good looks, but he was the man she had been dreaming of all of her life. Somehow, he must make her want him more than anything. She must want him so badly that she would be willing to risk her job for him. Only then could he tell her that together they would make the perfect couple, and that to complete their little family, it would be essential that they adopt the little boy that Himmler had named Liam. Heidi must want him so badly, she would be willing to find a way to adopt the child he wanted, if it meant he would marry her. He assumed he would be forced to bed her soon, to seal her feelings for him. And he was already trying to spin a story, in case he was unable to keep her from discovering that he'd been circumcised. The lie he told her about his circumcision had to be believable. His life and, more importantly, his son's life, relied on it. Heidi must never suspect that he was a Jew, and that Liam was really his son.

She was still talking about the Jewish question, as the Nazis called it. He was nodding, but not really comprehending much of what she was saying. Pitor was thinking of Jakup, and what he would do once he found him. This was going to be a dangerous mission, and he had no plan for where he might go once he had Jakup, or how he might keep his son safe.

"Would you like something else?" she asked. He didn't answer. "Konrad, are you all right?"

"Yes, I'm sorry. I was just admiring your beauty," he said, smiling. This seemed to satisfy her for the moment.

"You aren't eating. I mean, you've hardly touched your dinner."

He had tried to eat, but he couldn't. His mind was racing, flooding like a river overflowing with potential solutions to his problems.

The evening seemed long and drawn out for Pitor. He wished Heidi would stop rambling. It was unnerving him because he needed answers to his questions, and he wished he could just ask her to tell him where Jakup was. Pitor took a long deep breath and reminded himself to slow down. *I must not rush her, or she might catch on and refuse to tell me anything about Liam. She might even decide not to see me again.* Heidi was his only connection to finding his son, so he must court her carefully. It was essential that he make her fall in love with him. Finally, a waitress walked over to their table and informed them that the tavern was closing. Pitor paid the check. Then he stood up, and so did Heidi. He gave her his arm and led her outside. Then they walked hand in hand all the way back to Heim Hochland.

"I guess this is goodnight," he said, at the front of the building.

"Yes, unless you would like to come in. I have a little whiskey in my room if you would care for a drink."

"Don't you have a roommate? Or do you have your own room?"

"Gretchen and I share a room here. Even though she is married, the accommodations are better here. We have hot water for bathing, and better food. And on top of all that, Horst has a roommate that is moving out soon, then Gretchen will move in with her husband, but until then she mostly stays here. But, if I ask her, she will call Horst, he has a telephone, and he will pick her up. She can spend the night with him at his place. After all, on several occasions I've slept downstairs in the main waiting room so she and Horst might have some privacy in our room."

"I'd rather not do that on our first date. Let's plan a night when we can be together. I will get us a room. Or if you prefer, you can talk to Gretchen about allowing us to spend the night in your room. But if we do use your room, I think we should give Gretchen and Horst some advanced notice. That way she won't have to spring this all on her husband at the last minute. I mean that is, of course, if you will agree to go out with me again?"

"Of course I will go out with you again," she beamed. "What girl would refuse you?" she reached up and touched his cheek. "Where are you staying tonight?" she asked.

"Oh, I am ashamed to admit that I am staying in a rather horrible place. It was very late when I arrived in Steinhoring the other night, and this hotel was the only place I could find that had a vacancy. I'd never bring a girl who is as lovely as you to a place like that. I mean, I am sharing my room with another fellow, and that would be uncomfortable for both of you."

"Do you really think I'm lovely? I mean, I know you said it earlier, but I find it hard to believe. I've spent my entire life feeling like I was one of the lesser girls. You are like a dream come true for me."

"I can see that you are very lovely," Pitor said, tucking a strand of her hair behind her ear. It had been blown across her face by a strong gust of wind.

Heidi reached up and touched his hand. Then she took it into her own and kissed it. Her face was shining, and her eyes were lit like candles with a soft, loving glow. It was all he could do to restrain himself from asking just a few questions about Jakup.

She blushed. "I must tell you something," she said.

His heartbeat quickened. *Is she going to tell me about Jakup without me asking? She knows I want that particular little boy. Maybe she will volunteer the information without me saying a word about it.* "Of course. You can tell me anything," he said.

"I just have to tell you again, I mean I know I said it before, but I can't believe it. Never, not in my wildest imagination, did I dream that a fellow as handsome and accomplished as you are, would be interested in a simple, and plain looking girl like me."

He managed to hide the disappointment with a half-smile, but his lips quivered. "Is that what you wanted to tell me?"

"Yes, I just wanted to say, thank you for choosing me."

A few moments passed. There was nothing more he could do as far as Jakup was concerned, at least not yet. So, he cleared his throat and in a soft whisper he said, "It's a beautiful night. Look at the moon, it's full," he pointed at a perfectly round silver disk that hung like a Christmas ornament.

"You're right, it is," she said. "It's very dark out tonight except for the full moon. But the inky dark sky is what makes the moon look even brighter."

He turned her face towards him. "I had a nice time tonight," he said, reaching up and running his finger down her cheek. Then gently he removed a lock of her hair that had fallen into her eyes.

"Me too. I guess you could say this was the best night of my life."

"So, then I can count on you agreeing to see me again and maybe exchanging letters with me? I would love to correspond with you. Would that be all right?"

"Did you ever doubt it?"

"Well, I was hoping..."

"Of course, I'll see you again. Absolutely. And I will wait with bated breath for your letters."

He leaned down and kissed her softly on the lips. She closed her eyes, and he kissed her again.

"I can't wait to see you again." She whispered. Then she sighed.

CHAPTER THIRTY-THREE

That night, Horst and Gretchen sat at the table sharing a meager dinner of vegetable stew with noodles.

"I want to talk to you about Konrad Hoffmann." Horst said.

"Go on." Gretchen took a sip of water.

"I can remember him vividly from school. And, I am telling you, this man is not Konrad. He resembles him, but not enough to be him. They both have blond hair and blue eyes. But I am quite sure this is just not him. Whenever I bring up things about our days at school, he avoids the conversation. Konrad was fun loving and friendly. Everyone in school loved him. He was always ready with a quick smile and a hello. In fact, he was very popular because he was also the captain of the football team. This man is not like that at all, he is very quiet, dangerously so."

"But who is he then?"

"I don't know. However, I plan to find out." Horst said.

"I don't think he's a jew. He doesn't look like one." Gretchen said, "But, if you can find out who he is, and why he's impersonating Hoffmann, you can turn him in. That will help you rise up in the party, which will be good for us. We will have more money, and you will have a better position giving us both a better life."

He nodded.

"But how are you going to find out?"

"I don't know yet. So far, I am watching and waiting for him to slip up and make a mistake. He has to, eventually."

"I hope so," she said, smiling.

After they finished eating, Horst went into the living room and lit a cigarette while Gretchen cleaned the kitchen. As she washed the pots and pans, she thought about Heidi. *Damn her. She has gotten everything she wants out of life. She's so arrogant now that she has Konrad. Well, I hope Horst is right and Hoffmann is a fraud. That will bring her back down to earth, and I can't wait.*

CHAPTER THIRTY-FOUR

Heidi's position was a very good one for a little brown sister. It paid well, provided nice food and lodging, and to top it off, she was given a handsome and important looking uniform. Most of the German girls, whose appearances did not qualify them to be amongst the 'Chosen Girls,' ended up working long hours in factories. While the 'Chosen Girls' were honored to stay at the home for Lebensborn where they were treated like princesses and expected to produce perfect Aryan children. So, Pitor knew Heidi considered herself very fortunate to have landed this job, and he was intent on earning her trust. However, he also knew that she was falling in love with him, because she believed he was the kind of man she had always dreamed of. But the real question was, would she love him enough? He must make sure she would be unable to resist his request when he finally asked her to find out what had become of Jakup, or Liam, as they called him.

The following morning, Pitor boarded a train to Munich to return to work.

A few days later, Pitor composed and sent his first letter to Heidi.

My dearest Heidi,

I am writing to tell you that you are constantly on my mind. You and I enjoyed such a lovely evening together. At least I know I did. I hope you enjoyed it too. And I am looking forward to seeing you again soon. In fact, I have two days off from work at the end of the month. I would love to come to Steinhoring to see you. So, I am hoping you have time for me and that you will agree to join me for dinner. I will anxiously await your reply.

With deep affection, Konrad Hoffman.

He was pleased when he received a return letter a week later.

My Dearest Konrad,

I, too, had a wonderful time when we went out for dinner. Just send me the dates when you will be coming into town, and I will make arrangements to take some time off from my job so we can see each other.

With deepest affection, Heidi

Two more very affectionate correspondences were exchanged between Pitor and Heidi, and within them a date for a future meeting was arranged.

Pitor arrived, as promised, later that month. He checked into a nicer hotel than the one he'd stayed in during his previous visit. After unpacking, he walked over to Heim Hochland to meet Heidi for dinner that evening. When she saw him, she practically jumped into his arms and hugged him tightly. Then she kissed him passionately.

"I've missed you," he said, hating himself for being so deceitful.

"I've missed you too, Konrad," she said. "I'm so glad you came to see me again."

They took a long walk to a restaurant that was further away from Heim Hochland than the restaurant they'd gone to on their previous date. Heidi seemed so nervous she could hardly eat. But once they finished, the two of them slowly ambled arm in arm through the streets of Steinhoring. It was getting late, and the sky was lit up with stars. "It's such a beautiful night, isn't it?" Heidi asked, looking up into Pitor's eyes.

"Yes, it is," Pitor said, remembering warm nights like this when he and Mila used to sit outside the little house they lived in before their arrest. They would talk about everything going on in their lives and they would share their hopes and dreams for the future. Later, after Jakup was born, they would wait until he was fast asleep before they went out. Then they would whisper to each other and listen quietly to be sure they hadn't awakened their son.

"Pitor, is everything all right? You seem so distracted," Heidi said, breaking his thoughts.

"I was just enjoying the stars," he said softly. But he knew she felt ignored and he must not lose her interest, not now, not right before he was going to ask her about Jakup. He'd nurtured and grown her feelings for him. And he felt she was almost ready to reveal the answers to his questions.

Pitor stopped walking. Then he turned Heidi to face him and pulled her into his arms. He kissed her deeply and passionately, and he felt her melt. *She's almost ready.*

That night when Pitor returned to his hotel room, he felt bad about toying with Heidi's emotions. But he could see no other way.

When Pitor returned to work, he was told that he had been moved to Berlin. This location was much further from Steinhoring, and that made things inconvenient. But he had set his plan in motion, and he was going to carry it out. He would just get up earlier to take an earlier train the next time he went to Steinhoring. Each week he wrote Heidi a romantic letter professing his growing feelings for her. In each letter that he sent her, he inserted a single flower he had pressed between the pages of a book. He never had to wait long for her to answer his letters. And she always assured him that her feelings for him were growing, too.

Pitor's superior officers knew he was frequenting Heim Hochland, but they thought he was going there to visit the 'Chosen Girls,' which they highly approved of, but then one of his superior officers spoke to a friend who worked at Heim Hochland, and discovered that Pitor had been going to the home for the Lebensborn to court a little brown sister. Pitor was immediately called into the office by his direct boss, who was eager to discuss this situation.

"I'm sure that spending time with a little brown sister is flattering, because I imagine that she worships you like an Aryan God. But I am afraid that your seed will be wasted with her. If you impregnate her, you may very well have more children who don't quite fit the Aryan ideal. Hoffmann," His superior officer said gently, "you are a beautiful specimen of Aryan good looks. So, it would behoove you to consider sharing your precious seed with one of the 'Chosen Girls.' I am quite certain that any one of them would be honored to bed you and carry your child for the Reich."

Pitor would have liked to tell the man to mind his own business, but he knew he had to tread carefully. "Thank you. That's very kind of you to say, sir. But, I have found that I like Heidi. I realize she is only a little brown sister, but she *is* of pure German blood."

"Hmmm," his superior officer answered, shaking his head. "I suppose that's true. However, I am only trying to help you, and it would be far better if you chose a woman who had blonde hair like yours."

"I realize that," Pitor said. "Perhaps I will find a blonde in the future. But right now, I am quite taken with this young lady. We have been dating, and she is actually very nice, and very devoted and loyal to the Reich."

"Have you taken her to bed yet?" His superior officer asked, shamelessly.

"Not yet, no."

"Ahhh, well once you have had her, a handsome fellow like you will surely tire of this little brown sister. Just keep our conversation in mind, will you? And realize that you can bed any and all of the 'Chosen Girls' at the home, whenever you feel like it."

"You are probably right about my feelings for this little brown sister. And, of course, I will keep in mind that I may visit the 'Chosen Girls too," Pitor said.

His superior officer winked at him, and Pitor forced himself to smile and nod.

"Heil Hitler," his superior officer saluted, "you may go now."

"Thank you, sir. Heil Hitler."

CHAPTER THIRTY-FIVE

A few days later Pitor's superior officer called him into his office again, "I saw this scarf in the suitcase of one of the Jews who was transported to Birkenau last week. So, I took it for you to give to your little brown sister the next time you go to Heim Hochland. A nice gift like this should help soften her resistance. I am assuming she has been resisting your sexual advances, and the challenge to make her say yes is what is driving your interest in her."

"Perhaps you're right," Pitor said, feeling the softness of the silk in his hand and feeling sick about the fate of the Jewish woman who this pretty scarf had belonged to.

"Have you been to any of the camps yet?"

"No, I haven't," Pitor said.

"Terrible places. Filthy and disease ridden. I promised to go to Birkenau to see a friend of mine who is working there. The only redeeming part of the visit was I was able to bring back several nice gifts for my wife. They have this section in the camp that they call Kanada, where they sort through the possessions the Jews bring with them. The nicest part about it is that the Jews bring their finest possessions, because they don't realize that they are never going to see their things again."

"What happens to them?" Pitor asked.

"The possessions?"

"The Jews."

"Oh, they are liquidated."

"You mean killed?"

"That's a rather ugly word. But yes. They are gassed. It's over quickly and painlessly. We use a very effective substance called Zyklon B. Would you like to know more about it? If you would like to see a gassing, I can arrange for you to visit Auschwitz-Birkenau. I think you will find it fascinating."

"Oh no, thank you. I'd rather not."

"Dare I say you are a soldier with a weak stomach. That is rather odd. Don't you think?"

"It's not a weak stomach. I would just rather do my job than take time away from work for this. But I will go if you insist," Pitor knew he must not appear weak, because if he did, this Nazi would put him to the test.

"Ahhh, well, that is true. You are needed here. And I am sure if you take time off, you are going directly to Heim Hochland to see that girl. Let's hope this scarf seals the deal for you. Then once you've conquered her, you will be more apt to visit more deserving women."

"Yes, let's hope it does seal the deal. It's very pretty," Pitor said, looking at the rich midnight blue color of the silk in his hands.

"You know, something rather strange occurred when I returned from the camp. I brought this scarf back with me for my wife. But she didn't like it. In fact, she began shaking when I gave it to her. She said it upset her, because it reminded her of one of her teachers when she was a young girl still in school. She said her teacher had always worn silk scarves. I wonder if this was before Jews were forbidden to teach at Aryan schools. I mean, my wife's teacher might have been a Jew. Perhaps she was the same Jewess who the scarves belonged to. Who knows?"

"Yes, who knows?" Pitor said, feeling a little nauseated. His mother had owned a silk scarf that she'd worn on special occasions.

"Well, good luck with that little brown sister. I hope this satisfies the challenge for you."

"Yes, I hope so too," Pitor said. Then he folded it carefully and placed it in the breast pocket of his uniform.

"You'll see. Give her the present and she'll do whatever you ask of her."

"I really hope you're right," Pitor said, and he did hope so.

"I know I'm right. I like you, Konrad. You don't give me much trouble, and you are always willing to do any task I send your way. I want to see you succeed. In many ways you are like the son I never had. And I know for a fact that it's important to the Reich that our men are married, family men. Of course, if you do get married, it won't restrict your visits to any of our houses for the Lebensborn. Visiting women there, and spreading your seed for the Führer will always be honored as a noble cause. However, when choosing a wife, a man must be very selective. The woman a man is married to can help or hurt him when he applies for a promotion. A wife should reflect all the beautiful qualities of an Aryan hausfrau. She should be blonde and blue eyed, athletic build, an excellent housekeeper, a frugal and creative cook. Just take a look at Magda, Dr. Goebbels' wife. She is a perfect example."

Pitor nodded. Then he looked down at the ground. "I can see what you are saying is true. But you're right, I am quite taken with Heidi right now, and unfortunately, although her blood is pure, she is only a little brown sister. So, I will do as you have instructed me to do. I give her the gift and then hopefully seduce her. Once we've had sex, I'm sure you are right, and my interest will wane," Pitor said, hoping that agreeing with his superior officer would pacify him. At least for now, it was better to have the man on his side than to have him as an enemy.

"I knew you would see things my way. You're a smart fellow, Konrad. You are the only one of all the men under my charge who has not tried to go after my job. That alone tells me you have integrity."

"Thank you, sir," Pitor said. *You have no idea.*

"Well, that's all for now. Go on back to work."

"Yes, sir."

"Heil Hitler."

"Heil Hitler."

CHAPTER THIRTY-SIX

Pitor's next weekend off was a month away. He continued to write to Heidi. And he received letters from her at least twice a week. Then, he finally had three days off in a row. Getting up very early in the morning, he traveled by train from Berlin to Steinhoring to see her. The weather had begun to change. Autumn was here, and the ground was covered with an array of colorful leaves. The air was crisp and clean as he entered the home for the Lebensborn. Pitor carried the scarf in a box in his hand. The girl who was sitting at the front desk had seen him before, and she remembered him as Konrad Hoffman, Heidi's boyfriend.

"You can go on upstairs if you'd like," she said, smiling. "Heidi is working in the infant's room today."

"Thank you," Pitor said, and he saw the girl's eyes light up. He knew she found him attractive. *I am praying to you, God, please make this work.*

When he walked into the room with the screaming infants, he saw Heidi standing in a corner. She greeted him with a warm and very passionate kiss. He was fairly certain she would sleep with him when he asked. The only thing bothering him was how he was going to explain the fact that he'd been circumcised. *I'll have to hide it somehow, even though I am not sure how I am going to do that. However, I must find a way. It's the only choice I have. If she sees that I have been circumcised, she will become suspicious of me. She will question my purity and then, when I ask about Liam, who knows what she will do?*

"Dinner tonight?" He whispered softly in her ear.

"Yes. Of course. I can't wait."

He smiled, "I'll meet you out in front of the building at eight? Is that all right? Will it give you enough time to get ready?"

"Eight is perfect. I'll be here."

The infants were screaming so loud that Pitor forgot to give Heidi the scarf. He couldn't wait to leave the room, and he wondered how she could bear to listen to that all day.

"I'm going to go. I'll see you tonight," he said.

She laughed, "I know they're loud. But you get used to it."

He nodded as he left the room. *I would pick them up. I wouldn't just let them cry.*

HEIDI WAS WAITING for him when he arrived at eight o'clock. She wore a very provocative red dress. "I would love to cook for you," she said, staring suggestively into his eyes. "I am an excellent cook. I can make a meal with almost nothing. I was a very good student in the Bund Deutscher Mädels. I want you to know that. However, I don't have access to a kitchen here."

"It's all right," he smiled. "And I'll bet you are an excellent cook. I can tell."

"Oh yes, I am. I promise you that. I took all the courses available to me to learn how to be a good Aryan wife," she smiled broadly.

"I'm glad to hear it," he said, his mind was racing. *How am I going to keep my secret?*

"Shall we go back to either of the restaurants we went to before?" he asked.

"Yes, let's go to the first one, if you don't mind. It's closest."

"It's perfect," he said.

After dinner, they walked outside. The moon had risen, and there was a cool breeze shuffling the leaves on the ground.

"I asked Gretchen if she would spend the night with Horst at his apartment. She agreed. So, if you'd like, you could come up for a drink before going back to your hotel," Heidi offered, nervously.

"Sure," *I am afraid that we are going to need to be lovers before she will trust me enough to give me the information I need to find Jakup.*

They walked back to the dormitory like rooms where the little brown sisters slept. This area was not nearly as pretty or ornate as the rest of Heim Hochland. He'd caught glimpses of the rooms where the blond, blue-eyed girls were housed. Those rooms were charmingly decorated, bright and cheery. As Pitor followed Heidi up a long stair-case, he glanced inside a couple of the rooms where the occupants had left the door open. They were hardly bright or cheery. In fact, they were dark and dank. The furnishings were old and minimal.

"This is my room," Heidi turned to him, smiling. "It's not as pretty as I would like, but it's home." She said as she opened the door. He followed her inside.

It's still far better than the terrible apartments Mila and I were forced to live in when we were imprisoned in the Warsaw ghetto.

She poured them both a glass of schnapps. Then she raised her glass and said, "To the Reich."

"To the Reich," he said, clinking his glass with hers.

She poured them another glass. "To the future."

"To the future," he said.

Then she looked into his eyes and in a throaty, passionate voice, she said, "To our future." She poured another glass for each of them.

"I have a gift for you," he said, taking the box with the scarf out of the breast pocket of his uniform.

"For me?" she asked.

"Well, there's no one else here, so it must be for you," he smiled, teasing her in a warm and good-natured manner. Then he handed the box to her. Her eyes lit up and grabbed it eagerly and removed the lid. When she saw the rich dark blue gray silk, she gasped.

"Oh my, this is beautiful," she said, carefully lifting the scarf out of the box and brushing it across her face. "It's gorgeous. It feels like silk. Is it real silk?" she asked.

"Yes, it is actually. And it's lovely, but it's not nearly as beautiful as you," he lied, knowing he sounded very charming. He'd always known that there were two ways to a woman's heart. One was to say, "I love you," and the other was to tell her she was beautiful. "That's why I got it for you."

Heidi stood up and walked over to the mirror on the wall. Then she draped the scarf across her neck.

"The color is quite flattering on you," he said.

"I love it. Thank you."

Heidi folded the scarf and then tucked it safely into her dresser drawer. Then she sat down beside Pitor. Heidi moved closer to him so that their thighs were touching, and strategically angled her legs so that her dress rose up high on her thigh. He was worried, because he knew what she wanted and what was expected of him. Then, in a voice hoarse with passion, she whispered as she took her schnapps glass and raised it up, "To our future. To our future...together."

"Together," he said, feeling like a cad. The type of man he'd always despised.

They drank. The schnapps was good, decent quality. It burned his throat, but it warmed his soul and left him more confident than he was before drinking it. Her hands were cold and trembling as she reached over and took his hand in hers. He felt her body shake a little as she lifted his hand to her lips and then ran her tongue across his palm. All the while, her eyes were glued to his. Heidi wasn't beautiful, but when she smiled, her dimples and bright eyes made her look cute, in a pixie sort of way. Pitor could see her lips quivering as she managed a smile, and he knew she felt insecure about how all of this was going to turn out. However, he could see that she was determined to win his affection when, still looking directly at him, she placed his hand on her thigh where her dress had ridden up past her stockings to reveal skin.

If he hadn't needed her help, he would have taken his hand back and walked away. But not before he apologized for leading her on. And although he'd had his share of women before he met Mila, he had always been careful to be honest with them. Before he had sexual relations with anyone, he told his potential partners the truth. He made sure that they knew he was not in love with them. Then, if they still wanted to make love, he proceeded. And at least he felt he hadn't lied. He had never lacked for bed partners, even when the women knew he would not be with them forever. Some of his early encounters continued for several months and occasionally, one of the girls would tell him she'd fallen in love with him. That was when he broke things off. Pitor was a kind man at heart, and he hated to hurt anyone. That was why he vowed he would never lie to a woman to get her into his bed. But then there was Mila. He'd never lied to her. He'd never had to. The first time they met, they were just children, and nothing had happened between them. Not even a kiss. But from the first time he saw her, he remembered that his mother had told him that when he met his bashert, the woman who he was meant to spend the rest of his life with, he would know it. And the first time he laid eyes on Mila, he knew he had found her. Mila was his bashert. Pitor knew that he would have to wait for her to grow up before he could marry her. But he had no doubt that the day would come when he would make her his. And even though it was several years before their relationship began in earnest, he knew they would someday be together.

For a long time, he did not see her anywhere in town, although he was always looking for her. Then, on a very ordinary day, when he least expected it, he saw her again. This time Mila was all grown up and more beautiful than he'd ever imagined any woman could be. He was in love with her before he'd even spoken to her again, and he was already certain he wanted to marry her. In fact, he had never been so sure of anything in his life. Somehow, by some miracle, he'd won her heart. She'd gone against her father's choice for her husband, and she'd married Pitor. It had been a wonderful marriage, but not without difficulties. Mila had lost a child, and there had been ups and downs until Jakup was born. But through it all, Pitor and Mila had clung to each other and their love only grew stronger. Now, his precious love was gone. And all Pitor had left of his beautiful family was a memory, and hope that he could find Jakup again.

"Konrad..." Heidi said, pulling him back into the moment as she began unbuttoning her blouse. "If you would like to spend the night..."

He smiled at her. Then she reached for his manhood, and he bristled. He wasn't hard, and he wondered how he was going to achieve this. His entire body grew rigid with concern. Heidi must have felt him tense up because she looked at him weirdly. "Are you all right?" she asked him.

He knew he had to answer, and he did have an idea. So, he said earnestly, "Heidi, I have a bit of a kink. You might say."

"Oh?" she whispered.

"Yes, I hope you will understand."

"What is it?" She looked at him. He could see in her face that he had scared her. The passion had withered in her eyes. It had been replaced by worry as she looked at him, waiting to hear what he had to say.

"Well, you see," he said. "I don't like to be touched. I like to do all the touching. But you must not touch me. And...also, the lights must be off. I only make love in absolute darkness."

"You don't like to be touched? Not even to have your manhood kissed?"

"No, I don't like it. I'm sorry. I care for you. I do. And I can't say why I have this rather strange kink. I only know that I do. However, if you and I become lovers, I will promise you that you will not suffer because of this. I will pleasure you, and I promise you will not miss touching me. Will you give me a chance?" he asked, knowing he had to make love to her to make her trust him enough to put her job on the line for him. "However, if we decide to make love, you must promise me that you will not touch my manhood. I'm sorry, but that's the way it must be."

She shrugged. Then she nodded, "Sure. I mean I suppose if that's the way you like it, it's all right with me."

He reached up and touched her face. "You're beautiful." He lied, because he did not find her beautiful. "Has anyone ever told you how pretty you are?" Pitor knew no one had, and that was why his telling her this was going to mean so much to her.

"I don't think so. I mean...I can't remember," she said.

"Don't trouble that pretty little head of yours," he smiled, then he kissed her and fondled one of her small perky breasts. "Lie down with your head on the pillow," he whispered. She did as he asked.

Then he removed his uniform jacket and his shirt. He knew women liked the way his muscles rippled. Pitor let her admire him for a minute before he got up and switched off the lights. She stood up and pulled down the window-shade, so that no light from the moon or stars entered the room. She got back into bed and Pitor climbed in beside her. He massaged her upper thighs before lifting her skirt up to her waist and pulling off her panties. Then, slowly, he began kissing her breasts. Pitor took his time. But he could not achieve an erection. He forced himself to remember why he was doing this, and since he could not achieve an erection, he used his tongue and lips to do what his penis refused to do. It didn't take long for her to have an orgasm, and because he was experienced with women, he knew when she had finished. Relieved to be done, he lay down beside her. "Was it all right?" he asked, but he already knew her answer.

"It was wonderful. But...well? What about you?"

"I achieve pleasure by pleasuring," he knew that there were plenty of odd kinks out in the world. So, he was hoping she would believe him and accept this.

"Whatever is best for you," she said. He took her in his arms and hugged her. Then they lay side by side without speaking for several moments. "Konrad," Heidi said. "I hope this doesn't ruin things, but I have something I must tell you."

He shivered. *I can't lose her now. I am so close to gaining her trust.* "Go ahead. You should know that you can talk to me about anything." He whispered in her ear as he moved her hair out of the way.

"I think I am falling in love with you. I mean, I am not asking that you marry me or anything like that," she began to stutter nervously. "It's just that, I think about you all the time. I am always waiting for your letters to arrive. And when I receive one it makes me so happy." She took his hand and squeezed it. The room was dark but from the broken tone of voice he felt certain that she was crying and even though she was a Nazi, and he hated everything she stood for, he felt sorry for her.

Pitor didn't know what to say. He hated himself for what he was doing, but he knew she would never give him what he needed if he didn't make her love him. There was a long silence.

"Konrad, have you fallen asleep?" Heidi asked in a soft whisper.

"No, I am just thinking."

"I hope you aren't going to break up with me because of what I said. I don't expect anything from you, and I would never try to tie you down," she whimpered.

"I know that. And...I am not thinking about breaking up. I am..." he hesitated, then cleared his throat, "I am thinking that I might be falling in love with you as well."

"Oh, Konrad." She gasped. "Really do you mean it? Can it be true?"

She was terribly pathetic, and he felt like a jerk because he knew that eventually he was going to break her heart. "It's true," he said, turning her towards him and kissing her softly.

She lay in his arms for several minutes and neither of them spoke. Then Pitor said, "It's late, and I really should go now. I have to catch an early train in the morning because I am expected to be back at work the following day."

"It's all right. I understand. But I will miss you."

He touched her face. "I will miss you too. But I'll be back here in Steinhoring when I have more time off at the end of the month."

"You haven't even left yet, and already I can't wait until you return," she giggled.

"It won't be long. We are both so busy that time will pass quickly."

"It never does when we are apart. It only passes quickly when you are here," she said.

He wanted to go out on a limb and ask her about Jakup, but he was afraid it was too soon to press her for information. She might get wise and realize that there was something amiss. Then he would ruin his chances forever. *Regardless of how rushed I feel, I must force myself to slow down.*

Pitor stood up and turned on the light. Heidi lay naked on the bed, and as soon as the room was lit up, she covered herself with the blanket. "There's no need to cover yourself on my account. I find you lovely."

She smiled at him as she sat up, still holding the blanket over her small breasts. Pitor slipped on his uniform jacket, then he turned to Heidi and bent down to kiss her softly. "I'll write to you this week," he said, gently pinching her cheek.

"I'll be waiting for your letter."

Pitor smiled, then quietly he walked out of her room and closed the door behind him. He climbed quickly down the stairs and left the building. The sun had already begun to rise as Pitor walked back to his hotel room. Next time he came to see Heidi, he decided he would ask her about Jakup. If she still refused to get him the information he needed, he would break up with her. This, he told himself, would be so terrible for her, she would be willing to tell him anything in order to win him back.

CHAPTER THIRTY-SEVEN

Steffi was on a mission. She decided she was going to change Zita's appearance. Most of the neighbors who had seen Zita had seen a small, dark-haired girl who was very quiet. They probably would not recognize her now. She had grown into a beautiful young woman while hiding in the cellar. If Steffi could somehow bleach Zita's hair blonde, no one would ever mistake her for the little Jewish girl. One afternoon, Steffi went into town and bought a bottle of hair bleach that was made by a French company. That night, she bleached Zita's hair until the dark color had been lifted out of it, and it was left a shade of dark blonde. Then she cut Zita's hair into a shorter, more modern style. She taught Zita to use cosmetics to change her appearance and make herself look older. Once they'd finished changing Zita's appearance, Zita studied herself in the mirror. "I really do look very different. But I am still afraid that one of the neighbors will recognize me," Zita said, tucking a strand of her newly bleached hair behind her ear.

"How often did you see any of them before your parents were arrested?"

"Hardly ever," Zita admitted.

"And you were just a child. Most people don't even notice children. Especially busy farmers. Did your parents have many friends?"

"None except for you," Zita said. "You were my mother's only friend. And my father didn't socialize with anyone at all."

"Did you go to school or play with other children?"

"No, my brother and I weren't permitted to go to school because we were Jewish, so my parents taught us to read and write and do a little bit of arithmetic. Enough to go to the market and count our money. Since the other children who lived on the neighboring farms were not allowed to play with us, we were alone all the time. No one wanted to be around Jews. It was too dangerous. They knew that the Nazis wouldn't approve. And it just wasn't worth the trouble."

Steffi didn't say a word, she just nodded.

"That's why my mother sent Asher and I to you when she was being arrested. She knew you were the only person she could rely on and trust." Zita's voice broke a little when she said her brother's name.

"Exactly!" Steffi said with excitement, trying to break Zita out of her grief. "And that's why I promise no one will recognize you. We are going to tell them that you are my sister's daughter. We will say my sister lived in Switzerland, but she got sick and recently passed away. I will say I did not know where to find your father. He and my sister had recently broken up. So, you came here to live with me. What do you think?"

"I think it sounds good. So, I am your niece then?"

"Yes, you will need a new name, a German name, and we will also have to come up with a name for my imaginary sister."

"I like the name Emilia," Zita said, smiling.

"Emilia it is." Steffi smiled back at her. "And as for my imaginary sister, your mother? I think we should call her Liesel. For a surname, how do you like Brandt?"

"Emilia Brandt?"

"Yes."

"I like it," Zita said, looking in the mirror again. "Emilia Brandt," she repeated to herself.

Steffi nodded. "So, now you have a new name and a new identity. Let's pray to God that our plan works, and no one suspects anything. I wish we could just pick up and leave here, but I don't have enough money for us to start over somewhere else. At least if we stay on the farm, we will have a place to shelter us when the winter comes, and we have a little extra food from the garden that we can hide."

"Besides, maybe that nice man will come back. The handsome one who was wearing the Nazi uniform, but he was really Jewish." Zita said.

"Oh, you mean Pitor?"

"Yes. I couldn't remember his name. But he was nice. And he, like me, was posing as someone else."

"That, he was," Steffi said. "I, too, wish he would return, but I doubt he ever will. If he finds his son, he will probably take him and try to get out of here. Maybe he'll go to Switzerland. Or try to find a way to get out of Europe all together."

"I'll bet you are still on his mind," Zita said, smiling coyly at Steffi.

"Oh, I doubt that. I was just a girl he met along the way. It's all right. I am glad to have met him."

"You like him, though. I knew it when I saw you together. And... you still like him."

Steffi laughed, "You are quite the perceptive one. How did you ever become so insightful at your young age?"

Zita shrugged. At first, she smiled, but then her face dropped, and a tear ran down her cheek.

"What is it? Why are you crying?" Steffi asked, putting her hand gently on Zita's shoulder.

"I was just thinking of everything and everyone I have lost. I suppose losing everyone I love, and then living in constant fear has made me grow up faster than I would have if my life had been normal."

"Yes, that's probably true. But don't cry. Your maturity might just be the factor that saves both of our lives."

"Perhaps," Zita said, still looking down.

There was a long silence. Then Steffi pulled Zita close and put her arm around her. "From this moment on I will call you Emilia, even when we are alone you must think of yourself as Emilia, as if this is your given name now. I know you don't want to be someone else. But, if the Nazis even suspect you might be Zita, the child of my Jewish neighbors, we are both finished. So, it's terribly important that we both think of you as Emilia. The time may come when we are confronted by a Nazi who has come hunting for Jews, and we must be sure that even when we get nervous, we must never slip up and use your real name. Do you understand me?"

"Yes, Steffi. I understand. I am Emilia Brandt."

"And what shall we say happened to your papers?" Steffi said, more to herself than Zita.

"Umm. I lost them?" Zita chimed in.

"How about instead of saying your mother got ill and passed away, we can say she passed away in a terrible house fire. And everything you had burned, including your papers."

"That's good!" Zita smiled.

"Ok, so Emilia, tell me about you."

"Well," Zita began, "my name is Emilia Brandt, and I grew up in Switzerland."

"Where in Switzerland did you live?"

Zita stared blankly at Steffi. "I don't know. You never said."

"No, I didn't. So, it's very important that we create an entire background for you. And you must memorize it. If you can think of any questions that someone might ask you, we should discuss them in advance. Do you understand?"

"Yes, I hadn't thought about all of this before."

"But we must think of every possible question someone might ask about your past. Anyway, listen to me now. We'll start here and expand as we go along. You grew up in Lucerne Switzerland. Since I was there once when I was younger, when my parents took me with them on holiday. I'll tell you everything I remember about it."

"Oh yes, do tell me everything, please."

"Well, there were mountains, and I can still remember a very lovely lake."

"I'm sure there is more."

"There is, but I can't remember much. I was too young. But I remember it was very beautiful and not too crowded. I hope they don't ask too much about it, because I don't know if there are any books available at the library. And I can't think of any other way to find out information. So, this is the best we can do for now. But we can create details like your favorite teacher. And your best friend. Neither of these people need to be real. They can both be imaginary people, who we will create. However, you must be consistent with your story. It must never change. Are you ready to get started?"

"Yes. I am."

CHAPTER THIRTY-EIGHT

The day after Pitor returned to work, he received a letter from Heidi. He knew she would have had to send it at least two weeks before he went to visit her, because it had been forwarded from his location in Munich to his new post in Berlin. Her letter made it clear to him she was smitten with him. And he wished he could just come right out and ask her about Jakup. But he knew he must hold back and continue to go slowly. Everything that was important to him was riding on her, and he dare not make the wrong move.

"We have come to Berlin because the Führer is scheduled to speak at a rally next week. And it is very important that all his security be there with him and be focused. And that means you," Pitor's superior officer said.

"Of course. I will be there."

"Then, immediately following the rally in Berlin we will all be taking a little retreat to Wolfsschanze, known as the Wolf's Lair. You will like it there. It's a lovely place. My favorite in fact, because it is very safe, and the compound is well stocked with everything we might need. In fact, the Wolf's Lair is our Führer's favorite spot. He spends most of his free time there. Although, lately we have been unable to take time for relaxation, because we have been so busy. However, once we get to the compound, you will see why the Führer likes it so much."

"Will we be returning to Munich any time soon?" Pitor asked, anxiously.

"Oh Hoffmann, what am I to do with you? Please, don't tell me you are still thinking about that little brown sister," his superior officer said, as he slammed his fist on the desk and began shaking his head. "There will be plenty of women in East Prussia, just itching to climb in your bed. Forget about that one at Heim Hochland. She is only a little brown sister, and therefore she can be of no good use to your career."

"East Prussia?" Pitor said. "Is that where we are going?"

"Yes, that's where the Lair is located."

Pitor nodded. "I see." He said, trying to hide the worry on his face. He was on the brink of asking Heidi for the information he needed, and now he was being sent away. Traveling from Berlin to Steinhoring was a longer distance than Munich had been, but it was manageable. Now he was headed to East Prussia, and he wondered how long a train ride would be from there to Steinhoring. It wasn't going to be as simple to see Heidi in the future. In fact, it might be a long time before he was given enough time off to be able to return to Steinhoring. And, by then, he was afraid he would lose the momentum he'd gained with Heidi.

"So, Hoffman, you look like you're in a daze. Wake up and go back to your rooms to get your affairs in order, because we might not return to Germany for a while." Then he smiled at Pitor, "Don't be so upset. I promise you are going to like the Lair. And, you are still going to be an important man, just like you have been since your promotion. So, if you are still interested in that girl in a few months, and you are willing to take a long train ride, I will find a way to arrange a little time off for you."

"Thank you. It means a lot to me."

"Well, I like you Hoffman. You are my protégé and if you look good to the high officials, then I look good. So, you must promise me that if I help you to go and see the little brown sister, you will not do anything stupid.

"I promise," Pitor said, quickly.

"What I am trying to tell you is that you must not marry that girl. Am I making myself clear?"

"Yes, absolutely."

"Good. Now go and start packing your things," his superior officer said, then he raised his hand in a salute, "Heil Hitler."

"Heil Hitler," Pitor saluted.

CHAPTER THIRTY-NINE

Pitor walked back to his room in the living quarters in a daze. The last time he saw Heidi, he had not mentioned Jakup, or Liam as they called him, because he hadn't wanted to rush. But now he was leaving Germany and going to East Prussia. How long would it be before his superior officer was able to get him several days off in a row so he could return to Steinhoring? And would he be able to keep her interest through letters until he could see her again? *I am afraid I made a mistake by waiting. I was afraid of pushing too hard. But it backfired on me. So, the next time I see her, I will not wait. I will find a time that is right and then ask her about Liam. I didn't realize that something like this might happen, and now I am afraid that if too much time passes between our meetings, she will not be as crazy about me as she is now. And if she is not wild about me, she won't tell me what I need to know. Then what will I do?*

He knew he could not refuse to go to the Lair with the rest of Hitler's entourage. His superior officer would be furious if he even suggested it. And, for right now, he was sure that his position in the party was part of Heidi's attraction to him. If his plan was to be successful, and it must be successful, she had to want him more than any other man. She had to want him so badly that she would be willing to lose her job, if it meant winning his affection.

Pitor was stunned by the turnout of people attending the rally in Berlin. He had never seen so many people in one place at one time. When the Führer walked up to the podium, the applause and wild cries of approval were so loud, Pitor was afraid his ear drums would break. With each sentence the Führer uttered, the crowd grew more entrenched. Women watched him with mad desire in their eyes and sweat running down their brows. By the time it was finally over, Pitor was exhausted, and his head ached.

The following morning, the entire group boarded a train to East Prussia.

As his superior officer had promised, the Lair was a place where Hitler could escape the crowds who adored him, and relax for a while. It was a secure compound built to entertain, but also to protect the Führer. Pitor was not surprised at how intense the security was at the Lair, and because he had thought of murdering Hitler, he assumed others had the same idea. However, there had been attempts on Hitler's life, and somehow, not one had been successful. Now that Hitler was safe in the Wolf's Lair, it was even less likely that Pitor could ever achieve such an impossible feat. Security was everywhere. Hitler even employed tasters to assure his food was not poisoned. And, although he would never admit it, Hitler was afraid he was losing the war, and if he did, the German people would lose their love for him. But from what Pitor could tell, Hitler was too power hungry to change his tactics, and Pitor wondered if Hitler knew that trying to invade Russia had been a fatal mistake. He had sacrificed his troops by taking an unprepared German army into Russia at the start of a brutal Russian winter. The soldiers did not have warm enough clothes, and they were freezing to death even before they made it to the battlefields. And, due to the frigid weather, it had been far too difficult to deliver enough food to them to keep the soldiers from starving. Even so, Hitler refused to back down. The German army was falling on the frozen ground of the eastern front like autumn leaves. Meanwhile, Hitler was embroiled in a fierce battle with the British, the French, and the Americans on the Western front. He'd spread himself too thin. It was beginning to look like Germany was going to lose the war. For this... Pitor was secretly very grateful.

While the Führer contemplated world domination as he hid in his lair, located deep in the Masurian woods, Pitor continued to write letters to Heidi. However, because the location of the Wolf's Lair or the Wolfsschanze, as Pitor soon discovered that it was called, was top secret, and only those who were closest to the Führer knew its location, all the letters leaving the compound were opened and read before they were mailed. Any compromising information, regardless of how unimportant it might seem, was censored. This was achieved by carefully cutting the offending text out of the letters. And to make things even more difficult for Pitor, any letters leaving the lair were only brought into town to be mailed once a month.

Pitor was not permitted to give Heidi a return address, so she was unable to return his letters. This kept him worried and wondering if she was still interested. But all he could do was write to her and profess his growing affection.

Then finally, after almost three months, Pitor received a leave, allowing him to take off from his duties for four days. This would enable him to catch a train and travel directly to Steinhoring. However, he had not been given any notice. He was told about his time off the day before it was to begin. And because of this, there was no time to send a letter informing Heidi that he was on his way. His visit to Heim Hochland was going to have to be a surprise.

The following morning, he was awake and ready to leave before sunrise. But before he could go, he was forced to swear that no matter what happened, he would keep the location of the Lair a secret.

Pitor swore under oath that he would not reveal the location of the Lair. Then he was allowed to go.

Before he left, Pitor's superior officer stopped him in the hallway, and put his hand on Pitor's shoulder. "I arranged for your time off. So, I am hoping you will listen to me and do whatever you have to do to get this girl out of your mind. She is wrong for you. And quite frankly, I can't see what a fellow like you could possibly see in her. How could an ambitious fellow like you allow a worthless girl like this to ruin your chances for a bright future?" His superior officer growled at him. "I'm really getting tired of watching you walk around here like a lovesick puppy. I've been trying to help you with this for a while, but you refuse to listen to me. So, I've decided that perhaps it's time you thought seriously about finding a wife."

"I will try to find a woman who will be good for my career," Pitor said, hoping to pacify him.

"There are a lot of beautiful young women at Heim Hochland. Marry one."

Pitor nodded, doing his best to satisfy this man who had taken him under his wing, and was attempting to act as a surrogate father to him. Little did he know Pitor despised him.

"Well, go on now. You don't have much time. Make sure you are not late in returning," his superior officer said.

Pitor nodded.

"Heil Hitler."

"Heil Hitler."

CHAPTER FORTY

Quickly, Pitor left and went into town, where he planned to take the next train leaving for Munich. Once he was in Munich, he would transfer to a second train that would take him directly to Steinhoring.

As he stood on the platform waiting for the train, Pitor looked around. He noticed that no one, except a very young boy, made eye contact with him. *They are afraid of me. I wonder how many of them are traveling with false papers?* He thought, but it didn't matter. He had no intentions of finding out. All he wanted was to find his son.

It was late in the afternoon when Pitor finally arrived at Heim Hochland. He told the receptionist, a new girl who he had not seen at Heim Hochland before, that he wanted to surprise Heidi, and so there was no need to let her know he was there. "Is she still working in the children's room?" he held his breath; he had been worried for the last three months that she might have been promoted, or left her job altogether. And if this were the case, she might not have access to Jakup's file anymore.

"Yes, she's still here working with the toddlers," the receptionist said, as she glanced at his uniform. Pitor breathed a sigh of relief.

The receptionist let her eyes travel over him, and he had enough experience with women to know she was attracted to him.

"By the way, my name is Lottie. If you need anything, just let me know," she said.

He gave her his most endearing smile. Lottie was a pretty blond. But she was also very young. Perhaps seventeen. And Pitor knew that regardless of her age, his superior officer would be thrilled if he married her. This made him smile, because he had no intention of doing so.

"It's nice to meet you, Lottie," he said.

"My pleasure," Lottie said, then she looked away and carefully asked, "I know it's none of my business, but is Heidi your sister or a relative of some sort?"

"Heidi? No, she's not related to me," Pitor answered.

"I see. Well, is there anything I can get for you? Anything before you go up to the children's room?"

"No, thank you," he smiled, then he turned towards the stairs.

Lottie called out, "Do you know where you are going, or do you need directions?"

"I know where to go from here. Thank you for your help," Pitor said, then he continued over to the staircase and began to climb up to the second floor.

Heidi was not looking towards the door when he entered the room. She was busy washing a little girl's hands and face, all the while she was reprimanding the child severely. Heidi held the child inside a stationary bathtub, where she was scrubbing the little girl's face with a scrub brush that was dirty because it had been used for washing floors. The child was screaming. Her face was red and swollen. For a moment Pitor stood watching in horror. He had never seen Heidi behave this way, and he was shocked to see how vicious and cruel she could be to a toddler. From what he could overhear, Heidi was angry that the child had gotten into some ink and now she had ink on her hands and face. Several times, the child tried to break away from Heidi's grasp, causing Heidi to grow even more angry. So angry that she slapped the little girl's face, leaving a red mark on the girl's cheek. This only caused the child to scream louder. Then, the little girl bit Heidi's hand and this made Heidi slap her so hard that Pitor could hear flesh meeting flesh. The child was weeping loudly and shaking. But Pitor couldn't do anything to help. He stood quietly watching, wishing he could intervene because he hated to see any child feeling frightened or being hurt, but knew he must not. It was more important that he gained Heidi's trust. After all, he did not come to save the world. He came to find his son. The only sound in the room was the sound of the little girl sobbing. The other children had stopped playing and were standing or sitting with their mouths open as they watched Heidi, whose rage was growing stronger every minute. Pitor scanned the room for Gretchen, who was nowhere to be found. Heidi took the child by the shoulders and shook her hard. It was all Pitor could do to keep himself from trying to stop her. And even as he watched, he shivered to think of how far Heidi might take this anger. Then, like a miracle, Heidi's hair fell into her eyes. She turned her head and looked up to push the hair back. That was when she saw him. Almost immediately, the anger fell away from her face. It was replaced with a warm and welcoming smile. Gently, she took the little girl out of the tub and wrapped her in a towel. "Stay out of the ink," Heidi warned. Then she left the little girl whimpering as she sat on the floor.

Heidi smiled as she walked over to Pitor.

"You're here," she said in awe. "What a wonderful surprise."

"I came as soon as I had time off," he said, kissing her softly. But he was trying to hide how sickened he was by what he'd just seen. He prayed Jakup was not being treated this way by the adults who were raising him. *These Nazis are insane. They have their own ideas of how to raise children and so who knows what they could do to an innocent child?* A shiver ran down his spine. *All the more reasons to hurry and find out where my son is.*

It was as if Heidi knew by the look on Pitor's face that he was repulsed by what he'd just seen. "I'm sorry you had to witness that.

227

But, you see, if we don't discipline these children, they will grow up to be monsters. When we are trained to work with the children here at Heim Hochland, we are taught that if we are to raise good people, we must be very strict. And unfortunately, sometimes we must resort to violence to make them understand that they must listen to us and follow our instructions."

"That makes a lot of sense," Pitor nodded, putting his hand on Heidi's shoulder. He knew there was no point in arguing. "Where is Gretchen?"

"She'll be back soon. Why do you ask?"

"Well, I was hoping perhaps you and I might go outside for a walk when she returns." He said, "It's been so long since we last saw each other."

"I'd love to, but I don't think I can. Gretchen isn't expected to return for a few hours. By then it will be time for my shift to end and hers to begin."

"Dinner then?" He asked.

"Yes, of course, I'd love to have dinner with you," she gushed.

"I'll pick you up at eight, if that's all right?"

"Yes, that would be fine."

"In front of the building?"

"Yes, as always," she smiled.

He leaned over and kissed her softly. Then he left.

CHAPTER FORTY-ONE

At first, when Emilia began to live upstairs in Steffi's house, she had been very nervous. She had looked all around her, afraid of who might pass by every time she went outside to help Steffi with the chores on the farm. But as time slithered on, she became more comfortable. And nature took its course as she grew into a very attractive young woman with her long thick hair and slender but curvy body. Each month, late in the evening, the two women closed the shades tightly and Steffi bleached the roots of Emilia's hair. It wasn't long before they both became accustomed to seeing her as a strawberry blonde.

Although Emilia had become very helpful with the vegetable garden and the farm work, both she and Steffi decided it was far too risky for Emilia to go to school. Therefore, Emilia didn't have any friends. But she seemed to be happy just to be living a quiet and safe existence. Sometimes Emilia accompanied Steffi into town when they went shopping for supplies, or to pick up Steffi's ration cards. And then, it happened, on one such occasion, Emilia met a young man who worked at the general store. He was only a few years older than Emilia.

One afternoon, when the two women had gone to the general store to buy flour to bake bread, Steffi noticed this tall and lanky young man eyeing Emilia. At first, Emilia did not respond, and it seemed as if she was unaware of the young man's attention. But that was short-lived because the next time Emilia and Steffi went to the general store, the young man approached Emilia, and they began talking. Steffi could not hear what they were saying, and she tried to ignore it, telling herself that Emilia would not become involved with anyone because of her circumstances. But a week later when Steffi saw the same boy standing outside the window of her farmhouse, talking to Emilia and putting his arm around Emilia's shoulder, Steffi knew that somehow, they had met behind her back. And somehow, they had become familiar with each other. She hated to do it, but she knew she must address this with Emilia. It made her terribly sad to know that, for Emilia's safety, she must put a stop to this budding romance. But, if Emilia came to trust this young man enough to tell him the truth about herself, the results could be disastrous.

Steffi was braiding Emilia's long bleached hair as they sat in the living room of Steffi's farmhouse one late afternoon. "I know you like that young man who works at the general store," Steffi said. "His name is Gustav, isn't it?" she asked.

"Yes, it is. He's very nice, and it just so happens that he and his family recently moved into one of the farms just up the road from here," Emilia said. "The older people who owned the farm could no longer keep it up, so his family recently bought the place. They wanted to get out of the city, so they moved here from Nuremberg."

"That's nice," Steffi said, her tone of voice was cutting. She hadn't meant to sound so sarcastic, and she was sorry that she did. Even though times were hard, she had to remind herself that Emilia was only fifteen years old, and she had already lived a difficult life. "I understand your feelings. I really do. Gustav is handsome and he is the right age, only a few years older than you. But I am sorry to have to bring this up, however, you must not forget the danger that we face. You and I are living a lie. We are hiding you in plain sight. So far, we have been lucky. But we must not let our guard down. We must always be careful."

Emilia nodded, looking down at the ground as if she might start to cry. Steffi reached out and put her hand on Emilia's shoulder. Then, in a gentle, motherly voice, she whispered, "You are very young, and because you aren't in school and you hardly ever get into town, he is the first boy you've had contact with who is close to your age. I hope that the circumstances change, and Germany loses this war. Then you will have an opportunity to meet other young men. But Gustav is not right for you. I know you like him, but he is a German, and that makes him one of them. You must never forget this. So, no matter what he tells you, or how he treats you, you can never really allow yourself to trust him."

"You don't know him. If you did, you'd see that he's different than the others. He's not a typical German boy."

"Just because he is kind to you?" Steffi asked.

"Yes, he is very kind."

"He doesn't know you're Jewish. He might be different towards you if he knew. Does he belong to the Hitler Youth?"

"I don't know. We've never talked about it. But I believe it's mandatory, so I can't hold that against him. Besides, he might not hate Jews. We haven't discussed that either. He might not believe all this propaganda. Maybe I should ask him how he feels about Jews."

"No! Absolutely not. Don't ask him anything about that. There is no reason for you to discuss his feelings about Jewish people. Even a discussion like that could arouse his suspicion and we don't want him to suspect anything. Do you understand me?"

"Yes, ma'am," Emilia said, looking down at the ground like she might cry.

"Listen to me, from the time they are very young, the Nazis feed German children in the Hitler Youth hatred towards Jews. The children get swept up in it because the Hitler Youth groups are lots of fun. I know I was in the Bund Deutscher Mädels and it was very enjoyable. We had cookouts and played sports. We learned to be frugal and be good German wives. But they also spiced all this fun with fear and hatred of Jews. And most of the girls I knew believed every word of it. I didn't. However, we don't know what he thought, and so we have to assume he is your enemy."

"Like you said, we don't know that for sure. You didn't believe the propaganda. Maybe he didn't either. Besides, I attended a meeting of the League of German Girls, and I don't believe anything they say. The only thing they've ever taught us that's worthwhile is how to stretch our rations," Emilia said.

"When did you go to a meeting? I never knew you went."

"I was invited once, when we were in town. I wanted to see what it was, so I went out to a meeting when you were asleep one night."

"Are you crazy?" Steffi was angry now. "You must never do that again. Never. Do you understand me?"

Emilia nodded and looked away.

"And make sure you do not see that boy again. You must not risk it. Don't talk to him. Don't ask him how he feels about the Jewish people. Have you forgotten how dangerous our lives are? He only treats you nicely because he doesn't know you're Jewish. He believes you're a German like him. But if he ever found out the truth, he would think nothing of turning you in and collecting a reward. You must never forget that. Not only are you putting yourself in danger, but you are putting my mother and me in danger too." Steffi had been yelling, but now she was spent. The anger seeped out of her, and she sighed. "I hate to have to bring this up, but you must remember what that Nazi did to your brother. And what that group of horrible Gestapo agents did to your parents. You simply must never let your guard down. If not for your own sake, then at least for mine. If I am found guilty of harboring a Jew, I will be punished very severely. Perhaps even put to death."

Emilia looked directly into Steffi's eyes, then she looked away and Steffi thought she saw guilt in Emilia's face. "You're right. And I'm sorry for causing you all this distress. I won't speak to him again," Emilia said sadly.

"I'm sorry. I really am. I know you are young and it's natural for you to like boys at your age. So, I understand how difficult this is for you. But it's in your best interest to avoid any risks at all."

Emilia didn't say a word, she just nodded.

CHAPTER FORTY-TWO

Early the next morning, Emilia was outside pruning the bushes when she looked up to see Gustav riding up on an old rusty black bicycle. "Hello Emmie," he mouthed to her, trying to be quiet so as not to awaken Steffi. He got off the bike and took a small bouquet of wild-flowers out of the basket of his bicycle and held them in his hand.

Emilia stood up and spun around. A smile washed over her pretty face. Her hands were covered in dirt, but she wiped them quickly on the skirt of her dress. "Gustav," she said. Then she remembered her conversation with Steffi and the smile faded. "We must have a talk. You can't come around here to see me anymore"

"What is it? Why? Have I done something wrong? Have I offended you?" He said with worry in his eyes. His hands were shak-ing. Then, as if he remembered that he'd brought flowers, he handed her the bouquet. Emilia took the flowers, and her eyes glazed over as if she might cry. "Please tell me, what have I done?" he asked.

She shook her head. "There is nothing to tell. You've done nothing wrong. You've been kind and generous."

"So, what is it? Why don't you like me anymore?"

She wished she could tell him the truth, that she was Jewish and pretending not to be. In her heart, she was convinced that he would never betray her. But she knew she owed it to Steffi to keep her secret. "My aunt thinks I am too young to start seeing boys socially. I suppose she is afraid I might get into trouble."

"Trouble?"

"Gustav, please try to understand. With the war going on, I am just not ready to get involved with anyone. I can't have a boyfriend."

"Then, what do you say to the fact that I am not some fellow who is just interested in seeing you occasionally. Or who only wants to take you to his bed?" He cleared his throat. "How would you feel if I said I want to marry you? I love you, Emmie."

"Please, don't say that." She felt like she might weep.

"I have to, because it's true. I love you. Would you consider an engagement with me? Perhaps your aunt would be less likely to distrust me if I were your fiancé?"

Emilia had dreamed of this moment. She'd often thought of what it might be like to have a handsome young man propose to her. This was like one of the romantic scenes from one of the books she had read, and she was having a difficult time not being swept into the excitement and romance of it. But she couldn't ignore the conversation she'd had with Steffi, and she knew she had promised she would break things off with Gustav. Tears burned the back of her eyes as she was just about to tell him they must never see each other again. But before she said the words she knew he must hear, he moved close to her. Then, he took both of her hands in his. Gustav was a full head taller than Emilia, so when he looked into her eyes, he looked down. His gaze was so passionate and sincere that she melted. How could she ever make Steffi understand he was different than the others? He loved her. But regardless of her feelings, she knew that with all that Steffi had risked for her and for her brother, before he was killed, she must adhere to Steffi's wishes, even if doing so hurt her deeply, which it did.

"Emmie," he said, "please, listen to me. I have something I must tell you."

"Yes? What is it?"

Then he blurted out, "I've been conscripted in the army. I received a telegram last night. That's why I want to become engaged. I want you to be there waiting for me when I return."

"Oh no, Gustav. Can you get out of it?"

"I'm afraid not. I must go."

"The army? The war. Oh no, Gustav. Not you," she said, in disbelief.

"Yes, I have avoided it up until now, but I can no longer do that," he squeezed her hands. "Oh Emmie, I will be leaving here at the end of the week. And I had to come and tell you. I couldn't go away without seeing you first. I came to ask you to marry me. I know it's selfish, but I believe you have strong feelings for me too. And I thought that at least if we got engaged, I would know you were mine and you would be waiting for me to return."

"I don't know what to say," she said.

"Say yes," he smiled. "Please say yes." With one hand, he reached into his breast pocket and took out a small gold ring with a tiny blue stone in the center. "It was my grandmother's ring. My father's mother. She gave it to my mother when my mother got married. Now, it is only right that it should be yours."

Emilia pulled her hand away from him and turned her back to him, breaking free of his gaze. "I can't marry you," she said. "I'm sorry, but I can't."

"Please, you must at least tell me why," he said. "I deserve that, don't I?"

"You do. So, I will tell you. It's because my aunt Steffi needs me to stay here and help her with the farm. I cannot get married and leave her alone to tend to it by herself."

"Then, as soon as the war is over and I am free, I'll move in here with you. I will be a big help to your aunt. You'll see. She'll like me once she knows me better."

"And what about your parents? They need you on their farm."

"I have two brothers. I am sure that at least one of them will stay with my parents to help them with the farm."

She could hardly breathe. The idea of marriage to Gustav was like a dream come true, and yet she could not accept his offer. She'd been crazy about him since the first time she saw him, when Steffi took her to church so people would think she was a christian. He hadn't seen her then. In fact, he hadn't seen her until a month later, when she entered the general store. But by then, Emilia had found out a lot about him. She had asked a few of the women, who Steffi sat with in church, who he was. They told her he was a new boy in town whose family came from Nuremburg. She didn't need to ask anyone anything else. She could see for herself that he was devastatingly handsome with his strawberry blond hair, strong jaw and high cheekbones. All the girls had their eyes on him, or at least that was what Emilia thought. But after they'd spoken at the general store, he'd actively pursued her. Two days following their first meeting, he had come by the farm and introduced himself. Steffi was busy tending to her mother, who she bathed and fed each day. So, Emilia was free to take a walk with Gustav. They'd walked side by side, hardly speaking to each other. But the sexual chemistry between them was undeniable. When they returned to the farm, and he kissed her for the first time, she'd felt transported to another world. Heaven, perhaps. She was dizzy and lightheaded as she watched him ride away on his bicycle. He came to see her again, at the same time the following day, because she'd explained that was when Steffi took care of her mother.

Once again, she and Gustav went for a walk. But when they returned, he did not leave. He'd pulled Emilia behind the barn and kissed her passionately. Since then, they had seen each other at least twice every week for over a month.

"I won't say no to your marriage proposal. But I can't, I love you too much. But because of the circumstances, I must not say yes to you, either," she said. "We can write to each other, but I shouldn't take this ring from you because I can't wear it. I would have to keep it a secret until you return. If my aunt Steffi saw it, she would want to know how I got it, and if I told her she would be very angry. She would insist that I give it back to you."

"Then take it and hide it until I return. She doesn't need to know about our intentions for the future. At least not yet. We will tell her together when I return," he said sincerely. "I will make her like me. I know I can do it. Once she gets to know me, and she sees how much I care for you, she will change her mind about me."

"I don't know. What's the point in my taking this ring from you if I can't wear it?" she said. "I would have to hide it in my drawer. Then we would have to discuss this again when you come back," Emilia was worried about Gustav. He was not the type of man who would do well in the army. Gustav was not a fighter; he was a poet at heart, who had taught himself to play the guitar. His singing voice was hauntingly lovely. These were some of his traits that had charmed her. But now, she was afraid that they were the type of personality characteristics that would prove him to be too weak to survive a war. Emilia trembled when she thought of Gustav going away to a foreign land, where he would be forced to walk through minefields and where he would be shot at by enemies.

"That's just it. This war is real. And, although I love you and I will do everything I can to stay safe, the fact is, I may not make it back to you. I could easily be killed. At least if we are engaged, then we would both know that we had loved each other deeply and truly. And you would have the ring. It would be yours and it would always be a reminder of my love. So, you see, it means so much to me that you have my ring."

Emilia longed to tell him the truth. He loved her. She believed he truly loved her, and that he would love her whether she was Jewish or not. And she believed that people in love should not lie or keep the truth from each other. Her knees were weak, and she couldn't stop them from trembling. The right thing to do was to tell him the truth, and she would have told him, had it not been for Steffi. Even though Emilia trusted Gustav completely, she loved and respected Steffi. She knew how much Steffi had sacrificed for her and her brother. So, she would not betray Steffi's trust. Steffi had been very insistent that no matter what happened, she must never tell anyone that she was really Zita, a Jewish girl. And so she could not be honest with this man, even though she loved him. "Gustav, you must promise me that you will not die, you must return to me," she said. She was shaking him softly as tears fell from her eyes. "You must never even think that there is a possibility that you won't survive this. It's bad luck."

He shook his head and with a serious expression on his face, he said, "It's impossible not to think about. Anyway, this war is bad luck. And, as far as I can see, it's unnecessary too. In fact, Hitler is bad luck. He's the worst thing that's ever happened to Germany."

"You must not let anyone else hear you say that," she said, her eyes sharp with terror. "It would be considered treason."

"I know. But I love you, and love is synonymous with trust, isn't it?" he asked.

She shook her head and looked away.

"Now, I know that the soldiers who fought in the great war want to avenge Germany's loss, and the Führer says he wants to put Germany in her rightful place as the one world power. But I don't believe any of it. I think the Führer just wants to be the most powerful man alive, and he doesn't care how many young men he sacrifices to do it. Now, personally, I would be a lot happier to have things back the way they were before this war began. It's true that Germany was struggling financially. And for a while it looked like things might get better here. But they didn't. They've gotten worse."

She nodded. "I agree with you. But you must be careful what you say. No one can be trusted, so you must never tell anyone what you are telling me. I would die if you were arrested for treason."

"I know you're right, that I must not let anyone else know how I really feel. Only you," he sighed.

"You can tell me anything. You always can," she said, then in a soft voice, she added, "I wish you didn't have to go. I wish we could run away together."

"We can, if you will go with me."

"If we do, you will always be on the run. For the rest of our lives, unless we can get out of here. But, I know that the Nazis won't let you go easily, they will hunt you down for breaking their law."

"If they can find me. If they can find us," he corrected himself.

"I don't know what to do. I am going to have to discuss this with my aunt Steffi."

"Don't tell her. She won't want you to go with me. She'll forbid you from talking to me when she finds out how I feel. She will say our relationship is too dangerous. And she is probably right."

"Oh Gustav, what are we going to do? If we run, where will we go? Hitler seems to have his thumb over the entire world. And how can we get there?"

"Believe me, I've been mulling this over in my mind since I received the letter letting me know I was drafted. The truth is I have no answer to that question. I don't know how we would be able to afford to pay the passage to get to America, and even if we could, I'm not sure they would let us in. So, I was thinking of Switzerland. But it will be difficult to get there too. We would have to go through the alps on foot."

"I don't know what to do. I can't just leave Steffi like this, all alone to tend to the farm without any explanation of where I have gone and why. The only way I can go is if I discuss it with her, and she agrees to it."

"Don't bother. Your aunt is a good German. I can tell. I'm sure she is all for the Führer and whatever he says is what she believes. They are all like that. Besides, I know your aunt doesn't like me. And she will never agree to you leaving here with me."

"It's not that she doesn't like you, Gustav. She doesn't really know you. At least not the way I do. She is just very protective. I am sure you can understand that she is afraid for me," Emilia said, but she wished she could tell him that Steffi wasn't a follower of Hitler. However, she dared not.

He nodded. "I suppose the truth is that I am being selfish by asking you to run away with me. You are safe here on this farm with your aunt. And, because I love you, I want what is best for you. So, it's probably best that we don't try to run. I should probably go to serve in the military as is expected of me."

Emilia shook her head. "I am so confused, I don't know what to do."

She watched him as he paced for a few long moments. The sun illuminated his golden hair. Then, he turned to look at her and with strong conviction he said, "I have decided that I am going. I will not put you in danger. I will report for duty as is required. And, with God's help, I'll make it through. Then when I return, you and I can get married. But I ask you for one thing only. Will you keep the ring safe for me? Please?"

"I can't. I can't take your ring. You may need to sell it. You may need the money to survive."

He looked at her with pain in his eyes. Then, without waiting for her response, he put the ring in his pocket, then turned and mounted his bicycle and began to ride away. For a moment, she watched him. Then she began to run after him yelling, "Gustav, please stop. Gustav, Gustav."

He stopped and dismounted the bicycle. Then he turned to see her running towards him. She was out of breath when she reached him. He let the bike fall and took her into his arms. She began to cry. "I couldn't let you go away angry. I love you, Gustav."

"I love you, too," he said.

Then she took his hand and led him into the barn. When the door was closed and they were alone, he pulled her close to him, all the while whispering, "I love you, Emmie."

It made her entire body tingle when he called her by his pet name for her. Emmie.

They made love for the first time together on a pile of fresh hay. And when they finished, Emilia accepted the ring.

Meanwhile, Steffi was making bread in the kitchen when she glanced out the window and saw a bicycle lying in the field. She had seen this bike before, and she knew it belonged to Gustav. For a single moment, she was angry at Zita, because she assumed that Gustav and Zita were alone in the barn. But then her anger faded away as she thought about how she had wanted to be in love like this when she was a young girl. However, it was not meant to be. Love had evaded her. And even now, sometimes she longed for it. So, how could she blame Zita? *Young love is so brave, so unafraid of the dangers.* Steffi thought as she shook her head.

CHAPTER FORTY-THREE

Pitor had been worried about Jakup since his visit to Heim Hochland, when he discovered that Jakup, now Liam, had been adopted. Now that he had made the decision that tonight he was going to speak to Heidi about Jakup, he could hardly contain himself long enough to finish dinner.

The meal was expensive, but Pitor could hardly eat. He did his best not to watch her eating. Not to watch her take each bite and count the minutes until she took the next one. She was all dressed up, wearing rouge and lipstick and smiling at him as she made light-hearted conversation about a concert she'd attended with Gretchen the previous week. Heidi was eating slowly and rambling on about how much she had enjoyed the concert, and how she'd wished he could have been there with her. He could tell that the dress she wore was new because she was very careful not to spill anything on it. It was a traditional German frock with a bright blue dirndl skirt and a crisp white blouse. Her hair had been carefully curled. Pitor attempted to compliment her on her appearance, but his nerves were on edge. It was almost impossible for him to sit still and listen to her. Inside he was screaming, "Stop talking about nonsense and tell me where that little boy is, the one who Himmler named Liam!" But he forced himself to smile and appear calm. He knew he must not lose control of himself. If she even suspected that he had any previous involvement with Liam, she would most certainly want to know all about it.

Finally, the waiter brought coffee and dessert. "I'm so glad you came to see me. I've missed you and this has been such a lovely surprise," Heidi said.

"I was hoping you would be available for dinner tonight," he smiled, but his lips were shaking. "I didn't have time to write and make arrangements. I was given my leave only a few days ago."

She reached across the table and took his hand. "I must admit, you haven't come to see me in a while, and I was starting to worry you might have lost interest."

"Never," he said, knowing it was what she wanted to hear. "I've been moved. I'm stationed at a new location. And I haven't had any time to myself."

"Oh? Where is it?"

"I'm afraid I can't tell you. I would love to, don't get me wrong, but it's top secret."

"Sounds rather serious," she smiled, "and important."

"It is quite serious. As you know I have an important position working directly for the Führer. However, no matter what, you must never think I've lost interest in you. I can't always come to see you when I want to. But you should know that I will come as soon as I can," he said, smiling. Pitor thought about his promotion. He, Konrad Hoffmann, had been promoted to this very important job as a body-guard. However, he had only seen the Führer a handful of times. Still, it was a good idea not to tell Heidi that. She was impressed, not only by his good looks but also by his important position within the party.

He had given a lot of thought as to when it might be best to bring up the subject of Liam, and he'd decided that Heidi would be most receptive to answering his question right after they finished being intimate. So, after they left the restaurant, they walked for a while, then he said, "I hope I am not overstepping my boundaries, but I was wondering if you would like to come to my hotel room to have a drink."

She looked up at him and smiled broadly. "Of course I would. In fact, I have been waiting for you to ask."

He put his arm around her shoulder protectively, and she cuddled into him as they walked back to his room. Once they were alone, he turned off the light, then under the protection of darkness, he made love to her. After it was over, he sat up and said, "I am going down the hall to the bathroom." This gave him the opportunity to put his pants back on and hide his circumcision before she turned on the light.

A few minutes later, Pitor returned from the bathroom. Heidi lay naked in his bed. He wore a white undershirt and the pants to his uniform. Getting into bed beside her, he took her in his arms. Then he smoothed her hair and began to tell her the story he'd invented about Liam. Pitor hoped that it was a feasible explanation as to why he wanted to adopt Liam so badly.

"Heidi, do you remember that little boy with the curly blond hair. The one Reichsführer Himmler named Liam?"

"Yes, of course I remember him. Cute little fellow he was. But why do you ask about him?"

"I never tell anyone this, but I have come to care for you and to trust that you care for me too. So, I am going to ask for your help."

She sat up on one elbow and looked into his eyes. "What is it?" she asked. "You know I would do anything for you."

"Well, you see," Pitor hesitated for a moment, "when I was a boy, I had a little brother. You might say my brother was a miracle baby. He came to us as a surprise. My parents had not planned to have another child. At thirty-nine my mother thought her childbearing years were over. However, my brother was a special little boy. We named him Hans, and perhaps it was because I was only eight when he was born, little Hans adored me. I had always wanted a brother.

I'd secretly prayed for one. And Hans was perfect. He emulated everything I did. With each passing day, I grew closer to him. I remember that I got on the floor with him and taught him to crawl and then later when he was a little older, I taught him to stand, and eventually walk."

She giggled. "You sound like an adorable little boy. I would love to know all about your childhood. In fact, I'd love to know everything there is to know about you."

Pitor squeezed her upper arm gently. "Well, I was crazy about my little brother. In fact, I taught him lots of words. And he was always trying to speak to me. But then, a terrible thing happened. When he was just four years old, he caught the flu. My parents did everything they could for him. We didn't have much money, but they managed to get a doctor to come to the house. However, it didn't help, nothing did. Hans was too young and weak to survive. He was gone within a couple of days."

"I am so sorry," she said, reaching up and touching his cheek, then she asked, "But what does this have to do with Liam?"

"Well, I'll tell you… I guess this is rather odd. Hans bore a very strong resemblance to little Liam. And, because of this, I have not been able to put Liam out of my mind. I would like to adopt him."

"But he's already been adopted," she said. "There are other children you might want to consider. Of course, you would have to be married to adopt one of the Lebensborn children."

"I know. But I don't think that any of them would be the same as Liam. He just reminds me so much of my brother. I need you to help me with this."

"But how? What can I do?"

"Well, if you could find out who adopted Liam, perhaps I might speak with them and hopefully I can make them sympathize with me. There are other children who they could adopt, and perhaps they would?"

"Well, yes, there are other children. But this is a highly unusual situation. I don't think the couple who adopted Liam would be willing to consider this. And besides, I cannot give you the information you would need, if you were to try and find them."

He'd expected this. However, he had to keep his patience. He dared not get angry. Pitor reminded himself that she was smitten with him and if he could only tap into her feelings, he might convince her. So, he said, "I know you said that I would have to be married to adopt a Lebensborn child. And since I care deeply for you, I was thinking that you and I could get married and adopt Liam."

"Married? Really?" She said, and he heard the joy ringing through her voice.

"Yes, would you like that? I mean, would you consider marrying me?"

"Of course I would, Konrad. But I am still young, and we don't need to adopt. You and I could have a child of our own. Or if not, we might consider adopting one of the other children who is currently available. You can come and see them if you'd like."

Pitor felt himself losing patience and his tone of voice sounded a little too strong even to his own ear. "I don't want another child. I want that one. I want Liam. If you want to marry me, then you will get me the information I need."

"Well," she said, taking a deep breath. "I have to tell you something."

"What is it?" he asked curtly. Pitor had put time, effort and money into this situation with Heidi, and now he was feeling annoyed with her.

"It's about the little boy you like so much. It's about Liam."

"Go on. What is it?" he asked. "Tell me."

"He's got Jewish blood."

Pitor felt as if someone had punched him in the stomach. For a moment, he couldn't speak. *How could she possibly know this? And did anyone else know? And if so, who? Was Jakup in danger?* His heart pounded so hard it felt like a small bird had been locked in his chest and was now fighting for its life. "What? He's Jewish? Are you sure? How do you know this?"

"I am quite sure. And I will tell you how I know. Gretchen is my best friend and my roommate. As you are aware, she's been with Horst for several years. And, I know him, so I know he would never lie to her."

"Wait a minute. So, Horst told Gretchen this preposterous story about that little boy?" He said, trying his best not to sound too invested, but his stomach was turning with anxiety.

"Well, yes. But there's more to this story. However, I can't tell you the rest unless you absolutely promise to keep it a secret. If you ever tell anyone it could cost Horst his job, maybe even his life. And, even worse, if anyone ever found out that Gretchen and I knew the truth all this time, we would be in serious trouble as well."

"I promise you. I will never tell a soul," he said, taking her hand in his and then looking directly into her eyes. Pitor was trying to appear as sincere and trustworthy as possible. "Tell me everything."

"Well, as you know, Horst has a lousy position. I don't know why, but he has not had much success being promoted in the party."

"Go on."

"I guess his superior officers don't like him very much. Although, I don't know what he did to deserve this."

Pitor nodded. He didn't give a damn about Horst or his superior officers, but he had to be patient and let her tell him the story at her own pace.

"As you know, the Lebensborn girls, or the 'Chosen Girls' as they are often called, cannot produce children fast enough to meet Reichsführer Himmler's quota. So, although not many people are aware of this, German officers have been instructed to go to Polish neighborhoods where they have been told to find and take children who look Aryan. Then, they bring them back to Heim Hochland and to the other Lebensborn homes where we Germanize them," she smiled.

"Then you are saying Liam is Polish? Not Jewish."

"No. I am not saying that at all. I am saying, he is Jewish. Horst admitted to Gretchen that he was given a short amount of time to find a Polish child who fit Himmler's criteria. And, well, he was unable to find a Polish child in time. But as he was walking through the Warsaw Ghetto, he saw Liam. And of course, as you know, Liam looks very Aryan. So, Horst took him and brought him to us at Heim Hochland."

"Horst stole Liam from the Warsaw Ghetto?" Pitor finally knew who was responsible for kidnapping his son. He was furious, but at the same time, he was grateful. If Jakup had been in the ghetto during the uprising, he probably wouldn't have survived. At least as things now stood, Pitor knew Jakup was alive and, although it wasn't going to be easy, he might find a way to get him back.

"Yes, that's exactly what happened. No one else knows, so it's all right. Horst won't get into trouble, so long as no one finds out. But that's the reason why you don't want Liam. You are better off choosing another child. I realize he's just a little boy, right now. However, I can guarantee that as he grows up, his dirty Jew blood is going to rise to the surface and then he will turn into the dangerous subhuman Jew he was born to be."

Pitor was outraged. He could hardly breathe. His voice came out harsher than he wanted it to. "Find out who has him." Pitor growled. "Find out for me."

"But why?"

"Because I am asking you to, that's why."

"But, Konrad, now that you know that he is a Jew, why do you still want him?"

"Because I do."

She shook her head. He could see in her eyes that he was losing her. He had to find a way to spark her interest again.

"I love you, Heidi," he leaned down and kissed her. "Will you marry me? And please, will you help me find Liam? I know why you don't want to adopt him, but I must do it. He reminds me so much of Hans. And I believe that with you as my wife, we can change him. We can Germanize him together. And won't it be safer if he is with us? If the other family ever finds out, they will trace it back to Horst and to you. Don't you love me? Will you be my wife?"

At the mention of love and marriage, Heidi's entire demeanor changed. She wrapped her arms around Pitor's neck and held him tight. "Yes, I do love you. And, yes, I'll marry you." She said, her voice ringing with joy.

"But first, you must find out who has Liam and where they are living. Can you do that for me... darling?"

"You're right. If they ever find out, they will trace it back to Horst, and then to me. Oh, Konrad, you were just trying to protect me! I'd do anything for you, anything!" She threw her arms around Pitor's shoulders. "I want you to be happy. And if Liam reminds you of your brother, then I will do my best to find out where he is. I can't promise that the couple who has adopted him will give him up, but we can try," she said. "After all, my love, you are the Sturmschar-führer," she reached up to touch his cheek, "And my Fiancé..."

EPILOGUE

Gretchen was dreaming of receiving a home as a gift from the Reich when she felt Horst shake her shoulder gently. It was time to get up for work. *Another day.* She thought as forced herself to open her eyes.

"Are you awake?" Horst asked.

"Yes, I'm awake," She answered, annoyed because she was still so tired and there was no time to sleep. "I'll start breakfast."

The novelty of being married was wearing off quickly. At first it was fun because she had a husband, and Heidi didn't. And even though Horst wasn't much to look at, he was better than nothing. However, now, Heidi not only had a man, but she had a handsome, wealthy, and successful man, while Gretchen was stuck in poverty with Horst. She hated having to get up early in order to prepare food for her and Horst, while he took his time getting ready for work. *Why is it the woman's responsibility to cook? Once in a while it might be nice to have someone wait on me, instead of me having to serve Horst his every meal. I am sick and tired of spending my day off washing his clothes and cleaning his house. I could understand him expecting all of this from me if he earned enough money for me to quit my job and stay at home with a bunch of little children. However, he doesn't earn enough to buy decent food. At least not yet. So, I am constantly reminded of the mistake I've made by marrying him. Every morning regardless of how I feel, I have to get up and take care of everything, our breakfast, our lunches, and straightening up the apartment. I have to press his uniform then I have to hurry and get ready for a full day at work at the Lebensborn home. It is not fair. But we must follow the rules, and since the Führer says every German woman should be a hausfrau and she should have plenty of children, this is what is demanded of me. I wouldn't mind if I could be a hausfrau. But Horst doesn't earn enough for me to quit my job. We need every penny we both earn just to survive. So I must go to work every day. Then come home and take care of his needs and our apartment. And besides all of this, I am expected to get pregnant and have babies too.*

"Are you all right?" Horst asked, breaking her inner rant. "I mean, you're just lying there. Do you feel alright?"

"I'm fine," she said curtly.

"Then please get up, we are in a hurry. You should realize that," he said annoyed, looking at the clock on the wall.

She nodded, but she was too disgusted with him to look at him. Gretchen climbed out of bed and went into the kitchen where she filled a pot of water to make ersatz coffee. Then she took a small pad of butter and placed it in a pan. Butter was too expensive to waste even a drop. Besides the expense, it was not easy to come by, at least not for someone as low ranking in the party as Horst was. Careful not to burn the butter, she took it off the heat as soon as it melted. Then she quickly chopped a potato and began to sauté it with some chopped cabbage and a few pieces of an onion. By the time the food was ready Horst was dressed, sitting at the table and waiting for his wife to deliver his breakfast. She served him then herself and while he talked about the scarcity of things due to the war, she only half listened to him. Gretchen gobbled her food quickly. Once she finished eating, she washed the dishes then ran to the bedroom to get ready, so she would not be late for work.

There was no time to put on rouge, lipstick, or mascara. She did own a much-cherished tube of red lipstick that she had stolen from a Jewish owned store several years ago.

Once Gretchen had washed her face and put on a clean uniform, she and Horst walked side by side down the street, neither of them speaking. Finally they reached Steinhöring. Horst turned the corner and continued on his way to his job, while Gretchen headed up to the second floor to the children's room where she worked with the other little brown sisters, girls not pretty and Aryan enough in their looks to be considered acceptable to bear children for the Führer. From her position on the stairs, Gretchen could see the beautiful blonde Aryan pregnant women sitting at the long breakfast tables. These were the chosen ones. They were laughing and chatting with each other while dining on the finest of food. The rich smell of bacon and ham made her stomach growl. And as she looked down at the table, she saw cheese and large hunks of white bread. Jealousy and anger possessed her. She was always hungry. Horst was such a big man, and there was so little to go around, since the Führer had instated rations for Germans.

"Gretchen!" Heidi called out enthusiastically to her as Gretchen entered the children's room. "Heil Hitler!"

"Good morning," Gretchen said with less enthusiasm than Heidi, "Heil Hitler."

Heidi didn't seem to notice Gretchen's mood. She was too caught up in her own excitement. "I have wonderful news!"

"Oh?" Gretchen said, as she loaded a set of clean diapers onto a shelf.

"Yes, I have the most wonderful news." Heidi was beaming. Her skin and her eyes were glowing.

"You've already said that. So, what is it?" Gretchen asked. She was disgusted by Heidi, but curious to know what Heidi had to say.

"Well..." Heidi hesitated for effect, "Last night Konrad asked me to marry him." She paused again. "And, of course I accepted. I mean who wouldn't, right?"

"Yes, sure."

"So... We are engaged!" Heidi squealed.

"Hmmm..." Gretchen felt her heart sink. *Why does she get a husband like that? I am prettier than she is. Yet, she has a handsome man with an important job that pays well, and me? I got stuck with Horst.*

"And, well, I have to ask a favor from you. I really need your help with this."

"Oh, what could you possibly need from me?" Gretchen asked, bitterly.

"I'll explain," Heidi said. "Do you remember that little boy who Reichsführer Himmler named Liam at the last naming ceremony, the one who you said Horst took from the Jewish ghetto when he couldn't meet his quota of Polish children who looked Aryan? Do you remember that little boy? He was blond and blue-eyed. He looked so Aryan it was impossible to believe he had any Jewish blood."

Gretchen whirled around to face Heidi, "So, what about that child?"

"Well, he was under your charge if I remember correctly."

"That's right. So what?"

"So, because you were in charge of him, you are the only one who will have access to his adoption records."

"Of course I do. You know that. You know how all of this works. So what?" Gretchen asked.

"I know this is going to sound strange, but Konrad liked that little boy. He wants to adopt him. Konrad said he reminds him of his younger brother who died."

"He's not his younger brother. He's a Jew. And besides that, he's already been adopted. Tell Konrad to forget about him. Tell him to leave that child in the past. There will be others that you can adopt, or you can have one of your own."

"I know. And you're right. I tried to tell Konrad this, but he is insistent that he must have Liam. So to try to discourage him I had to tell him the truth about everything. I told him how Horst found Liam in the Jewish ghetto, and that he would never have taken a Jewish child because you cannot escape Jew blood. But I explained that Horst could not fill his quota so when he saw a child that looked as Aryan as Liam, he took him."

Gretchen's face turned white.

"Gretchen, you look so upset. But don't worry. Konrad doesn't care that Horst took him. He wants that little boy anyway."

"Who else did you tell about what Horst did?" Gretchen felt the anger rise in her. "Don't you realize that if the wrong person should find out and bring this information to the authorities, not only would Horst be terrible in trouble, but you and I would be in trouble too. We would be considered accomplices. Heidi, we knew about what Horst did, and we kept it a secret. We allowed Liam to be a part of our naming ceremony and then to be adopted by an SS officer. What we did was wrong. And all three of us could end up in a prison camp for this, or we might even be shot for treason. You little fool."

"Gretchen please try to relax. You're worried for no reason. Konrad will never tell a soul. In fact, he promised me that he would do whatever he has to do to protect Horst. So I am certain he will protect all three of us. So here is what I need from you." Heidi tried to smile, but Gretchen looked at her with eyes beaming with hatred. Heidi cleared her throat, then she went on, "All I need from you is the name of the couple who adopted Liam, so we can get in touch with them. Konrad says he is willing to pay them a nice sum of money for the child. And since they haven't had the little boy for very long, I am sure they are not attached to him yet. So, once Konrad pays them, we can help the couple find another little boy to adopt."

"I can't give you that information. You know it's strictly against the rules," Gretchen growled at her.

"If I don't get the information I need, Konrad will be disappointed in me. He might call off our engagement," Heidi began wringing her hands as she looked at Gretchen with distress in her eyes. "Please Gretchen, do this for me. I promise you won't get into any trouble. We have always been best friends. I would do it for you if the situation were reversed. Please, I am begging you. I don't want to lose Konrad. He's the best thing that's ever happened to me."

I hope he sees you for the failure you are and calls off the wedding. Why should you have such a good life while I have to struggle? Gretchen thought, but in a calm voice with a bitter and angry undertone she said, "I'm sorry Heidi. I can't do this. Not even for you."

Heidi was angry now. She stomped her foot on the ground and said, "Not even if I threaten to turn you and Horst in? I could go to the authorities and tell them what Horst did. I can tell them that you told me that you knew what he did all along, but you were hiding it because he's your husband and you love him. Don't make me do this, Gretchen. Don't make me betray you," Heidi growled at Gretchen.

"How dare you!" Gretchen was livid. Her face turned red, and she clenched her fists. "You would never do that. You can't be that stupid. It would implicate you as well."

"No, it wouldn't. You know why? Because I would tell the authorities that I just found out. I would tell them that you just told me. They would never know that I have known all along. And if you try to tell them, I will deny it. They will believe me, because I have no reason to lie. But you do. Horst is your husband after all. And I promise you that once they find out what you and Horst did, they will never trust either of you again."

"Damn you. Damn you to hell," Gretchen said, flinging one of the baby's hairbrushes at Heidi who ducked out of the way.

"I don't care what you say, or what you do. Just give me the name and contact information for the couple who has Liam," Heidi demanded.

"Fine. You win. I'll get the name and address out of the file for you," Gretchen glared at Heidi as she turned and walked out of the room and went straight to the file room. Her hands and legs were shaking as she jotted down the name and contact information for the couple. Then she quickly returned the file and put the paper on which she had written the information into the pocket of her uniform. As she headed back towards the children's room, she saw

Heidi in the window. She was smiling as she was changing one of the babies. *Tonight I will have to discuss this entire situation with Horst. He is going to be furious with me for telling Heidi that he took the child from the Jewish ghetto. I wish I didn't have to tell him, but I do because Heidi is no longer someone we can trust. She is an idiot who will say or do anything for Konrad, and her stupidity could cause our demise.* A shiver ran down her back. *Something must be done immediately to stop her and her* Sturmscharführer *before they can get in touch with Liam's adopted parents.*

A NOTE FROM THE AUTHOR

Dear All,

I always enjoy hearing from my readers, and your thoughts about my work are very important to me. If you enjoyed my novel, please consider telling your friends and posting a short review on Amazon. Word of mouth is an author's best friend.

Also, it would be my honor to have you join my mailing list. As my gift to you for joining, you will receive 3 **free** short stories and my USA Today award-winning novella! To sign up, just go to my website at... www.RobertaKagan.com

I send blessings to each and every one of you,
Roberta

Email: roberta@robertakagan.com

ABOUT THE AUTHOR

I wanted to take a moment to introduce myself. My name is Roberta, and I am an author of Historical Fiction, mainly based on World War 2 and the Holocaust. While I never discount the horrors of the Holocaust and the Nazis, my novels are constantly inspired by love, kindness, and the small special moments that make life worth living.

I always knew I wanted to reach people through art when I was younger. I just always thought I would be an actress. That dream died in my late 20's, after many attempts and failures. For the next several years, I tried so many different professions. I worked as a hairstylist and a wedding coordinator, amongst many other jobs. But I was never satisfied. Finally, in my 50's, I worked for a hospital on the PBX board. Every day I would drive to work, I would dread clocking in. I would count the hours until I clocked out. And, the next day, I would do it all over again. I couldn't see a way out, but I prayed, and I prayed, and then I prayed some more. Until one morning at 4 am, I woke up with a voice in my head, and you might know that voice as Detrick. He told me to write his story, and together we sat at the computer; we wrote the novel that is now known as All My Love, Detrick. I now have over 30 books published, and I have had the honor of being a USA Today Best-Selling Author. I have met such incredible people in this industry, and I am so blessed to be meeting you.

I tell this story a lot. And a lot of people think I am crazy, but it is true. I always found solace in books growing up but didn't start writing until I was in my late 50s. I try to tell this story to as many people as possible to inspire them. No matter where you are in your life, remember there is always a flicker of light no matter how dark it seems.

I send you many blessings, and I hope you enjoy my novels. They are all written with love.

Roberta

MORE BOOKS BY ROBERTA KAGAN
AVAILABLE ON AMAZON

A Million Miracles Series

I'll Never Cry Again

Searching for Jakup

Margot's Secret Series

The Secret They Hid

An Innocent Child

Margot's Secret

The Lies We Told

The Blood Sisters Series

The Pact

My Sister's Betrayal

When Forever Ends

The Auschwitz Twins Series

The Children's Dream

Mengele's Apprentice

The Auschwitz Twins

Jews, The Third Reich, and a Web of Secrets

My Son's Secret

The Stolen Child

A Web of Secrets

A Jewish Family Saga

Not In America

They Never Saw It Coming

When The Dust Settled

The Syndrome That Saved Us

A Holocaust Story Series

The Smallest Crack

The Darkest Canyon

Millions Of Pebbles

Sarah and Solomon

All My Love, Detrick Series

All My Love, Detrick

You Are My Sunshine

The Promised Land

To Be An Israeli

Forever My Homeland

Michal's Destiny Series

Michal's Destiny

A Family Shattered

Watch Over My Child

Another Breath, Another Sunrise

Eidel's Story Series

And . . . Who Is The Real Mother?

Secrets Revealed

New Life, New Land

Another Generation

Made in United States
North Haven, CT
08 July 2025

70465383R00156